Praise for Mystic Siren

"A perfect recipe for exploring the dark side would be sitting in front of a roaring fire late at night with a warm drink and this book, listening for the things that go bump in the night. A great mood-setter that keeps you guessing."

Frank Hayes,
author of *Shattered Dreams*

Praise for the AJ Bugbee Mysteries

"If you like your crime fiction with a special dark twist, I can't recommend the AJ Bugbee series, by Jan Bogue and Bill Keller, highly enough. The stories have enough suspense to keep you reading all night, and the characters are so real they'll be like old friends by the time you're done. You'll be *dying* to read the next book!"

Steve Hamilton,
New York Times bestselling author of *Dead Man Running*

Also by Janis Bogue and William Keller
Mystic Bridge
Mystic Siren

MYSTIC FIRELIGHT

Janis Bogue and
William Keller

This is a work of fiction. The characters, places and organizations are either fictitious or used fictitiously.

To Lyn and Bill Desautel, Lisa Schwartz, and to Mom

ACKNOWLEDGMENTS

Thanks to Frank Hayes, for friendship, inspiration, and keeping the digressions and the Ands in check. To Steve Hamilton, for generosity and showing what it takes. To Mary Bossenbery-Russo, for not giving up on us, even when we kept breaking our promises.

And to Dad, for taking us firelighting.

Bud and Cal Bogue, preparing eels for smoking

1

The cry was faint and fair away, but it found her, tugged her out of sleep. Melody opened her eyes, shifted the pillow between her legs. Jack stirred then, too.

"Hey." He spread a hand across her rounded belly. "You okay?"

"Yeah, just another baby dream."

He slid his fingers gently up and down, following her shape.

"Sorry I woke you," she said.

"Shhh."

Melody turned and backed up to him. She glanced at the clock, which showed just after midnight. They were quiet. The room was dark and still. She closed her eyes.

Another cry.

"Jack?" Melody raised herself up on an elbow.

"I heard it, too."

They were both upright now, scanning the big bedroom, which was made bigger by moonlight. From outside, through the open window, came the sound again. A child's cry.

"I wasn't dreaming," Melody said.

Jack slid out of bed. "No."

Melody threw back the covers. "Where is it coming from?"

Already at the closet, Jack was pulling on a pair of jeans. "I don't know. By the water, it sounds like."

"By the water?"

"I'm going out." He slipped his bare feet into shoes.

"I'm coming with you."

***

Melody and Jack stood at the edge of the yard, aiming their flashlights out across the cove. Fog hung low over the water, glowing in the moonlight. All was quiet.

"Do you hear anything?" Jack said.

"No, nothing. Maybe it was just – "

From somewhere in the mist, the cry came again – the sound of a young child, lost and afraid.

Both lights swung toward the spot, but that only seemed to pull the fog closer.

Another cry.

"My God, Jack!" Melody said. "There's a kid out there."

"Stay right here. Keep your light trained on the end of the dock."

Melody found the wooden slats with her beam, followed them out into the water. Jack moved quickly along that illuminated path. Though he was a big man, and no longer young, he stepped easily into the small utility boat that was tied there. In a few seconds he had freed the line and was heading out into the cove. The sleek electric motor barely hummed. The fog took Jack in.

Jack steered the boat forward, aiming his light just above the surface. Looking back toward the shore, he saw Melody's light, judged the distance. He cut the motor and glided. There was nothing but a soft silence, the occasional clap of water against the hull, his jacket whispering as he turned left and right. He worked the beam back and forth in front of him.

The cry again. Short, stifled.

Jack gave the motor a burst, then killed it. He switched off his light. Immediately, a faint yellowish glow appeared not far in front of him.

"Hello!" Jack waited for a response.

More snuffly cries.

His boat floated through the chilly cloud. He kept his eyes on the yellow light.

"Are you okay?"

The water tapped, tapped against the hull. Jack switched his flashlight on again. A small open boat leapt into view. It was rotating, slowly, its stern swinging toward Jack. Mounted there, just above the

2

water line, was a sputtering lantern.

"Hello?" Jack said. "I'm here to help you."

The boat spun silently. A head rose up over the side – a small girl with a pink bow in her black hair. She began to cry in earnest, loudly, uncontrolled.

Jack edged his boat up to hers.

"It's okay," he said. "It's okay." Gripping the other boat's gunwale with one hand, he pulled alongside. The girl was alone, sitting on a tackle box. Next to her, running almost the length of the craft, was a wooden pole. Jack traced it with his light, followed it to the end, to the barbed prongs. They were wet and foul. They had been used – had been plunged into the shallow water and then, at just the right depth, jerked sharply back, setting the hooks into the soft flesh so that the catch could be lifted, writhing, into the air.

Jack pointed the light down into the boat. He saw them, the night's bounty. Narrow, with dark backs and silver bellies, some a yard long, they surrounded the girl, tangled and twisting at her feet.

Eels.

2

At the same hour, in another dark bedroom, Amelda Brown was wakened by the sound of the closet banging shut.

"Roland?" She switched on the light. Her husband was working his legs into a pair of jeans. His ample stomach was still fully exposed to the chilly air.

"Sorry, didn't mean to wake you."

"What are you doing?"

"I have to get to the hospital."

"What?" Alarm crossed her face, then vanished. "Have you been listening to the scanner again? You're not chief of police anymore. You don't have to run out for every emergency. That's what retired means." When her husband didn't respond, she added, "Whatever it is, you'll just be in the way."

Roland yanked a T-shirt over his head. "It's George Bugbee. They've just taken him to the E.R. Heart attack."

"Oh, shit." Amelda threw the covers aside. "Give me a second to catch up."

***

Officer AJ Bugbee's Jeep raced into Westerly, red light flashing on the roof. His girlfriend Claire sat next to him, her hands gripping the seat and the door. They had the dark midnight streets to themselves. They flew.

"Do you think your dad will still be in the emergency room?"

Claire said. "Or will they have already taken him somewhere?"

"I'll have to check at the desk. I don't want to call Mom right now." AJ made the last turn into the lot.

"Drive up to the door," Claire said. "I'll park and meet you inside."

AJ stopped under the portico. He jumped out.

Claire circled around the hood. She drove to an empty parking spot, then jogged back up to the hospital with her phone to her ear. "Hey, Dave," she said. "Hope you weren't asleep. We're at the Westerly hospital. It looks like AJ's dad had a heart attack."

"Jesus. Is he okay? Maybe I should come over."

"No, I don't think so. Not right now. I just wanted you to know. And could you open the market in the morning? You and Sela?"

"Sure, of course."

"Great, thanks. I gotta go. We'll keep you posted."

"If you can. I'll be thinking of all of you."

The glass doors parted and Claire hurried inside.

3

When AJ came back into the emergency room waiting area, it was crowded with friends – not just Claire, and Roland Brown and his wife, Amelda, but, despite Claire's advice, both Dave Sela and Dave DaSilva, known to their friends as the Daves.

"How is he, AJ?" Claire said, going to him.

"Stable. They're saying it was a heart attack, like we thought. He's going to have an X-ray, then they'll take him upstairs." AJ skimmed the row of faces. "Jesus. I didn't know I'd be giving a press conference."

"I hope you don't mind, AJ." Roland was on his feet. A big man with a shaved head, he looked every inch the chief of police that he'd been until recently. "I heard on the scanner that they were bringing your dad in. I just wanted to be here, see if there was anything I could do."

"Thanks, Roland."

Everyone was standing, now.

"*Is* there anything we can do?" Sela said.

"Don't worry about the market," DaSilva said. "We got that covered."

Sela shot DaSilva a look. "I think that's the least of AJ's worries right now."

"Claire called and asked." DaSilva said, his Adam's apple bobbing in his throat. "I just don't want him to have to even think about it."

"Thanks, all of you guys," AJ said, raising his hands. "I appreciate your concern. It will mean a lot to Dad to know you were here. But you can't see him yet. And I – I think I just need some air."

No one followed him as he bolted for the door.

"I guess we need to leave him to his thoughts," Amelda said.

AJ, as he worked his way out of the hospital, didn't look like someone deep in contemplation. He kept his eyes up and moving, alert, watchful, searching.

Outside, he took a few steps past the light that spilled from the entrance. He studied the landscaped drive and the parking lot. His eyes paused on a big spruce tree. The branches were lit from behind.

"Hey," he said. "Come on out. I can see you."

Ben Shortman, ghost and former ghost hunter, and AJ's oldest friend, appeared from behind the tree. "How's your dad?"

"He had a heart attack. But he's stable."

Ben only nodded.

"What are you doing lurking out here?" AJ said.

Ben came around onto the sidewalk. "With all of the people inside, I thought it would be better if I stayed away. Less complicated for you. I knew I wouldn't be able to keep my mouth shut. I'd be yapping at you, and you'd have to pretend that you didn't hear anything… Since we decided to keep it quiet for now, that I was back again. And since your mom and dad still don't even know about your ability…"

A man came up the walk, moving at a brisk jog. "How ya doing?" he said, nodding at AJ and nearly powering through Ben, who to him was invisible, inaudible, impossible.

"Excuse me," Ben said to the man's back. Turning to AJ, he added, "I know he can't see me, but it still seems rude." He glanced down at himself, as if to confirm his presence. "I'm the same, aren't I? You'd tell me if I didn't look right? No one else can."

AJ stared back at him. He seemed to be taking it all in – the shorts and T-shirt that never changed, the perpetual two-day stubble, the full sleeve of supernatural-themed tattoos, all of which gave off a colorful glow.

Before AJ could comment, Ben said, "Maybe you should just tell everyone that I'm back again. Claire will be okay with it. The others – DaSilva – we'll figure it out."

The two men were quiet for a moment. A seagull squawked from some distant perch.

"I want you to be straight with me," AJ said.

"Of course."

"Are you here for my dad?"

"What? What are you talking about?"

"If you are, just say so."

"I have no idea what you mean."

"You helped Elizabeth to – I don't know – move on or whatever. Are you here to do the same for my dad?"

"No. AJ. That's crazy."

"I'm serious," AJ said.

"No! Elizabeth's spirit had been stuck in Claire's house for over a hundred years. And *we* – you, me and Claire – helped her move on. It's totally different with your dad. He's alive. I'm not the grim reaper, AJ."

"You sure about that?"

Ben turned away.

"You don't know why you're back, this time," AJ said. "I'm just thinking – "

Ben spun around again. "Shhhh."

"What?"

"Do you hear those cars? I'd swear one of them is Melody's. It always ran a little rough."

"I don't hear any car. But Claire might have called her." AJ tipped his head. "Okay, I hear something. You can recognize Melody's car? That's kind of creepy. You really were crazy about her, weren't you?"

Ben let that go. "Here they come."

An ambulance sped up the drive, followed by an old sedan.

"Told you it was her," Ben said.

"You didn't mention that the other car was an ambulance."

"I didn't know," Ben said, looking concerned.

When the sedan had come to a stop in front of him, AJ went around it. He opened the door.

"Is she all right?" Ben hovered behind.

"Are you okay?" AJ said, as Melody labored to shift her center of gravity and get to her feet. "Is Jack?"

"AJ? Yeah, I'm fine. He's fine. What are you doing here? Did somebody call you?" She hurried toward the ambulance.

"It's my dad," AJ said. "He's stable now, but he had a heart attack."

"Oh, AJ. I'm so sorry to hear that." Melody hugged him.

Ben followed them down the walk. "Who's in the ambulance? Where's Jack?"

AJ, the only one who could hear Ben's questions, seemed to ignore them. They reached the back of the boxy vehicle. The big doors swung open. Jack jumped out. A medic handed him a bundle – a long, upright shape wrapped in blankets.

"What the…" Ben said.

"What's going on?" AJ said.

Jack acknowledged AJ with a puzzled look but said nothing. He and Melody started toward the glass doors.

"We'll fill you in later," Melody said. "At least, what little we know."

AJ and Ben stayed there on the walk, watching the couple hurry away. A little girl with big brown eyes and a ragged pink bow peeked over Jack's shoulder. Her eyes seemed to find Ben's face, hold, get even a little bigger. Then she and Jack and Melody reached the entrance and all three disappeared.

"What the heck's going on?" Ben said.

AJ kept looking toward the entrance. "I have no idea."

4

Claire and Melody took a cab from the hospital.

"The baby's kicking," Melody said, as they wound through the sleeping streets of Westerly. "Here." She took Claire's hand and placed it on high up on the curve of her abdomen.

"Oh!" Claire said. "I wonder what she's trying to tell you. Or he."

"I think it's something about food. I know I'm hungry."

The cabby checked the rearview mirror. "Are you first-time moms?"

Claire and Melody smiled across the seat at each other.

"It will be my first," Melody said. "We're not a couple. But it's nice that you're open minded."

The driver's eyes found the mirror again. "I'm learning it from my kids. They say that everybody has a right to be themselves, and I can't argue with that. It's a free country, right? At least, it's supposed to be. Anyway, I meet all kinds of people in this job, so I try to be ready for anything."

"I like that attitude," Melody said.

In silence, they crossed the short bridge into Pawcatuck, leaving Rhode Island for Connecticut, then picked up Pequot Trail, which took them away into the country. The headlights lit up shrubs and ragged stone walls.

"Here's your checkered flag," the cabby said after a while, tapping the screen of the GPS. "You must be near that murder house."

"Murder house?" Claire asked, sounding like she knew better.

"Yeah, that big old place where they thought some rich guy killed a girl, then it turned out it was another guy, who tried to kill the new

10

lady who bought the house."

"Actually, that lady would be me," Claire said.

"And that rich guy," Melody said, "is my partner."

The cabby checked the mirror again. "When I stick my foot in my mouth, I like to get it all the way in and bite down hard."

"It's okay," Claire said. "I guess the house is kind of famous."

"A little bit," the cabby said. "Hey, at least you can't complain that life is dull."

They turned off the road onto Claire's lane. The headlights tunneled into the dark woods. They came to a stop under a floodlight mounted on the garage. Ahead, the big house cast a black shadow, made blacker by the few glowing windows.

"That's a nice big house," the cabby said. "I bet it's a beautiful spot in the daylight. You'd never guess there was a murder – "

Melody interrupted him with her credit card.

The two women crossed the lawn in the glare of the cab's headlights. The greyhound met them at the door.

"Hey, Buck," Claire said, scratching him behind the ears. He panted, quietly appreciative.

Melody slipped past them. "Believe it or not, I have to pee again."

A few minutes later, in the kitchen, Claire offered Melody some herbal tea.

"Sure." Melody pulled her dark hair back and fastened it with an elastic. "I'm actually a little hungry."

"Right! I'm sorry. How about an English muffin?"

"That sounds great. Do you have peanut butter?"

"Yep. Do you want jelly? Or honey?"

"No thanks. Just peanut butter for me."

They took seats in the living room, mugs of tea and plates on the coffee table in front of them. The dog stretched out on the floor.

"Thanks so much," Melody said, after her first mouthful, "for the food, for letting me come here. I really didn't want to go back to the house alone."

"You've helped me out so many times. I'm glad I can do something for you."

Melody wrapped her fingers around her mug. "I wonder if they're still looking for that little girl's parents." She turned toward the window behind her, which was as dark as if it had been covered with tarpaper. "Or whoever had her out in that boat."

"I can't imagine how she ended up alone in a boat full of eels."

Melody stared down into her tea. "I don't want to imagine it. That's why I'm here instead of at home."

**

AJ left his father's hospital room for another, one flight up. He found Jack sitting in a shiny, under-stuffed chair. In the bed, the girl was visible only as a shock of black hair on the pillow. Jack stepped out into the hall. "How's your dad, AJ?"

"Sleeping, when they give him half a chance."

"They say a hospital is no place to rest."

"They're right about that," AJ said.

"I want to thank Claire for looking out for Melody."

"I know she's happy to help." AJ nodded toward the open door. "What's going on with the little girl?"

"Well, she actually does seem to be getting some sleep."

"So, can you tell me what happened? How did you end up with her?"

"It was the weirdest thing." Jack looked both ways down the gleaming hallway. His silky hair glowed white in the fluorescent light. "We were in bed when we heard crying." He described following the sound outside, taking a boat into the fog, seeing the glow of the lantern, making his way alongside the other craft, where the girl sat, alone, bawling. Then seeing the eels squirming at her feet.

"No sign of anyone else? Another boat?" AJ said.

Jack shook his head. "I called out a few times. No response."

"Did you talk to the girl?"

"I tried to. At first she couldn't calm down, then she just went silent. She didn't speak at all in the ambulance, and hasn't said a word to anyone here, either. The doctor thinks it's trauma, emotional trauma. He doesn't see any physical problem that would prevent her from talking."

"They're letting you stay with her?"

"She started wailing every time I tried to leave. I had to cut off my conversation with the detective – Nardi, I think? – because she was so upset. Finally, they asked if I'd sit with her until she fell asleep. Now, I'm afraid to go." Jack peered back through the open door. "Maybe it's because of the way I found her, maybe it's because I'm

12

about to become a dad for the first time, I don't know. I feel kind of protective of her."

AJ clapped him on the shoulder. "I'll find you here tomorrow, then. I'm going to try to talk my mom into heading home. I don't want her spending the night in a chair."

"Okay. See you in the morning."

AJ took a few steps down the hall, then turned. "You're a good man, Jack," he said.

"Thanks. There were a lot of years when no one around here would have said that."

"I'm sure some would have stuck up for you."

"Yeah, I guess some. Not your boss, though."

"My old boss. No, not Roland Brown. Not then." With a wave, AJ headed for the elevator.

***

Claire's phone beeped to signal the arrival of a text. "AJ is at his mom's," she said, scanning the screen. "He's going to stay with her tonight, stop here in the morning, then take her in to meet with the cardiologist." She typed a reply.

"How is his mom doing?" Melody said. "I didn't see her."

"She looked scared to death."

"Aw. That's too bad."

"I think it's harder for her than it is for him," Claire said. "He's —"

"In denial?"

"George just bulls ahead. She worries."

"That's probably a good combination in a relationship," Melody said. "A bull and a worrier."

"Do you and Jack have that combination?"

"Actually, we don't have a worrier. We could probably use one."

"Whenever you need a little worrying," Claire said, "you can bring me in."

"I might take you up on that. So you're the worrier between you and AJ?"

"I don't know." Claire looked at Melody, then looked away.

Melody touched Claire's arm. "When I first met AJ, I would have said he was a worrier. There was a distance in his eyes, like he was seeing something awful that you weren't seeing. Then I found out that, in fact, he was... It's partly a curse, seeing what he sees. But the longer he's with you, the less I find that look in his eyes. You've been really good for him."

A smile flashed across Claire's face. "It's mutual." She glanced at the phone again. "We should go to bed. Tomorrow may be busy for both of us."

"Yeah, I'm exhausted." Melody began rearranging the cushions on the sofa. "Do you have a spare bed pillow?"

"You're not sleeping down here. You can try out the new mattress in the guest room."

Melody dropped the cushion. "You don't have to ask me twice."

Claire gestured at what remained of their snack. "We can pick this stuff up in the morning."

The women went up the stairs, disappearing as the steps made a half turn. The dog followed closely behind them.

In the front hall, a faint glow brightened, grew, then took shape. Ben Shortman moved to the landing, the very spot that had changed everything for him a little over a year before. He cocked his head, listening, as laughter came from above. Suddenly Melody reappeared, hurrying down, chasing Ben out of the way.

Claire's voice followed her. "Are you going to want pickles with that?"

"I might!"

Melody dashed into the kitchen. With the jar of peanut butter in hand, she climbed the stairs again.

Ben watched her every step until she was out of sight. Then, like a light being turned off at a dimmer switch, he faded and was gone, leaving only his voice hanging in the air. "Sleep well, Melody."

5

When AJ crossed the yard to Claire's front door, the only light was low in the sky and filtered by trees. He was a shadow among shadows. He pushed on the knob, moved the greyhound back with this hand. "Shhh, boy. We gotta be quiet."

The dog studied him soberly.

"Ben?" AJ said, in a whisper as he stepped into the hall. "You here?" He looked up the winding stairs, then down at the floor, as if Ben's body might still lie where Sela had found it the night that Ben went from ghost hunter to ghost. He tried the living room. Nothing. "It sure is hard to keep track of you."

AJ led the greyhound into the kitchen. After filling the dog's bowl, he went upstairs.

As he opened a dresser drawer, Claire rolled toward him on her pillow. "Hey," she said.

"Sorry. I was trying not to wake you."

Claire sat up. "That's okay. How's your dad? Did you get any sleep?"

"Dad's doing okay. I slept some. Mom was up and down all night. I'm worried about her." His clothes for the day were draped over one arm. "I have to shower and then stop at the market before I pick up Mom. Melody's in the guest room?"

"Yeah," Claire said. "And Jack?"

"Still at the hospital, as far as I know. He seems to have really bonded with that girl."

"How did she end up alone in a boat full of eels? At night?"

"They were firelighting. You do that at night."

"*Firelighting.* Someone said that yesterday at the hospital. What is that?"

"It's an old school method for getting eels. You attach a lantern on the stern of a small boat, right at the water line, then pole yourself around in the shallows with an eel spear – a long pole with barbs at one end." AJ spread his arms to indicate size. "You look for eels that show up against the bottom and try to hook them with the spear. If you manage to get one, you toss it into the boat."

"Right where your daughter is sitting." Claire shook her head. "Who does that?"

"Hopefully, we'll get our answer soon."

"Yeah," Claire said.

"Go back to sleep. One of us needs to be rested today."

"Don't run yourself ragged, AJ. You can't cover everything."

"I know."

"Give my love to your mom and dad."

"I will."

"Call me, or text me."

"I will." AJ headed for the shower.

***

When AJ got to the Bay Market, there were extra cars in employee parking, the rough patch of hard ground behind the building. He squeezed the Jeep in beside the dumpster, sending a gull screeching into the air. As he approached the back door, he could hear raised voices.

"Who told you to do that?"

"No one told me! It's called being a self-starter!"

Inside, AJ found the Daves – Sela and DaSilva – glaring at each other across a counter. Roland Brown was quietly peeling potatoes at a sink, while Detective Wheeler leaned against a refrigerator, wearing his windbreaker, a to-go coffee in his hand. Ben, invisible to all except AJ, kept an eye on everything from just inside the plastic strips that separated the kitchen from the front counter.

"What's going on?" AJ said.

Ben was the first to answer. "These two have been in charge for, what, thirty minutes? And they're already at each other's throats."

"Everything okay?" Sela said.

"I don't know anything new," AJ said. "Everything okay here?"

"It doesn't look like it," DaSilva said, "but we've got it under control."

Sela rolled his eyes.

Roland Brown knocked his peeler against the sink. "I thought the boys might need some help, so I stopped by."

This time, both Daves rolled their eyes.

"He really doesn't know what to do with himself since he retired, does he?" Ben said, continuing the commentary that only AJ could hear.

Wheeler raised his cup. "I'm just here for the free coffee."

"He wants to ask you to help him look for that little girl's parents," Ben said. "Or their ghosts, anyway. But he wasn't sure this morning would be a good time."

"Help yourself, Sam," AJ said.

Ben continued. "He's had a team out looking for bodies in the water near where the girl was found, but nothing so far. No calls to the station from someone who's missing a daughter, either."

To the Daves, AJ said, "What were you two arguing about?"

"DaSilva took too many porgy from Larry."

"Porgy Night was a hit all summer," DaSilva said. "We always ran out."

"That's the idea. Sell them all. It's not like we sold out in ten minutes. And you doubled the order!"

AJ raised his hands in front of him. "That's fine, Dave. But we just need you to keep the doors open, okay? You don't need to get too creative."

"Okay," DaSilva said.

"Roland," AJ said, "I appreciate the help. Make sure you take something home for Amelda."

"Can I recommend the fried porgy?" Sela said. "We're running a special."

AJ turned toward Wheeler. "I'll help if I have time, Sam. Is there anything you want me to do?"

Wheeler raised his cup. "Family first, AJ. But if you can... We haven't found a body, but I was thinking if someone drowned out there where Jack found the girl, the ghost might be in the area."

"I'll try to get over there. I'm going to get Mom, then head to the hospital. Do you guys need anything from her? For the market?"

"We're good, AJ," Sela said. "Don't forget, we ran this place while they were on that Alaska cruise."

"The place ran itself," DaSilva said.

"Okay. I have my phone if you need to reach me." AJ went out the back door.

Ben was waiting on the wooden steps. "Listen, I'll take a look around over at Melody's, and keep an eye on things here, too."

"Can you be in two places at the same time now?"

Ben seemed to think about that. "Never tried…"

"Seriously, I appreciate it."

There was the sound of approaching footsteps. Beth, the young woman who worked the counter, hurried across the back lot. Ben slipped out of the way. Beth gave AJ a hug.

"I heard about your dad," she said. "Hope everything's okay."

"Thanks."

Beth continued on. As she went through the kitchen, she caught Sela's eyes. "Poor AJ."

Sela nodded. "He'll be all right. I mean, as long as his dad is."

"Yeah." Beth paused at the plastic strips that divided the kitchen from the counter. "It seems like he might be losing it a little, though. He was out there talking to himself."

The two Daves looked at each other across the kitchen. For the first time that morning, they seemed to be thinking the same thing.

6

"A roadblock?" Melody stretched to see around the police car that was parked at an angle across the pavement. "How am I supposed to get home?"

They were at the top of the last road on Wamphassuc Point. At the end of the road, out of sight down the hill, was Jack and Melody's waterfront house.

Claire brought the car to a stop. "Is that your neighbor?"

Between the cruiser and a two-story cottage, a woman was having words with a cop.

"Yeah, that's Alice," Melody said. "Can you pull over?"

Claire edged the car left and they got out. Alice hurried over.

"Melody, are you all right? Where's Jack? What's happened?" She pointed to the policeman. "He won't tell me anything."

Melody put one arm around the woman's waist. "Alice, you remember Claire." She motioned across the car.

"Yes, of course. Good morning, Claire. I didn't mean to be rude, but when I saw all of this commotion…"

"I don't know that officer," Claire said. "but let me see if he'll let us through."

"Go to it," Alice said.

Claire approached the policeman. "Hi. I'm Claire Connor. Officer Bugbee's, um, partner. Girlfriend."

"Good morning, ma'am." The cop's expression, under a uniform cap that he wore with the bill pulled low over his eyes, remained as stern as ever.

"AJ and I were at the hospital when they brought the girl in. Have they found anything?" Claire gestured down the hill.

"Sorry, I really can't comment on that."

Claire studied the man. He was no older than twenty-five. Fit. A bit of swagger even in his stance. "That's Melody Johnson," she said, pointing behind her. "Is it okay if I bring her down to her house?"

"Yes, no problem."

"Thanks." Claire started back toward the car.

The cop added, under his breath, "And you can take the old bat with you."

Claire spun around. "I'm sorry, what was that? Officer..."

"Adams," the man said, suddenly red-faced. "I just... She..."

Without saying any more, Claire returned to the car. Melody was in the passenger seat again, twisting around so that she could talk to Alice, who had climbed into the back.

Claire worked the car around the cruiser, then drove down the hill. Melody led them into the house. While she and Alice lingered inside, Claire continued onto a deck that overlooked the cove. Last night's fog had already burned off, and the water sparkled under the early sun. Jack's turquoise sloop was anchored a little ways out. Other boats dotted the shimmering surface.

Detective Wheeler was coming up the yard toward them. "Claire!" he called out, warmly.

"Is it okay for Melody to pick up a few things?"

"Yes, that's fine." Wheeler climbed the steps to her level. Up close, he looked like a man who had been awakened by a phone call in the middle of the night – his cheeks were stubbly and his hair pointed in all directions. "I saw AJ earlier this morning. I hope they get good news about his dad today."

"Me, too," Claire said.

Melody and Alice joined them. "Did you find anything, detective?" Alice said.

"Nothing yet. Officer Romano is taking a last look." He pointed toward the shoreline. "Then we'll be done here."

"So you don't know who the little girl belongs to?" Alice said.

Melody jumped in. "This is our neighbor, Alice Garrison."

"No, we don't," Wheeler said. "You live in the cottage?"

"Yes," Alice said.

"Did you hear or see anything unusual last night?"

"No. But then, I took a pill to help me sleep – I do that sometimes – and was dead to the world from nine until dawn. I didn't even know anything had happened until this morning."

"Here's my card," Wheeler said, "in case anything else occurs to you." He passed the card to her. "Excuse me." Pulling a vibrating phone from a pocket of his windbreaker, he went a few steps across the deck.

"I should get ready to head back to the hospital," Melody said. "I'm sure Jack will call soon."

"Would you mind if Claire ran me up to my place?" Alice said.

"No, that's fine."

Melody led them through the house again.

When they were at the car, Alice said, "I'm going to the hospital to see that little girl."

Claire seemed doubtful. "I don't think there's anything you can do. She wasn't speaking to anyone. They're not sure that she *can* speak."

"Yes, Melody told me. That's why I want to see her. Speech problems are kind of my thing. I taught at the Mystic Oral School for a number of years."

When Claire gave her a blank look, Alice continued, "I guess you aren't from around here. Mystic Oral School for the Deaf. It's closed now. I worked there, and then in the public schools, with hearing and speech challenged children."

"Oh. You should try to see her."

"I'd like to. There are so many possible causes for the girl's silence. According to what Melody told me, she can cry, so it's unlikely a purely physical problem. It could be simple delayed speech, sometimes called late talking. It could be an issue with hearing or cognition. Autism – more and more common these days, I'm afraid. Einstein syndrome. I want to be sure she gets the right care."

"Einstein syndrome?"

"A kind of late talking that's found with the extremely intelligent."

"I just assumed it was the trauma of last night..."

"Yes. There is that, too." Alice looked through the windshield toward the water. "In all those years of working with kids, I saw a lot. Good parents and bad. All kinds of bad. I can tell you that even the worst parent or guardian that I encountered wouldn't have

21

abandoned a small child in a boat in the middle of the night."

"A boat full of eels." Claire said with a shiver.

"Right. I think something bad happened in that boat. And it happened right in front of her."

7

AJ came out of the hospital into the sunlight. As he stared vaguely across the parking lot, he let out a long breath. His face went slack. Then a voice at his shoulder made him jump.

"What's the news?"

"Jesus, Ben."

A man coming up the hill gave AJ a doubtful look.

"Bee," AJ said, swatting at the air.

Ben moved off the sidewalk to let the man pass. "Take out your phone so you can talk to me without looking like a crazy person."

AJ put his cell phone to his ear.

"So how's your dad?"

"He may need bypass surgery. He probably will."

"Shit." Ben reached for AJ, then let his hand drop. "Bypass is serious, but they're good at that stuff now. My uncle had it done a few years ago and he came out of it better than ever. If you wanted to talk to him, I'm sure he'd be glad to – "

AJ's cell phone buzzed in his ear, startling him. He pulled it away, tapped the screen. The quick conversation was mostly *okay, okay,* on his end. "That was my mom," he said, when he'd finished. "She wants me to run home to get a few things for Dad."

"Okay. Guess there's not much I can do to help with that. Do you want me to – "

AJ was already headed toward his car. He turned. "Sorry, Ben. I've got a lot on my mind."

Ben kept pace with him. "I know. And, I know we agreed that it would be best for DaSilva, for everyone, if we kept my comeback a secret, at least for now. But maybe, with everything that's going on… Maybe I could be helpful if people knew. Maybe that's why I'm here – to help someone. Like the first time, I helped you figure out how I died, and I helped free Elizabeth. This time, plenty of people need help – you, your dad, that little girl…"

AJ looked back at him but kept walking. His phone buzzed. "Hi, Claire," he said, the phone to his ear again. He continued down the hill.

Ben stayed on the grass, out of anyone's way, the bright sunshine overwhelming the glow that came from every part of him. He watched AJ get into the Jeep, back it out of its parking space, then make for the street. Turning toward the entrance, Ben saw a woman shepherd a frail man through the glass doors. At the moment the doors closed, there was no motion anywhere outside the Westerly Hospital. The emergency entrance was quiet, the parking lot was still, the flag drooped against the pole. No motion except the invisible swiveling of Ben's head as he took it all in.

"Why the hell *am* I here?" he said. "Or, why the heaven? I could use a hint…" He scanned the grass and the sky and the parking lot again. "Anything?"

8

Melody rode alone in the hospital elevator, holding a cup of coffee in one hand, fixing her still-damp hair with the other. When the doors parted, she could see Jack in the hall, talking to a woman who clutched a leather-bound notebook to her chest. The conversation ended. The woman passed by Melody with a wordless nod.

"Hey!" Jack said, seeing Melody for the first time.

"What's going on? I take it no one has come forward to claim the girl? Other than Alice, I guess."

"No. The caseworker from DCF, Ms. Holt – the woman who was just here – is still hopeful that they'll find someone who's looking for the girl in the next twenty-four hours."

"I hope she's right."

They both stopped at an open door. Inside the spare room, Alice sat on the bed, the girl tucked under her arm, a large picture book open on their laps.

As Alice read, the girl occasionally cast a glance toward the doorway.

"She's keeping an eye on you," Melody said.

"Yes, she is."

"When did Alice get here?"

"About twenty minutes ago."

"The girl seems to like her."

Jack laughed softly. "Alice didn't give her time to think. She just walked in and acted like they were old friends."

Melody reached into her oversized, orchid-color bag, and

25

produced a stuffed bear. "Can I give her this?"

"You bought that for the baby."

"I know, but our baby will have lots of stuffed animals," she said.

Jack put an arm around her.

"Jack, Melody," Alice called from the bed. "Can you come in here?"

Melody slipped the bear back into the bag. She followed Jack into the room.

The book that Alice was reading to the girl was a reprint of an early edition of *Peter Pan*. The open page showed Tiger Lily in a fringed buckskin dress, her long black hair decorated by a single feather.

"Who is that?" Alice pointed at the figure.

Holding her hand open, the girl tapped her chin with her thumb. She gave the page a kiss.

"Was that sign language?" Melody said.

Alice nodded.

"Great!" Melody said. "If she knows sign language, then we can communicate with her. We can find out what happened, where her home is."

"I don't think so. From what I can tell, she's been taught just a few signs. That's sometimes done with children who can hear and are capable of speech but are speech-delayed for some reason. I'm not sure we can have a real conversation."

"Oh. So what is that sign?"

The girl repeated the motion – the open hand, the tap on the chin.

"I used to know a little ASL," Jack said. "Isn't that the sign for *mom*?"

***

AJ took the path into the park behind the Westerly library, a big yellow building with a clay tile roof. When he saw Claire waiting for him by the fountain, his pace quickened. They found a bench. She leaned to kiss him, crinkling the bag in her lap.

"Lunch," she said, holding up the bag. "Montini's."

"Great. I'm so hungry."

She passed AJ a sandwich wrapped in deli paper. "I saw Sam this morning, at Melody's. They were checking the water, and the shoreline."

"What did they find?"

"He said they didn't find anything."

"I meant to see how it was going with Jack and the girl this morning, but I didn't get the time."

"You have enough to worry about."

They started in on their sandwiches.

"I didn't realize how hungry I was," AJ said. "Thanks for this."

"They are good, aren't they?" Claire let him take a few more bites, then asked, "So, can you tell me what's going on with your dad?"

"The doctor says he may need bypass surgery. He recommended a surgeon in Hartford."

"Okay." Claire put her sandwich on the bench beside her. "When would that happen?"

"Right away, I guess. As soon as they can move him and get it set up." AJ watched the fountain water rise sparkling around a stone figure.

"How's your dad taking that news?"

"He's not showing much. He just keeps saying everything will be fine. Mom is terrified."

They stared at the water splashing in the fountain.

"Mom asked if I could take time off from work."

"Of course," Claire said. "They'll have to give you time when your dad has the surgery."

"No, she means an extended period of time. She's worried about the market."

"Oh."

"The doc said after the surgery, Dad's going to be pretty limited for a good long while. No lifting, no driving. Maybe up to two months or so. He said Dad could go back to work in a few weeks, if he was careful, but Mom worries that he doesn't really understand how hard Dad works. How physical it is."

"It sounds like they will need your help. Or someone's. Maybe they could hire – "

"It's not just about having an extra hand. Apparently they've been talking about retiring for years, or at least cutting back. They were planning on asking me if I might be interested in the business. I guess this thing with Dad just moved the timetable up a little." AJ finally looked at Claire. "Honestly, I thought it would be another ten years before I had to think about this."

"They seemed so happy at work," Claire said. "I thought they'd keep going until – "

"They dropped dead behind the counter? I guess we're lucky that didn't happen."

Claire only pressed her lips together.

"When they took that cruise," AJ said, "the first real vacation they've taken in – how long? – I guess it made them realize that they should enjoy themselves while they still can."

For a while the only sounds were the rhythmic splashing of the water in the fountain and the hum of traffic going by on Route 1.

Claire slipped an arm across AJ's waist. "I'm sorry. It's a lot to think about. You can talk it out with me."

"Thanks. I will." AJ dug into his sandwich. When it was gone, he said, "I should get back."

"Can I come with you?" Claire was already wrapping up what was left of her sandwich.

"That would be great," AJ said. "My parents would love to see you. And maybe we can stop in and see how the little girl's doing."

"Melody's neighbor, Alice, was going to come to the hospital to see her. I guess she worked with hearing-impaired kids. She's probably there now."

"Good. Who knows, maybe she's got the girl talking."

9

Dave DaSilva sat at the one picnic table behind the Bay Market, his eyes half closed. Sela came out of the back door, carrying two beers. He passed one across the rough wood. "Something to perk you up."

"I need it," DaSilva said. "I slept for shit last night." He took a long sip.

"You're worried about George."

"I guess. And AJ. This place." He glanced toward the low building. "And that girl."

"George is going to be fine," Sela said. "It's all going to be fine."

"Yeah, I know."

Sela's cell phone buzzed. "Don't recognize that number," he said, checking the screen.

"Must be a telemarketer. I never answer if I don't know the number. It just encourages them."

"Yeah, but with George in the hospital – it could be... Just in case." Sela put the phone to his ear. "Hello?"

He was suddenly erect and alert, swinging his legs out from under the table. "Yes. Yes, *Mystic Afterlife.*" He made a beeline for the edge of the parking lot, as if he had urgent business in the reeds.

DaSilva kept his eyes on Sela. After a minute, the call ended. Sela immediately tapped his screen, talked into the phone again. After another minute, he came back to the table. As he sat down on the bench, Ben Shortman appeared nearby, then slid closer, silent and invisible, the definition of stealth.

"So guess who that mystery caller was," Sela said.

"I have no idea," DaSilva said.

"Guess."

"Jesus. I'm too tired to guess. Who was it?"

"The Mystery Channel."

"What?" Ben said.

"From TV? What did they want?"

"They want a pilot. Or maybe more like a demo."

"Of *Mystic Afterlife?*"

"Our spooky little cable access show, yeah. You remember Jack took our highlight reel to someone he knew at NBC?"

"Yeah, and we never heard anything."

"Right, nothing," Ben said.

"NBC wasn't interested," Sela said, "but I guess that guy passed it on to someone he knew, and that guy passed it on. It's been making the rounds. And it finally ended up with someone at The Mystery Channel, who just called me."

"Holy shit," Ben said.

"No shit," DaSilva said.

"None. Absolutely none." Sela grinned across the table. "They want to get in on the whole paranormal thing."

"So, what, we send them one of our old episodes?"

"No. Jack already showed them a few of those. She wants something new. Something with 'a little more,' she said."

"A little more," DaSilva said.

"Yeah."

"You mean, she wants us to fake some kind of supernatural encounter."

"I don't think we have to fake anything. We just need to get some better footage."

"Okay, sure," DaSilva said. "We just have to get incredibly lucky. Luckier than in all of the years we've been doing this."

"Well, yeah."

"I wish Ben were still here. He could give us something."

"Now you're talking," Ben said.

"When do they need it?" DaSilva said.

"As soon as we can get it," Sela said. "I negotiated a week."

DaSilva put his head in his hands. "Ahhhh," he moaned.

"What's your problem? This is good news. This is great news."

DaSilva looked up. "How is it great news? They need something in a week? We've been trying for literally years to find the kind of footage you're talking about. Now we have to get it in a week? What are the chances? And right now, when we're doing extra shifts here?"

"Don't freak, DaSilva. We just need one good half hour. We can get that. I already called that inn that we've been talking to. I explained that there's a rush, told them why we need it soon."

"You did?" DaSilva said.

"Yeah. They're really excited. And it turns out that this is a good time for them. They're mostly empty. In fact, that's why they need us to come back. They need more business. They're pinning all of their hopes on the whole haunted inn thing."

DaSilva seemed to think that over. "Okay. Maybe we can pull this off."

"That's the spirit!" Sela raised his bottle.

"Hey, I'm the spirit," Ben said. "If your plan doesn't work out, I definitely can be the backup plan."

DaSilva hadn't moved to join Sela's toast. Sela lowered his bottle. "Now what is it?"

"Ben should be here for this. This is his dream – taking our show big time. I feel like I'm stealing it, or something."

"You're right," Sela said. "It does suck for Ben. But this is our dream, too. It's what we were all working for. And he would want us to jump on it."

"Damn right I would," Ben said.

DaSilva nodded. "He'd be pissed if we didn't."

The two Daves touched bottles across the table.

"Something cool is going to happen," Sela said. "I just know it."

"Hey, don't jinx it." Ben made as if to rap the table, his knuckles sinking deep into the wood.

Just then Beth poked her head out of the back door. "Do either of you know anything about some eels George was going to buy?"

"No," Sela said. "I guess we could take a few if they're fresh."

"No, it's – Mike's here. He said he was supposed to pick up some eels to smoke."

Sela shook his head. "Dave, do you know anything about that?"

"No," DaSilva answered.

Sela motioned with his hand. "Send him out."

A minute later, a man came through the back door. His face was tanned and lined from countless days outdoors. "Hi, guys."

"Hey," the Daves replied, in unison.

"Sorry to hear about George," the man said. "When you see him, tell him I hope he feels better real soon."

"I will," Sela said. "He's tough. This isn't going to stop him."

"You're right."

"So what's this about eels?" Sela said. "They're not something we usually deal with."

"George called me late yesterday and asked if I could smoke up some eels for him. He said he'd let me know when I could pick 'em up today."

DaSilva put down his beer. "We had all of our deliveries. Nobody brought eels. Did George say who he was getting them from?"

"He just said a young dude came in and asked if George could use some eels. I guess the guy seemed kind of down on his luck. He had a cute kid with him, a little girl. George felt bad for them and told the guy he'd take a bucket or two."

Sela looked at DaSilva. "I didn't see any of that happen, did you?"

"Must have been after we left," DaSilva said.

"Yeah. Sorry, Mike. The eels never made it here."

"All right. Like I said, give George my best." Mike went around the building toward the front lot.

"That girl Jack brought in to the hospital – " DaSilva said.

"That could that have been her and her dad who came in here."

"Yeah. So if that was them, then – "

"Where the hell is the dad now?"

***

June Bugbee and AJ and Claire surrounded George's hospital bed, where George lay propped up, laughing over a story from Claire's recent book tour. Her phone rang.

"Sorry! I should have turned that off. I don't think they want cell phones in here." Claire reached into her purse.

"Don't worry about it," George said. "The doctor sat right there and took a call on his cell. I think we're safe."

Claire checked the screen. "I'll be right back." As she walked away down the hall, she put the phone to her ear. "Hey, Dave. What's going on?"

"Are you with AJ?" Sela said.

"Yes. We're at the hospital."

"How's George?"

"He's doing pretty well. Is everything okay there?"

"Yeah, yeah. It's just that we think he – George – may have talked to that girl's father. The girl Jack found."

"You're kidding."

Sela told her about the conversation with Mike. "We were going to call Sam Wheeler," he added, "but then we thought Sam would right away want to talk to George, and we didn't know if this was the right time, with George in the hospital..."

"Let me put AJ on." Having circled back to the room, Claire stuck her head in. She motioned for AJ to join her in the hall, then gave him the phone.

He moved away toward the nurses' station. After a brief exchange, he came back to where Claire was waiting.

"What are you going to do?" Claire said, taking the phone back.

"Ask Dad a few questions."

George frowned anxiously. "Is everything okay? Did something happen at the market?"

"The market's fine," AJ said. "Dad, did a guy come by there yesterday wanting to sell you some eels?"

"Yes. June and I were just closing up."

"Did he have anyone with him?"

"He had a little girl," June said. "She was so cute. Black hair, big brown eyes. She was maybe three or four."

AJ and Claire exchanged a glance over the bed.

"What's going on, AJ?" George said.

AJ told them about Jack's midnight rescue of a girl in a drifting boat, eels writhing at her feet.

"You think it's the same girl?" June said. "The girl in the boat and the one who was in the shop?"

"From your description, yeah," AJ said. "It sounds like the same girl."

Claire stood up. "I could take June downstairs to see the girl that Jack brought in."

"She's here?" June said, getting to her feet. "Let's go."

"Come right back up when you've seen the girl," AJ said.

"Oh, we will," June said. "I'm not leaving George any longer than

I have to."

***

As soon as Claire and June got off the elevator, they could hear a child crying. They found Jack standing in the hall, watching Alice have an intense conversation with Ms. Holt from the Department of Children and Families. Inside the hospital room, Melody sat on the bed holding the girl, who sobbed uncontrollably, her face buried in Melody's shoulder. Alice and the woman ended their conversation, and the woman hurried past, her hard soles loud on the shiny linoleum.

"Jack, is everything okay?" Claire said.

Jack turned. Seeing June, he said, "How's George?"

"Stable and in good spirits." June gestured into the room. "Is she all right?"

"Well, they just tried to run some blood tests." He shook his head. "It didn't go so well."

The girl's laments picked up momentum.

"So," Claire said, "yesterday, a man came into the market about some eels. He had a little girl with him. We'd like to see if this is that same girl."

"Okay. Hang on." Jack went into the room. After a minute, the girl fell quiet. Jack stepped back into the hall. "June, you can come in."

As June approached the bed, the girl continued to hide her face in Melody's shirt. June took a seat. "Hi, sweetheart," she said.

The girl kept her face pressed to Melody's shoulder.

"The other day, the cutest little girl came into my shop," June said. "Was it you?"

Still no reaction from the girl.

"There was a man with her. Her father, I think."

At this, the girl slowly lifted her head. She peeked out from Melody's shoulder. When she found June, her eyes were filled with tears.

"It is you," June said. "I'm so glad to see you again."

The girl stared back at her.

"It's definitely the girl from the market." June said, in a hushed voice. "No doubt."

34

The girl took a long shuddering breath. She raised her hand, fingers spread. She touched her thumb to her forehead.

"Dad," Alice said. "She's signing *dad*."

10

"I'm sorry that I had to bother your dad," Wheeler said, as he and AJ took the elevator down.

"It's fine," AJ said. "I know he felt bad he didn't have more details – a license plate, or a last name."

"Who looks at license plates besides cops?" Wheeler said, as the elevator door opened. "We got a description and a first name – Eric. It could be an alias, but it's a start."

They passed a small waiting area. Inside, Jack Westbury was talking to Ms. Holt and two doctors in white coats. He came out into the hall.

"So the girl's letting you out of her sight?" AJ said.

"Yeah. She's really taken to Alice, and Melody, too. It turns out Alice and her husband were foster parents for years, until he got sick. So Ms. Holt is making arrangements for the girl to go into emergency foster care with her."

"If Ms. Garrison hasn't done this in a while," Wheeler said, "is she set up for it? Especially for a kid that age?"

"Melody and I will help her get ready," Jack said.

"Good, good." Wheeler pulled his cell phone out of a pocket. "I'm not going to try to talk to the girl again, but I could use a picture. Since she's so comfortable with you, could you take one for me?"

"Sure." A moment later, Jack passed Wheeler's phone back to him. "How'd I do?"

The detective studied the image. "Perfect, thanks." He continued staring at the screen.

"What are you thinking?" AJ said.

"I'm thinking that your mom is right – she doesn't look like the daughter of someone with blonde hair and blue eyes."

"Well," Jack said, "with what we know about her mother – "

"That she's a character from *Peter Pan*?" Wheeler frowned. "I'm sorry. I just think we have to take that picture of Tiger Lily thing with a whole shaker of salt."

"Okay, sure," Jack said. "But it would make sense that the mom *is* Native American, and the girl takes after her."

Wheeler said nothing. He and AJ got in the elevator again, headed for the ground floor.

"What are you thinking?" AJ said. "It's not just that the mom isn't Tiger Lily."

Wheeler checked the lights above the elevator door. "What if this Eric isn't the girl's father? How does that change things? I mean, there's the usual explanations – she's adopted, or he's a stepdad. But what if…" He hesitated. "We've been thinking that the girl ended up alone in a boat because something happened to the adult who was with her. He went overboard. Or – "

"He was taken."

"Right. Well, what if, to start it all, the girl was taken? Whoever was with her in the boat had snatched her?"

The silver doors slid open. The two men went into the lobby, crossed it in silence, and exited through the big glass doors. AJ stopped there. "If she knows sign language, then she's been mute for awhile."

"Yeah," Wheeler said. "Of course, the experts still can't tell us if the cause of her issue is trauma. All they can say is that they haven't found anything physically wrong with her."

A slight breeze made the flag in the little landscaped lawn flap against itself.

"I wish I could help, Sam."

"There is one thing," Wheeler said. "I'm sure you haven't had a chance yet, but if you could you take a look around at Jack's place, by the shore… I mean, if someone died there, out on the water, wouldn't their ghost still be around?"

"I think so. Probably. Honestly, I don't know a lot more than you do about how this stuff works. But I should be able to get over there, once my dad is settled in Hartford." AJ pushed his hair back from his forehead. "I have to talk to the chief about my schedule."

"I wish we didn't have to work around him," Wheeler said. "It was a lot easier with Roland." He flashed a pained smile. "Can you picture Gaines's face if you told him you were working the spirit world for information?"

"No, actually, I can't."

"Hey, I have an idea. Arrange a haunting. If only Ben was still around..."

"Yeah, if only."

"I'll talk to you later." Wheeler continued on toward his car.

When AJ went back inside, he found Claire hurrying across the lobby.

"I was looking for you," she said.

"Is everything okay?"

"Fine, yeah. They're ready to move your dad."

"When they said an hour, I figured it would be more like three."

"They're right on schedule. Should I drive there, too?"

"You don't have to. I'm not going to stay long. I want to try to get Mom home early. Then I have to go to the station and talk to the chief about my hours."

"Make sure you ask for enough time off, okay?"

AJ didn't answer.

"I wish Roland were still the chief."

"Don't we all," AJ said. "Alice is going to have the girl," he added. "At least for a while."

"Yeah, Melody told me. That's good. She'll be safe there."

"As safe as she is anywhere."

11

George Bugbee, almost as soon as he was in his new bed in Hartford Hospital, started making noises about being tired.

"Are you just trying to get rid of me?" AJ said.

"I'll see you when you come back for your mother," George said. When he closed his eyes, then, it was deliberate and unconvincing, but he did look tired, washed out, his hair skewed, his bulk almost lost in the loose and faded hospital gown.

"See you soon, Dad." AJ tapped the stiff bed cover.

It was an hour's drive back to Stonington – south on 9, then east on 95, across the arched bridge over the Thames River. AJ continued past the exits for Mystic and took the one for the Stonington Borough – the quickest way to the precinct.

To get to Chief Gaines's office, AJ had to run a gauntlet of well wishes and concerned looks. When he finally stood at the open door, he took a deep breath, then knocked on the jamb. "Chief? Can I talk to you?"

"Come in."

Chief Gaines, who could still measure his tenure in weeks, sat at the desk tapping on a laptop keyboard. Everything about him was precise – his collar, his crew cut, the movement of his fingers.

"Sorry about the last-minute schedule change today," AJ said.

The chief looked up from his computer but left the lid raised. "Your father sure picked a bad time to have a heart attack. This is quite a problem we have on our hands."

"The girl."

"Yes. And one lost little girl is not going to be the end of it, I guarantee you. You'll need time off. That's what you want to talk to me about, right?"

"I'll need the next two days for sure. They're evaluating test results and coming up with a plan."

"Don't you have four or five brothers who could be dealing with your dad?"

"No, that's Manzella. I don't have any brothers or sisters. It's just me."

The chief scowled, as if he were annoyed by his mistake. "We're going to be awfully thin. And we can't afford to have this blow up in our faces, after last summer's horror – the murder of a teenage girl, a woman burned alive. I'm not sorry that I missed all of that. Of course, I inherited it, anyway, because all of that makes this new horror even worse, even more urgent, than it would otherwise be. The town won't tolerate a failure. These good people are not used to violence, and it's our job to make sure that they never get used to it."

The stern expression on AJ's face said it all – the chief was right.

"You've always had things your way, haven't you?" Gaines said. "Close family friend of the chief's. Make your own hours. Special treatment in terms of assignments – almost like you were a detective rather than just a beat cop."

"Chief? I'm not sure I – "

Gaines held up a hand. "I think I have a pretty good picture of how things worked before I got here. Let me be clear that there won't be any special treatment now. That kind of thing can wreck the morale of a force." He let out a heavy, impatient sigh. "All right. I'll see that your next two days are covered. But if you find out that you need more time, tell me ASAP."

"I know Romano is looking to pick up more hours."

"That will be up to me."

"Right." AJ turned to go. "Thanks."

"Hope this is all over quickly."

From the doorway, AJ squinted at the chief, as if trying to decide what to make of those words. All the way through the station and back into the sunlight, he seemed to still be thinking about it.

***

"Hey, you're home early," Claire said. She was on the couch in the living room, a sheaf of papers in her lap. "How are you doing?"

"Okay."

"Can I make you a sandwich or something?"

"I'll get it. Want to keep me company?"

They talked in the kitchen as AJ put his meal together.

"I have to go back over to Hartford in a bit and get Mom."

"That's a lot of back and forth."

"Yeah. I wanted to stay over there, but I had to talk to Chief Gaines, and I wanted to do that face-to-face."

"How did that go?"

"He said Dad picked a bad day to have a heart attack."

"You're kidding."

"He never even asked how Dad was doing."

"How long does he expect to get away with treating people like that?"

"I guess it's worked for him so far. It got him that job."

Claire filled a glass from the faucet. "He got the job because there was a panic over what happened over the summer."

"Yeah. People wanted a hard-ass."

"Exactly. But it's going to catch up with him."

"He also said no more special treatment."

"What does that mean?"

"He's not wrong. Roland did treat me a little differently, because he knew about my...ability."

Claire opened the door to the back porch and AJ went through carrying his plate and the glass.

"How'd you and Melody and Alice make out?" he said. "Is Alice going to be ready for the girl?"

"Alice is something. She generated a complete list of things to buy and do in about five minutes."

"That was probably a good education for Melody."

"I could see her mentally taking notes," Claire said. "I took a few notes myself."

AJ's and Claire's eyes met across the table. They both seemed to be about to say something, but neither did.

AJ ate for a while in silence. Claire watched him.

"Before I head back to Hartford," he said. "I thought I'd have a look around at Jack's."

"For a ghost. The father's ghost."

"Yeah, if he was the father."

"Right, or stepfather."

AJ only glanced across the table.

"Wait," Claire said, "you think that man the girl was with… Oh, God. You think maybe she wasn't his? He could have abducted her?"

AJ held up a hand. "Don't repeat that, but Wheeler raised it as a possibility. It might explain a few things, like why she's not talking."

"It could also explain why he took her eeling. He didn't want to let her out of his sight."

"Some folks wouldn't think having her out in the boat was so unusual. My dad took me eeling when I was about seven or eight. Right of passage, I guess. I can still picture those things squirming around on the bottom of the boat."

"There's a big difference between an eight year-old and a three year-old."

"True. But if whoever took that girl out in the boat had grown up eeling it might not have seemed odd to them."

"I keep thinking about her being out there, alone. It makes no sense unless the guy fell overboard and drowned. That could happen, right? A fisherman drowning?"

"Sure, though most people who fish for money can swim at least well enough to get back to their boat."

"Maybe he was drunk."

"Maybe."

Claire's phone chimed. She tapped the glass. "Melody sent me a photo. The girl is in her new bed at Alice's and I guess she's refusing to get out even for food or TV."

"She's been through a lot. The bed makes her feel safe."

"That poor girl." After tapping out a reply, Claire said, "They're leaving Alice's for home in a few minutes. Do you want me to ask if you can come over?"

"Sure. I wouldn't stay long. If the ghost is there, I'll see him pretty quick."

Claire tapped on the phone again. A few seconds later, she said, "Melody says come anytime. You can take their boat."

"Tell her I'll be there soon." AJ finished off his sandwich.

"You sure you don't need a little time to rest first?"

"You know what they say…"

"'You'll rest when you're dead.'"

"We both know that's not always true," AJ said. "I was thinking 'no rest for the wicked.'"

"Oh." Claire typed the message, then put the phone down. She touched his hand. "If you're not too tired when you get home, maybe you can show me just how wicked you can be."

***

As Jack led AJ down the grassy slope, the sun was low behind them, and the cove was in shadow.

"Glad to hear the girl is settling in," AJ said.

"So are we." A smile softened Jack's square face.

They went the length of the weathered dock. Jack bent as if to step into the boat that was tied up there, but AJ stopped him.

"It might be better if I went alone."

"Are you sure?"

"Yeah. Besides, you look like you could use some rest."

"That's an understatement." Jack studied AJ for a second. "Not like you don't have some sleep to catch up on, too. How do you keep going?"

AJ shrugged.

Jack clapped him on the back.

AJ climbed into the boat, then Jack gave him a quick explanation of the electric motor. Jack freed the line. Soon AJ was slipping across the water. When he was a hundred yards out, he made a slow pass back and forth, looking across the cove at the boats anchored with their sails furled, then toward the shore again, at Jack's dock and lawn and the woods that surrounded them. The motor barely made a whisper. Everything else was still.

"Eric," AJ said, softly. "Are you here? Eric? Talk to me. I want to help you. The girl is safe. She'll be fine. But we need to know – what happened out here?"

There was no answer.

After making a few more passes, moving steadily further out, AJ swung east, around Wamphassuc Point. He studied the narrow beach. The houses came quicker now, one lush lawn meeting the next, docks like sparse quills. When he had passed a fifth dock, he steered the boat in a big sweeping one-eighty. As he went back around the point, he cut the motor. His eyes strained to pick out something – some movement, some color, that glow that he knew not only from Ben, but from others that he'd encountered at crime scenes and in the most ordinary places, going back as far as he could remember. But there was only the flat, dark water, the waves slapping against the hull. He was alone.

He started the motor up again and made for the dock. Melody and Jack were waiting by the house. As AJ climbed toward them, Melody called out, "Did you see anything?"

"No. Nothing."

Melody put an arm around Jack's waist. "I'm sorry, I guess."

AJ came up onto the deck. "I don't think you're going to have a ghost here. I wouldn't worry."

Melody squeezed Jack a little tighter. "It's not ghosts that I'm worried about."

12

Two big men, two versions of the same heavy face, stared at each other across the gleaming restaurant table, lips clamped shut. Two men named Daniel Frost. Father and son.

"Why are we here, Dad?" the younger man said. "How's this going to help us find Eric? What, he's going to just wander through the door?" When there was no response, he continued, after a quick scan of the room. "This isn't exactly his kind of establishment. Even if he didn't have a little girl with him."

All around them, couples and families dressed in crisp but casual clothes talked easily, raised their cocktails, owned the place.

"We're here because I want a steak," the father said. "Anyway, I wouldn't know where Eric would eat, never having been out to dinner with the man."

"Well, but you know this would be a little out of his price range. He never could hold down a job."

"Maybe you have too low an opinion of him. He can't be all bad. He took care of Fern for the last three years. And your sister, too."

"Yeah, I'm sure that was no picnic."

"Don't talk about her like that. You have to remember..." The older Daniel's voice trailed off. He looked down at his glass.

"Sorry, Dad. I know. I don't think Eric was a bad guy. More like one of those guys who can't seem to catch a break. And he always picked the wrong people." When his father's eyes narrowed, he added, "I'm not talking about Rose."

The waitress took their order. The second she had left the table, young Daniel turned toward his father again. "So what are we going to do? We've walked all over this town. I've driven you down every tiny street in Stonington. We've checked most of the marinas and docks. You still think we're going to find them? Is this some kind of Indian thing?"

There were long-established bags under the father's brown eyes, but there was also something in his stare, now, something in the longish cut of his graying hair, and in the careful reserve of his posture, that conveyed that he was tired but relentless. "Okay, Daniel Junior," he said. "Tomorrow, we'll do it your way. We'll go back around and show people the picture. See if anyone's seen them."

"Good."

"We can try the marinas in the morning. Maybe hit some of those lunch spots."

"Actually, I already went to a couple of those places."

"When did you do that?"

"The day we got here. You crashed. I didn't want to just hang out at the motel."

"So you showed that picture around. When I specifically told you not to."

"You said not to show it around in bars. I went to restaurants. And an ice cream stand. Places where you might take a little girl."

The father seemed to be considering that. "I guess you had no luck."

"No."

Salads came, with little stoppered bottles of dressing. The men ate quietly.

"That was a good thought about the ice cream," Daniel said. "Kids love ice cream. You and your sister sure did."

Daniel Junior put his fork down, leaving one cherry tomato in the bowl. "I'm glad you've decided to use the picture. What about the other thing?"

The father played dumb.

"C'mon, Dad. We can't do this on our own. We need to contact the police. They could put out some kind of alert."

"No."

"Dad, Eric mailed you a hundred-thousand dollars. In cash."

"Yes." Daniel raised a finger in front of him. "And the last postmark is why we're here."

"The point is, you know he's involved in something. And as long as you have the money, you're involved, too."

"Two minutes ago, you said that he's not a bad guy."

"I know. But how did he come into that kind of money?"

"He must have been getting paid under the table somewhere."

"Yeah? What would he have been doing that paid like that?"

"Construction. Or driving a truck."

"Yeah, that's it. He was driving a truck."

The waitress replaced the salad bowls with the entrees – a burger and a steak.

The men ate quickly, heads down. Their plates were mostly empty before either spoke again.

"I just think we could get this resolved much faster if we had help," Daniel Junior said. "Official, law enforcement help."

The father's hand hit the table, making the dishes jump. "No police." He glared at his son. "Tomorrow we take the picture around."

Daniel Junior pushed his plate aside. "All right, Dad. Whatever you say."

13

The floodlight on Claire's garage showed two vehicles – Sam Wheeler's sedan and Roland Brown's SUV. AJ approached them with a last burst of speed, the tires digging into the gravel.

Buck met him in the front hall. Together, they went through the house to the kitchen. The greyhound immediately plopped down under the table.

"Hi," Claire said, looking up from the glass of wine she was pouring.

"What's going on?" AJ said.

"Roland and Sam said they needed a private place to talk to you." Claire ran her fingers down AJ's arm.

"How long have they been here?"

"Maybe twenty minutes?" Claire gave him a peck on the lips. "How's your dad? Has he met with anyone on the cardiac team yet?"

"Not until tomorrow. He's doing well. Mom's really getting worn down, though."

Claire studied AJ's face. "What about you? Do you want to talk to these guys? I could send them home."

"AJ?" It was Roland, from the porch.

Claire leaned in again. She touched his hair as they kissed. "Talk to you later," she said.

After pouring himself a half glass of wine, AJ went out.

The screened-in porch seemed small, with darkness and a chill pressing in from three sides. Wheeler and Roland sat at the table, a long-neck bottle in front of each of them. Ben hovered to the side.

AJ filled the others in on his dad. Then there was a long silence. He rubbed the stubble on his chin. "So, how's everything else?"

"The Daves handled things well at the market today," Roland said.

"Yeah, I talked to Sela. Less fighting today, I guess."

Roland nodded. "Sela bit his tongue a few times, so yeah, less fighting."

Ben moved behind Roland into AJ's line of sight. "Don't sell DaSilva short. He might have some good ideas about the market."

AJ only raised his eyebrows.

"I hope you don't mind us showing up here," Wheeler said. "We couldn't use my house – it's my wife's turn to host the book club."

"Yeah, and Amelda doesn't want me anywhere near police work, so my place was out, too." Roland turned the bottle in front of him. "She thinks I'm at a bar with friends."

"He's actually using a bar as a cover story," Ben said.

"This town's too small for us to discuss the case at an actual bar," Wheeler said.

"Especially if the discussion includes you-know-what," Ben said.

AJ raised his glass. "Here's to small towns. Sam, tell me what's going on."

"I needed Roland's help," Wheeler said. "With a child involved, I wanted to make sure that I was thinking of everything, and doing everything the right way."

"And he wanted my advice on how to deal with Chief Gaines," Roland added.

"I can relate to that." AJ looked across the table at his former boss. "Anyone who didn't appreciate you before, Roland, definitely does now."

"Who didn't appreciate me?" Roland's smile faded quickly. "I feel bad about leaving you guys to – "

"Don't," Wheeler said. "You did what you needed to do."

There was another pause.

"AJ," Roland said, "I know you need some downtime, and we're getting in the way of that."

"It's okay. I'd like to get caught up on this case."

"We have the boat," Wheeler said. "A guy turned it over to us a little while ago. I think his first instinct was 'Finders, Keepers,' but then he thought better of it. We traced the registration number, and located the owner. He's been away, didn't even know the boat was missing."

"Are you going to get anything from the boat itself?"

"I doubt it. The guy who found the boat was pretty grossed out by the eels. After he got rid of them, he gave the boat a really thorough cleaning."

"I don't blame him." Ben shuddered.

"Any other leads?" AJ said.

"Well, with the girl's reaction to seeing Tiger Lilly in the book, we wondered if her mom might sometimes wear native dress. Maybe at public events."

"That's a good idea."

"Seemed like it. I visited both the Pequot and Mohegan reservations."

"And?"

"Dead end," Wheeler said.

"Did you try the Pequot Museum? They do that kind of thing."

"Didn't get to it today. I asked Gaines for Nardi's help, but apparently he can't spare him."

"Why not?" AJ said.

"Gaines has him doing online research for a missing child matching ours."

"Okay, that's good. But I thought he hired the research specialist, Joan, for exactly that kind of work."

"So did I," Wheeler said. "But she's compiling and organizing stuff in his office."

"So she's not so much the department's research specialist as his personal research specialist. "

"Right," Wheeler said. "She told me she'd try to take over for Nardi, free him up."

Roland groaned softly.

"Anyway," Wheeler said. "Romano hit the marinas but had no luck – nobody remembers seeing a man with a young girl that fit the description. Manzella did canvas the Wamphassuc Point houses earlier in the day, before you were out there, to see if anyone had seen or heard anything the night before. A lot of the residents weren't home."

"Will you recanvas?"

"Sure. At least once."

"We should check if any of those houses are empty," Roland said.

"Even for a little while – if the owners are away. The post office can tell us if they're holding mail for anyone."

Ben made a face. "What's he talking about?"

AJ kept his eyes straight ahead. "You're thinking our guy Eric and the girl might have been staying in an empty house."

"Yeah. I don't think they're local," Roland said. "In fact, I think they're traveling. Eric comes into the market asking about selling eels, then steals a boat to get the eels… He's improvising. Like you might do if you were passing through, and just trying to make gas money to get to the next town."

"All right," Wheeler said. "So we should also check our lower-priced motels."

"If we have any of those," AJ said.

"We checked the KOA," Wheeler said. "Tomorrow *The Day* is running a story. We'll see what that does for us."

The men fell quiet. Beyond the screen walls the insect sounds were steady and loud.

"So what the hell happened to Eric?" AJ said.

Wheeler held up his bottle. "I know what the simple answer is."

"He'd been drinking," AJ said, "and he just fell overboard."

"Wouldn't be the first time," Wheeler said. "A guy stands up in a boat to pee, ends up in the water."

"It's almost poetic," Ben said. "A fisherman dying with his rod in his hand."

"Except that we didn't find any bottles or cans in the boat," Wheeler said. "No body in the water, either." He took a long pull of his beer.

"My gut tells me someone else was involved," Roland said.

Ben drew an arc in the air in front of him. "If that gut talked to me, I'd listen."

"Could be," Wheeler said. "We don't even know if Eric's a victim or a perpetrator."

The greyhound came out from the kitchen, padded silently over to Ben, paused there for Ben to deliver some intangible strokes, then continued on to the table. He rested his head on AJ's knee.

"Good old Buck," Ben said. "He's the only one who treats me just the same as he always did."

Roland cleared his throat. "I know you don't like talking about this stuff, and I know maybe I pushed you too hard in that direction when you were working for me. God knows, Gaines won't. I'm glad for that, at least."

"Jesus Christ, Roland, come out with it," Ben said.

Roland continued. "Sam says you didn't see a ghost at Jack Westbury's place. Does that mean…"

"I don't know if that means anything," AJ said. "It does seem like if someone meets a violent end, they stick around."

"So, since you didn't see his ghost…" Wheeler watched AJ intently. "Maybe he's still alive."

"Or maybe," Roland said, "he went straight to hell."

***

"We won't have many more nights out here," Claire said. She sat next to AJ on the porch, facing the woods. On the table front of them, a candle burned in a glass bowl.

"Probably not." AJ put his hand on hers.

She turned her hand and squeezed. "You're cold."

"Yeah, it's getting chilly out here. Time to go inside." He didn't budge.

"Your dad will get through tomorrow fine," Claire said after a while. "And then he'll be better. We're moving in a good direction."

"I know." AJ made a conscious smile. "I should get to bed. Mom's going to want to be at the hospital early."

"Right."

They brought the bottles and empty glasses into the kitchen.

"I'll clean up," Claire said. "See you in a bit."

They kissed. AJ went upstairs.

When Claire was done at the sink, she went on into the sitting room.

Ben waited by the fireplace. "Hey, Claire. I tried to give you and AJ some privacy. Sounds like AJ went to bed. He's going to have an early morning."

Claire picked up a stray pair of shoes from in front of the chair.

"You know, AJ actually asked me if the reason I came back was to, ah, escort his dad to the beyond or whatever. I didn't really know how to take that."

Claire tested the locks on the doors at either side of the room.

"I actually don't know why I came back. Suddenly, I just was back here again. I don't know how long I'm staying, or what happens next. I don't really even remember where I was, while I was gone. It's pretty weird. That's why AJ and I decided not to tell anyone about me for now. DaSilva took everything so hard, before, and... It just seemed like we should wait. There were too many questions. Right? Does that make sense?"

Claire went to the front hall. She set the shoes down there, neatly perpendicular to the wall.

"Actually, I've changed my mind on that. It would be a lot easier for me if everyone knew." Ben followed Claire into the living room. "I hope you don't mind me hanging around here for a while," he said. "It just feels like home, you know?" He stopped by a shelf of DVDs. "I wish I could get you to pop one of these in," he said. "It's a long night when you don't sleep. Maybe if I..." Ben reached for the shelf. He swiped at a plastic case, his finger sliding through the corner. Finally the case trembled, then dropped to the floor.

Claire let out a breath. She went to the spot. "That's weird."

"*The Devil Wears Prada?*" Ben frowned over Claire's shoulder as she picked up the DVD. "I should have read the label first."

Claire slid the case into the open slot on the shelf. She headed for the stairs.

"Wait!" Ben reached for the shelf again. "I'll find something else."

Claire had already disappeared around the turn in the stairs when a half-dozen cases tumbled to the floor. She came back down quickly. "What the hell?"

"Sorry," Ben said. "I'm still getting the hang of this."

Claire pushed at the shelf with one hand, testing. She looked down at the DVDs. "Knock once for Siskel, twice for Ebert," she said.

"Very funny." Ben leaned close. "Do you know it's me? You do, don't you?" He watched Claire gather up the movies. "That's a good one. Really, any one of those. I don't even care."

Claire turned in place, checking the room.

"I'm right here," Ben said.

Instead of putting the DVDs back on the shelf, Claire stacked them on the coffee table. One more time, she looked around the room.

Ben got in front of her gaze. "Why don't you say something to AJ about your suspicions?"

For a long moment Claire stared through him. Then she went back into the hall, climbed the stairs, went around the corner, and disappeared.

14

Daniel watched the street come down out of the morning sky. It dropped toward him, growing more opaque as the change in the angle closed the holes in the grid. The hum of the engine that controlled the drawbridge shifted to a deeper pitch. Within a minute, parallel had swapped places with perpendicular. Where there had been open space over the river, there were now two lanes and sidewalks, handrails and lampposts. The gate lifted.

Daniel stopped partway across. The massive counterweights hung over his head. Cars rattled the grate. A sailboat motored out toward open water and the sunrise.

He continued on into downtown Mystic. The shops were still locked and dark. The street was mostly empty. A little further ahead, a young woman stepped out of a door. After unfolding a sandwich board listing breakfast specials, she disappeared inside again.

Daniel walked up to the sign, stood over it for a second, then followed the woman into the Honey B Dairy. As soon as he was seated at a small table facing the window, a waitress came over to him.

"Hi!" she said, holding up a silver carafe. "Coffee?"

"Please." He watched her fill his cup. "I'm ready if you're ready," he said. "To order, I mean."

"Absolutely." She set the pot down. "What would you like?"

"I'll have a special that I saw on the board outside. The number one with bacon."

"Okay. Can I bring you the paper?"

"Sure. Might as well pretend to be interested in what's going on in the world."

"Well, you'll find out what's going on around here, anyway." She headed for the kitchen.

Daniel sipped his coffee and stared out at the street. The waitress came back with a folded copy of the New London paper, *The Day*. He smiled at her but then faced the street again. He sipped the hot drink. After a while, as if whatever departing boat he'd been watching in his mind had finally disappeared over the horizon, he put his mug down and opened the paper. He read the headline. *Young Girl Found in Boat with Eels*.

He donned a pair of half glasses. Bending toward the page, he read, then reread.

"Here you go." The waitress was back with his breakfast.

Daniel didn't look up.

She set the plate down. "More coffee?"

He kept reading.

She refilled his mug. "Pretty good acting job."

He didn't respond.

"Pretending to be interested in what's going on in the world," she said.

Still, he didn't answer.

"Are you all right?"

"Sure, coffee," he said.

Shaking her head, she left the table.

Daniel finished the story, then gazed out the window again. His face was different now – tight, like he was pushing hard against some heavy thought. Across the room, a woman shouted a hello to the waitress. Startled, seeming to notice his plate for the first time, Daniel moved his meal in front of him and began to eat.

The waitress came back with a pot of coffee in each hand. She topped off his mug, then looked down at the paper. "That's a strange story, isn't it?"

"Yes. Yes, it is."

"Poor kid, abandoned in the middle of the night, and with a bunch of eels. That will scar you for life. Can you believe people eat those things? They give me the creeps."

Daniel said nothing.

"That guy that found her?" the waitress said.

"Jack Westbury." Daniel pointed at the page.

"Yeah. He's loaded. For years everybody thought he got away with murder – and I mean that literally. But I guess he didn't really do it. Now he lives in a big house right on the water, right by where she was. That's why he was the first one to her, I guess."

"It doesn't say what happened to the girl," Daniel said. "I guess she'd be with the police?"

"I guess. They wouldn't just let Westbury keep her. He's about to become a dad, anyway – his girlfriend's pregnant. That's a story in itself. She's half his age. Used to work here. She still comes in once in a while, with him."

Daniel watched the waitress head toward the kitchen. After taking a few more bites of his egg, he called his son. "You need to get up," he said, turning toward the wall. "I found them. But we have a problem."

***

Daniel waited on a bench by the river. When he wasn't checking the pedestrians coming across the bridge, he studied the measured movement of the boats on the water and the crisscrossing of the gulls overhead. Cars hummed on the grate, their brake lights glowing. The bridge rose. When it fell again, it revealed Daniel Junior crossing from the other side.

"What's going on?" Daniel Junior said, when he was close. "You said you found Fern?"

Daniel held out the newspaper, which was folded to show the story about the girl in the boat.

Daniel Junior skimmed to the bottom of the page. "Jesus, Dad. What the hell happened? Where did Eric end up?"

"I don't know."

"Well, at least we won't have to fight about one thing anymore. The police are already involved. We'll go talk to them, tell them what we know. We can start whatever the process is – the DNA test or whatever – to get Fern."

"It's not that simple."

"Why? Because of the money that you got from Eric?" Daniel Junior's voice was suddenly sharp. "Jesus, Dad. Just hand it over."

"I'm not talking about the money."

"What is it, then?"

His father didn't answer. Above them, two seagulls squawked as they competed for position on the bridge.

"Dad?" Daniel Junior scowled, but even then his skin stayed smooth, with no hint of the lines that were fixed on his father's face.

The older man got to his feet. "Let's take a walk."

They headed away from the bridge. The father began to speak. As they reached the inn that butted up against the boardwalk, he was still talking. He went on talking, interrupted by questions from his son, as they passed the condos, came to the end of the walk, and turned around.

By the time they were back at their starting point, the frustration that had been rising in Daniel Junior seemed to have gone. He looked calm and resolute. He took his phone from his pocket. He began tapping the screen.

"What are you doing?" Daniel said.

"Getting help."

"I said no police."

"Jesus Christ, Dad, I got that. We need a different kind of help right now. I think I know where we can get it."

15

AJ stopped the jagged pulse of the alarm clock. He rolled toward Claire's side of the bed. Empty. So was Buck's round cushion. AJ sat up. He swung his legs over the side. "Claire?"

Barefoot, in boxers and a T-shirt, he padded down the cool hallway. At the top of the stairs, he paused to take a deep breath. Then, as if a question had been answered, he went down, across the landing, through the hall, past the blueprint that hung there, into the kitchen.

Claire was peering into the oven, surrounded by a warm, sweet scent.

"You're up early," AJ said.

Claire jumped. "I didn't hear you come down."

Near the door to the porch, Ben loitered, the dog at his feet. He waved.

"Sure smells good."

"Maybe it's my imagination," Ben said, "but I think I can smell it, too."

Claire closed the oven door. "I'm making low fat banana applesauce muffins for your mom and dad. When are you leaving?"

"About forty-five minutes."

"These should be ready." She leaned back against the counter. "I don't know what's up with Buck. He's been lying in that corner the whole time I've been down here."

"Guess he likes watching you bake."

With a shrug, Ben slid back through the porch door. Buck stood, then pressed his nose against the jamb.

Claire pointed with an oven mitt. "See, he's acting a little weird."

"Maybe you hurt his feelings," AJ said.

"Yeah? I'll give him a muffin to patch things up. Though I know you don't like him eating people food."

"Special circumstances."

They both stood looking at the dog.

"I hope the muffins are okay," Claire said. "I wanted to do something. I want your parents to know that I'm thinking about them."

"They get that. They really like you, you know."

"Do they?" Claire's smile sharpened her chin. "I'll put the recipe in the container so June can see that the muffins are healthy."

"They'll both appreciate it." He gave her a quick kiss. "I need to get ready."

"Okay." Claire checked the timer on the stove. "My plan is to have these all packed when you're ready to walk out the door."

"That would be great."

AJ was upstairs when Claire's phone buzzed on the counter. She picked it up. "Hello? Oh, hi. No, I was up."

Ben slid close to Claire, his head near hers. For an instant, parts of their upper bodies occupied the same space. Claire swiped at her shoulder as if to brush off a bug.

"Oops," Ben said, retreating. "Sorry. Just trying to hear how George is doing. I guess that's not AJ's mom."

"England?" Claire said. "What do you mean? Oh. I don't know. I mean, yes, of course! But now's such a bad time. AJ's dad had a heart attack. He'll probably need bypass surgery. We're finding that out today, as a matter of fact. Could we put things off just a week?" She raked her hair with her fingers. "I know it's a huge opportunity."

Ben floated up behind her. "AJ wouldn't want you to miss a good opportunity."

"Okay, yes," Claire said. "I'll call you tomorrow. Yes. Okay. Thanks." She closed her eyes for a second. "Okay. I know. Bye." As she lowered the phone, it chimed. She checked the screen, which was black. "Shit. Damn battery." She plugged her phone into a cord and set it on the counter.

Ben drifted backward across the room. "I'm sure it's me draining the battery. I don't have any control over that. Other than staying away, I guess. But, you know... I don't know where else to go. I did try hanging out with Melody, but I felt like a stalker, and when Jack's around – I don't really need to see the two lovebirds. Anyway, what's in England?"

The timer sounded, and Claire slid the muffins out of the oven.

AJ came back downstairs, his hair damp and finger-combed. He swerved into the living room, where he gathered a couple of magazines from the coffee table. In the kitchen, he found Claire biting into half a muffin, while Buck gobbled the other half from the floor.

"These are really good," Claire said, through a mouthful.

"Can I try?"

She held a chunk toward him. "Do you want eggs or something?"

"I'll have a muffin at the hospital. They are delicious." AJ watched Claire shift the muffins one by one into a plastic container.

"Keep the lid off until you're there," she said, "so they can cool a little more, okay?"

Ben met them at the front door. "I'm not going to follow you, so... Good luck with everything, AJ. I'd say give your parents my love, but you'd better not."

Nodding, AJ followed Claire outside and across the damp lawn. "You sure you're okay driving the Jeep today?" he said.

"It'll be fun." Claire set the muffins on the passenger seat. "I might give it back to you covered in mud."

"Perfect."

As AJ drove away down the lane, Claire went back inside. When she reached the kitchen, Ben was bending over the batter bowl, sniffing. Buck observed him from the middle of the floor.

"I really think I can smell it," Ben said.

Claire laughed. "What are you looking at, Buck? You want to lick the bowl?" She copied his gaze, then moved toward the counter, until her face was just inches from Ben's.

He stared back at her. "Well, this is awkward."

Claire addressed the dog again. "You really are a little weird today, boy."

"There is something weird here," Ben said. "But it isn't the dog."

Claire poked around in the cupboards, then tried the fridge, and the freezer. "I should have kept some of those muffins," she said.

"Are you a nervous eater?" Ben said. "I saw ice cream. Why don't you have some of that?"

Claire opened the freezer again. "It's time for dessert somewhere."

"Huh." Ben backed away as Claire retrieved a spoon and a bowl. "You should text Melody, see if she's up. If she is, call her, and tell her what the whole England thing was about. I can eavesdrop."

Standing at the counter, Claire typed something into her phone.

Ben watched over her shoulder. "Well, call me Mr. Subliminal," he said.

16

Melody and Jack walked up the private road in the morning sun. She carried a basket that was covered with blue checked cloth. They moved in step, shoulders touching now and then, passing in and out of shadow, through maples that were tinged with red. After a few minutes, they came to Alice's clapboard-sided cottage.

A door swung open. Alice squinted out at them. "Good morning!"

A small, uncertain face appeared at her knees. The girl peeked, then retreated.

"Hello!" Jack said. "I'm glad to see you." He stepped closer. In an instant, like a squirrel leaping from one branch to another, she was at his side, her arms around his legs. Laughing, he scooped her up. She clung to him, her face against his neck.

Melody peeled back the cloth that covered the basket. "Can you smell anything?"

The girl took a long, whistling sniff. Her eyes widened.

"You know what I have in there, don't you?" Melody said.

"Well, I don't," Alice said. "What are you hiding?"

"Homemade peanut butter muffins. I talked to Claire this morning and she'd baked muffins. It inspired me."

"You had better bring those right inside," Alice said.

In the kitchen Jack put the girl down. She stayed close to him, one hand on his leg. Her eyes were fixed on the basket.

"That child is obsessed with peanut butter," Alice said. "I think she'd eat it at every meal if I let her."

"We have that in common," Melody said. "Since I've been pregnant, I can't get enough of the stuff."

"The poor girl must have done the sign for peanut butter a hundred times at the hospital, but they were too afraid of allergies to give her any. I was convinced that if she knew the sign, she was used to eating it and I was right." Alice pulled a chair that had been fitted with a plastic booster away from the table. "Why don't you get up, honey?"

Cautiously, the girl left Jack's side and climbed onto the seat.

"I made scrambled eggs," Alice said. "And there's coffee. It's decaf, so you can have some, too, Melody."

"Great. I will." Melody put the muffin basket on the counter, then set her orchid-colored bag next to it.

"I'm sorry the table isn't ready," Alice said. "I was getting so much help this morning that I didn't get everything done. And then the speech therapist was here. She's agreed to make house calls for a while, so that everyone is in a place that feels safe."

"Any progress?" Melody said.

"Hard to say. She's sticking with signs, but she's quite engaged with her surroundings. I think there's a chance that she'll be one of those kids who doesn't say a word until one day she lets fly with a string of complete sentences."

"That happens?"

"It's not common, but yes."

Jack laid out the utensils while Melody and Alice prepared the plates. They worked easily together, despite the close quarters. In just a few minutes, they were sitting down to eggs and coffee, the muffins uncovered in the middle of the table, sharing their sweet smell.

Melody slid the basket toward the girl. "Would you like to try a muffin?"

The girl plucked one from the pile.

"They smell yummy, don't they?"

The girl pressed the muffin to her nose.

The basket made it around the table. The meal began in earnest.

"Have you seen today's paper, Alice?" Melody said. "There's an article on the front page that you'll want to read."

"I bet there is. I looked online before I went to bed – there wasn't anything yet. I meant to try again this morning but didn't get a chance. Somebody's been keeping me very busy." Alice bent toward the girl.

The food disappeared rapidly from their plates. When they were finished, Alice said, "Sweetie, would you like to watch a show?"

The girl followed Alice into the living area. A few minutes later, as a British voice described the antics of a polar bear cub, Alice took her seat again. "She just fine now with staying in the living room while I'm in the kitchen."

"So you think she'll be able to do the visit we talked about?"

"I'm hopeful." Alice glanced toward the other room. "Something else happened. I was doing my usual, calling her honey, and sweetie pie, pumpkin, mint julep – "

"Mint julep?" Jack said. "Where did that come from?"

"My father used to put on a Southern accent and call me that. So anyway, she came up to me, pointed to herself, and made the sign for F."

"Just F?" Melody said.

"That's all she seemed to have. Maybe it's all she remembers, or all that she learned."

"So you think her name begins with F?"

"Yes," Alice said. "I tried Florence, Fiona, Fredericka. Then I just went blank."

"Fran," Jack said. "Felicity."

"Wait." Melody went to the bag that she'd left on the counter. After digging in it for a minute she produced a small booklet. "*Baby Names A to Z*. I picked it up at the grocery store yesterday. Let's see what other F names we can find."

When Melody was back at the table, Alice peeked over her shoulder at the open page. "Could they make that print any smaller?" Alice said.

"Most of these are kind of weird. Falala? Really? Faelyn is pretty. Do you want to try any of these on her?"

"Just read a few out loud, like you're doing," Alice said. "Not like you're calling her, but just loud enough that she can hear you over the TV. Skip the really odd ones."

"Fay," Melody read. "Faith." She looked into the other room for a reaction. "Falon." She let the name hang in the air. "Fatima. Felicia. Fern."

Jack put his hand on Melody's arm. "That got her attention."

"Fern?" Melody said, a little louder.

The girl jumped up from her place in front of the television, ran straight to Melody and hugged her.

"Is that your name?" Melody stroked the girl's hair. "Should we call you Fern?"

The girl moved a fist as if she were knocking on a door.

"That's *Yes!*" Alice said. "Your name's Fern."

The girl knocked on the invisible door again, beaming.

"What a beautiful name," Alice said. "You know what? I think we need another round of muffins to celebrate beautiful Fern's beautiful name."

"You get started," Jack said. "I want to give our friend Ms. Holt a call. Sam Wheeler, too." As he went toward the door, he added, "Fern, make sure to save a muffin for me."

Fern took one from the basket. She set it next to her placemat.

When Jack returned a few minutes later, Melody was cleaning the dishes. At the table, Alice sang and signed the alphabet as Fern tried to follow along, her hand struggling to keep up. Jack joined Melody at the sink.

"Anything new?" she said.

"Not yet. The police will be making a statement soon."

"Think that will be on television?"

"Maybe on the local cable access channel."

"Alice has been trying to coax Fern's last name out of her. No luck so far. That may be too much to ask."

Leaning close, Jack spoke in a whisper. "Are you still up for giving Alice a break?"

"Absolutely."

"You sure we can handle it?"

"Pretty soon we'll be doing a lot more than that," Melody said.

"Are you nervous about it?"

"No, not nervous. Terrified."

"That's my girl."

"Honestly, I can't wait," Melody said. "I can't wait to meet this kid. Our kid."

"Me, either."

They were quiet for a moment, content with looking into each other's eyes.

"You think Fern will be able to leave Alice?" Jack said.

"Are you kidding me? The way she loves you? If I were Alice, I'd be worried about ever getting her back here. I do wonder about Fern's reaction to our house, though. The last time she was there – "

"It was pitch black and foggy. There were police cars, the ambulance, all kinds of emergency lights. It will seem like a different place today." Jack went to the table. "Fern, would you like to go play at my house?"

The girl jumped down from her booster and ran to Jack. She hugged his legs.

"I'd say that's a yes," Alice said.

***

They were all standing in the road in front of the cottage. Melody held Fern's hand. Jack carried a tote of Fern's essentials that Alice had given him.

"I'll just take my walk up the hill," Alice said. "When I miss even a couple of days, I feel it. I have my phone. If there's any problem, let me know."

"Okay," Melody said. "We'll be fine."

As the others went downhill toward the water, Alice went in the opposite direction. She wore walking shoes and moved with a smooth, practiced gait. The road was empty, the large houses along it spaced far apart, separated by woods. The only sound was the gentle *swish* of her windbreaker.

She'd gone almost a mile when a car shot onto the road just ahead of her, a young woman at the wheel. Alice watched the car zoom away toward Route 1. When she reached the spot where the car had emerged, Alice stopped. A narrow, paved lane ran away through trees, as bent and shiny as a black snake. For a long time, Alice stared at that immaculate ribbon of asphalt, as if she were considering following it. Instead, she took out her phone and tapped the screen.

"Hello, Detective Wheeler?" she said. "It's Alice Garrison, Jack Westbury's neighbor. Could you call me? No emergency. Probably nothing at all. But do call me back, please."

17

In a dingy motel room, a slightly overweight man in a worn golf shirt sat on the end of a twin bed flipping channels. Every now and then he checked the blue face of an oversized watch. The door opened. "Jesus Christ, Bobby," the man said, jumping to his feet. "Where've you been? And who the fuck told you you could take my car?"

"I got food." Bobby came in holding a bag. "I woke up starving." He was tall, thin, with hair cut straight across his forehead in a kind of Frankenstein style. "That free motel breakfast is crap."

"So you thought you'd just take my car," the other man said. "Without asking me."

"I'm sorry, Chad, but I couldn't ask you. You were asleep." Bobby set the bag down on a little round table next to a half-missing six-pack of Coke. "I also went out to the camper."

Chad dropped the TV remote on the mattress. "You did?"

"Yeah. I decided to check for the phone charger one more time. And guess what I found under the seat?"

"You got the charger? Let's plug it in! See if the phone works."

"I charged the phone a little bit in the car. There's the regular plug and the cigarette lighter thing."

"And?"

"There were a bunch of calls and texts from some guy named Demon."

"What kind of texts?"

"Just regular boring stuff. But he calls Eric sweetie sometimes. Do you think Eric's gay?"

"Jesus Christ. This guy named Demon calls Eric sweetie?"

"Yeah." Bobby shifted from one foot to the other. He sucked in his cheeks, making his already narrow face look gaunt.

"Let me ask you, Bobby – who did Eric come here to meet up with? Who were we going to try to talk to next, since Eric can't help us anymore?"

"That girl Devon, who lives down here."

"Devon. That's right."

"Yeah?"

"Devon. Demon."

"Oh," Bobby said. "So Demon's like a nickname."

"Yeah, like a nickname. Jesus. Let me see the phone."

Bobby handed him a basic model cell phone. "She left messages on voicemail, but you need a password. Her number's there. We could call her."

"Right, from her boyfriend's phone. And say what, exactly?"

"I don't know. We just found Eric's phone. We want to give the phone to her, so that she can give it back to him."

"Right. We say we're going to drive down to Mystic to give her the phone."

"Maybe we say we're already nearby."

"We just happened to be in the neighborhood."

"I don't know." Bobby twitched with frustration. "Weren't you going to call that girl back home -- what's her name? The one who told us about Eric following Devon here? See if she could give us Devon's address?"

"Don't you think I tried that already? She's not answering." Chad plugged the phone into the wall. "Anyway, since we have Eric's phone, we're way past that now. We just have to think."

Bobby went to the table and opened the food bag, releasing a salty sausage smell. "We could call my cousin," he said, looking up suddenly, inspired. "He can go to the bar where Devon worked and ask around. He's a good talker, and the girls like him. They'll tell him whatever he needs to know. Maybe he can get her address."

"Forget about the address!" Chad elbowed Bobby aside, reached into the bag, then tossed a wrapped breakfast sandwich to him. He took another one for himself. They each pried a soda bottle loose from the plastic yoke. He took the only chair at the table. Bobby sat down on the edge of a bed.

A buzz made them look up from their sandwiches.

"Is that you?" Chad said.

"I guess." Bobby pulled an enormous black phone out of his pocket. "No. Not me. Must be you."

"Jesus. It's our buddy's phone."

Bobby reached behind him.

"Give it to me," Chad said.

Bobby passed the phone to Chad.

"It's Devon." Chad read the message out loud. "'Where are you? So sorry about what I said. I've got the money. Let's make plans. Text slash call me.'"

"So she does have the money!"

Chad seemed to be rereading the message again.

"What do you want to do?" Bobby said.

"We have to play this right."

"You should text her back."

"Of course I'm going to text her back."

"Ask her where the money is!"

"No," Chad said. "We're not going to ask that."

"Why not?"

"Because he wouldn't ask that. We have to sound like him."

"It's a text message. She won't hear what we sound like."

"Christ, you are such an idiot."

"Well, what should we say?" Bobby was leaning over Chad, now, in position to read the text as Chad typed it.

"Give me some room!" Chad shoved Bobby out of the way and stood up.

"Ask her where *she* is?" Bobby suggested.

"Shut up a second and let me think." Chad went to the window, looking for inspiration in the scruffy, semi-circular parking lot. He typed a message.

Bobby came up behind him. "What did you say?"

Chad read. "'Thought you were mad. I'm not. Let's meet up.'"

"That's good," Bobby said. "Did you use the letter *u* instead of the word *you*?"

"No, I didn't use the letter *u*."

"Don't you think you should? Because she did."

"That was her, not him."

"I bet he would use the letter. You could check his old texts."

Chad pressed Send.

Bobby shook his head. "I think he would have used the letter."

Just a few seconds later, the phone buzzed again.

Chad read from the screen. "'Come back to the Bartletts' house. We can leave from there.'"

"Leave?" Bobby said. "Ask her where they're going. And where's the Bartletts' house."

Chad ignored him. "Cool! When?" he said, as he typed.

"Ask where the Bartletts' house is," Bobby said.

"It's where the camper is, dumb ass."

A text reply came back right away. "'I have to pick up a few things,'" Chad read. "'Be there around one.'"

"We'll be waiting," Chad typed.

The phone buzzed again.

Bobby craned his neck to see. "What'd she say?"

"Smiley face," Chad said, making one himself.

18

Ahead of schedule, at a little past twelve, Devon went down the Bartletts' long drive. She slowed as she passed the garage, then continued around the boathouse. An old pickup camper was parked there.

"Eric!" she said, as she got out of her car. When there was no answer, she went toward the back of the camper. "Eric! Fern!"

She was just raising her hand to knock on the door when she heard footsteps. She turned. Chad and Bobby were coming toward her.

"What the fuck?" she said.

"Sorry if we scared you, Devon," Chad said.

"What are you guys doing here? Where's Eric, and Fern?"

"They're at a motel."

"What? Why?"

Bobby closed in. He towered over her. "Don't play dumb. You know why we're here."

"What are you talking about?" Devon clutched the end of the scarf that was draped around her neck.

"We're here to talk about the money," Chad said.

"What money?"

"Our money."

"I don't know anything about your money." Devon took a step in the direction of her car.

Bobby blocked her path. "Bullshit. Eric didn't have the money on him, and we searched that piece of crap camper, and it's not in there.

He must have given it to you."

"Given what to me?" Devon backed away from Bobby. She worked an end of the scarf with her fingers.

"The money, for Christ's sake," Chad said. "Are you paying attention at all?"

"He didn't give me anything. I didn't think he had any money. Maybe he used it to buy the camper. He said he paid cash."

"Yeah, right," Chad said. "He paid a hundred grand for this thing." He kicked at the fender. Mottled chips of metal fell to the pavement.

"Wait, a hundred thousand? He took a hundred thousand dollars from you guys?" Devon covered her mouth with her hand. "He told me he only took what you owed him."

"Uh huh," Chad said. "I thought you didn't know anything about our money."

"That's all I know."

"We read that text. You said you had the money. What is it, you're watching it for him? Is it in the house?" Chad nodded uphill toward the sprawling structure.

"I'm just looking after the property, for the owners," Devon said. "I never go inside the house. I don't know where your money is."

"Come on, now. Eric must have told you something."

"He didn't tell me anything. If you want to know where the money is you'll have to ask him yourself." Devon looked from one man to the other. "Where is he?"

Bobby and Chad exchanged a glance but kept silent.

Devon took a quick step toward her car. "I'm out of here."

Chad grabbed her arm. "Hang on."

"Let go!" Devon tried to jerk her arm free. "You asshole!"

"I'm an asshole? We just caught you lying to us."

"I'm calling the cops." Devon tried to work her cell phone out of her pocket. Chad knocked it away. He hooked an arm around her and yanked her back toward the camper.

"Chad, take it easy." Bobby's hands were raised in front of him.

Trying to squirm free, Devon yelled, "Stop! Chad! Stop!"

"Chad," Bobby said, still in the peacemaker pose. "Think about what you're doing."

Chad threw open the camper door. He tossed the woman inside. Then he slammed the door shut.

On the other side of the thin aluminum, Devon screamed. Chad leaned hard against the door, which rattled as Devon pounded against it.

"Chad! Jesus." Bobby shoved him out of the way. The door flew open and Devon fell hard to the pavement, crying and gasping for air.

Chad tugged her to her feet. "Where's the fucking money?"

"I don't have it!" Devon could barely get the words out through her violent, sobbing breaths. She kept looking back at the camper.

"But Eric told you he took some money from us," Chad said. "What else did he tell you?"

"All he said was he took what you owed him." She glanced at the camper again. "Where's Fern?"

With his free hand, Chad drew a gun from his waistband. He pointed it at Devon.

She pulled back as far as Chad's grip would allow. "Shit! I don't have the money."

"But you know where it is." Chad pressed the gun against her ear.

Devon's breathing was quick now. "Eric said he sent money to Fern's grandfather."

"Damn," Bobby said.

Devon turned toward him. "I have a little money in the car. I'll give you whatever I have. Just please let me go."

"All right," Chad said, lowering the gun. "Go get the money from your car." He released her.

As Devon took a step, Chad raised his arm. He brought the gun down hard on her head. She fell.

"Jesus, Chad!" Bobby looked down at the woman. The scarf had draped itself across her face.

"There's some rope in the camper," Chad said. "Tie her up."

"Is she dead?" Bobby knelt over her.

"She's just knocked out. Will you please be of some use? Get that rope."

"No." Bobby stood up.

"What do you mean, *No?*"

"We already killed Eric. If you're going to kill her, too, I don't want any part of it."

"Son of a bitch." Chad went to the camper and climbed inside. He came back with some clothesline and a threadbare dishtowel. He tied

Devon's hands behind her. After ripping the dishtowel in half lengthwise, he pried Devon's lips open and gagged her, turning her over so that he could knot the cloth behind her head. She remained limp.

"What are you doing?" Bobby said, when Chad was done.

"We're taking her with us. She's going to help us get that money back."

"How?"

"I don't know yet."

"Great. And if she can't, then what? We just let her go? She knows about Eric, now. Thanks to you."

"If we scare her bad enough she'll keep quiet. That's why I showed her what happened to her boyfriend."

Bobby seemed to be thinking about that. "Yeah. Yeah, that could work."

Chad gave Bobby the smile of a man who was heading to the clubhouse with a birdie on the last hole. "See? Come on. Go get the car." He motioned in the direction of the garage, where a long gold sedan was just visible.

"Then what?"

"Then we get the hell out of here. After we take care of one last thing."

19

Alice went up the hill, cupping Fern's impossibly soft hand in her palm. "Did you have fun at Jack and Melody's house?"

The girl smiled.

"Did you know that I used to live there? Not too long ago. The cottage suits me better now. Nice and cozy."

They walked along together. Behind them, the cove came into view – the same cove on which Fern had drifted in the dark, crying. Today, it sparkled in the afternoon sun.

Alice said, "Did you have a nap at Jack and Melody's house?"

Fern shook her head.

"I see."

A chipmunk raced across the road in front of them, its tail as upright as a flagpole.

"That little chippie was fast," Alice said. "I bet you're a fast runner, too. Why don't you see how fast you can run to that big rock?" She pointed.

Fern found the rock with her eyes.

"I'll time you." Alice let go of the girl's hand. "Ready, set, go!"

Fern looked up at Alice, then at the rock.

"Do you want me to run with you?" Alice said.

Fern nodded.

"Okay! Ready, set, go!"

Alice set off at a brisk walk. Fern began to move. Alice picked up her pace. Fern took off, suddenly, arms pumping.

Slowing, letting the girl open up some distance, Alice counted in a loud voice. "One, two, three, four, five, six, seven, eight! Wow! Now run back."

After patting the big rock, Fern struck a pose, her fists in front of her. She dashed past Alice.

They walked a little further up the hill. Alice pointed to another large rock, one big enough to stand out from the stones that littered the ground.

"You want to run again?"

Fern made the sign for *Yes*.

"Okay. Ready, set, go!"

Fern bolted, doing her best beginner sprint. Alice counted. Fern's fists moved violently through the air, as if boxing with it. Her soles slapped against the pavement.

They continued up the road that way, Fern sprinting from rock to rock, Alice running alongside her less and less. The blue sky and bright sun brought out the first signs of color in the trees. The air was warm. Fern was tireless and smiling now as she ran. Racing ahead, she had almost reached the cottage when there was a loud boom.

Fern stopped suddenly, her eyes opened wide. Alice went to her, scooped her up and hurried through the door.

Somewhere up the road, beyond the trees, there was another boom.

Alice lifted the kitchen phone from the dock. She held the handset for a few seconds, then put it down again.

Another boom rattled the windows. Fern clutched Alice's legs.

"It's okay, honey," Alice said. She had just grabbed the phone again when a car came to a stop in front of the house. Fern followed Alice to the door. Jack's SUV was there in the road, Melody in the passenger seat. Jack looked across the roof.

"Did you hear that?" Alice said "It sounded close."

"Yes, it did," Jack said. "I don't think any of us needs a front-row seat to whatever excitement that's about to cause. What do you say we go for a ride?"

"That sounds like a good idea."

Fern raced back into the house.

"I'll get her seat," Jack said, heading toward Alice's car.

"Okay. I'll go see what she's up to." Alice found Fern in the room that had been made her own, a stuffed bear under her arm, trying to tug the quilt from the bed.

"You know we're just going for a ride? We'll be back here soon."

Fern kept tugging on the quilt.

"Okay. We'll bring the quilt. But we have to try to keep it clean."

After getting situated next to Fern in the SUV, Alice leaned toward the front seat. "Have you called anyone? Any authorities?"

"Jack called," Melody said.

"I don't think I was the first," Jack said.

The road was a straight shot toward Route 1. They passed widely spaced private drives, including the one that Alice had peered down earlier that morning. They went left onto Route 1 heading south, toward Mystic. A police car raced by.

Melody pointed out the window. "Jack, look."

Jack swerved onto the shoulder. They all twisted in their seats.

A dark, shaggy plume of smoke rose out of the trees.

"I'd guess that's coming from the Bartlett property," Alice said. "It's weird – I had a feeling about that place this morning. I even called Sam Wheeler. He hasn't called me back."

Jack checked the rearview mirror for Alice's face. "He might have been tied up with the TV thing."

"What do you mean?"

"The news conference that the SPD is holding."

"Oh, that's right."

In the distance, a firehouse siren swooped and howled. Fern pulled the quilt over her head.

"It's okay, Fern." Alice placed her hand on the quilt. "Don't be scared."

"Oh, sweetie," Melody said, peering over the seat back.

A fire truck roared toward them, its horn blaring.

"Let me get us off of Route 1," Jack said. He took the next right, into the woods. After a few minutes, the sirens faded. Jack switched on the radio. Mozart.

Melody tried another station. "We need some kids' music."

Jack looked across the seat at her. "You're right."

Alice rubbed Fern's arm through the quilt and stared out the window. "Maybe it was their furnace or something."

"It's the 'or something' that has me worried," Jack said, softly.

"Do you think it's connected somehow with – " Melody stopped.

"I don't know." Jack's voice was barely more than a whisper.

"That doesn't make any sense, does it? I guess I'm being paranoid. We probably should have stayed home."

"No, it's good to get away from the noise and everything. For all of us, but especially for..." Melody touched Jack's knee. "You have good dad instincts already."

"I like the luxury of being chauffeured around," Alice announced suddenly. "Such a nice vehicle, too."

Melody half turned toward the back. "Doesn't it feel like safety on wheels? This soft leather, the quality of everything. You feel kind of untouchable, don't you?"

"Indeed," Alice said.

"And the rings on the steering wheel always make me think of the Olympics."

Fern peeked out from under the quilt. Her sweaty hair was stuck to her cheeks.

"I'm not sure it's working for all of us," Alice said.

Melody's purse chimed. She dug out her phone. "It's Claire. She wants to talk, but I think I'll text her." For a few minutes she was intent on the glass screen. "She's invited us there."

"It might be good to land somewhere for awhile," Jack said. "Alice, what do you think?"

Melody half turned again. "They have a dog, Alice, but he's very mellow."

"What kind?"

"A retired racing dog. A greyhound."

"They're quite large." Alice looked at Fern. "Has he been around children?"

"No, I don't think so. But he's a gentle dog."

"We'll have to see."

***

Claire met them at the edge of the gravel driveway, with Buck on a leash. Jack lifted Fern out of her car seat. She immediately reached down toward the dog. Buck sniffed in her direction.

"It's clear they want to get to know each other," Jack said.

Alice gave her okay with a nod.

Jack lowered the girl to her feet.

Claire crouched down to Fern's level, keeping the dog close. "This is Buck. He used to run races, but now he lives with us. You can pet him."

Buck studied the girl, his head cocked, his long face keenly curious.

Fern reached out again. Buck licked her fingers. Fern laughed.

The sound from the silent girl's mouth appeared to stun the adults. They all stared at her.

Buck pressed his nose into Fern's palm.

"He probably smells peanut butter," Melody said. "We had peanut butter muffins for breakfast and peanut butter sandwiches for lunch."

"Gee," Claire said, "I wonder whose idea that was."

"Don't blame me," Melody said. "This girl is a Jiff devotee."

"Well, that's a good way to get in good with Buck. Should we go inside?"

They were heading for the kitchen when Buck broke from the group. With Fern following close behind, he entered a long room. There by the fireplace, with his glowing tattoos and permanent stubble, was Ben. Fern stopped.

"Uh oh," Ben said.

The dog crossed the wide-plank floor and plopped down at Ben's feet. Ben gave the dog's flank an impossibly gentle stroke. Buck twitched his ears.

"Here you are," Melody said, appearing around the corner.

Fern pointed at Ben.

"Shoot," Ben said. "Hey, sweetheart, want to see a magic trick?" His colorful glow brightened, then faded, then faded some more. Soon there was only the fireplace's stone and soot where he had been.

Fern clapped her hands. Buck howled, showing his canines, bringing Alice racing into the room. "What was that all about?"

Claire was right behind her. "I don't know. He's been weird lately."

Fern touched her forehead with an open hand.

"What man?" Alice said.

Fern pointed toward the dog.

"Oh. Dog," Alice said. She slapped her thigh and then snapped her fingers, making the sign. "Dog. He is a boy dog, though."

Fern looked back at her, smiling.

Melody squinted at the air over Buck's head. "You don't think...
Remember that Buck was like AJ – he could see – "

"What, Ben?" Claire said. "No. AJ would have told me."

"Was he barking at Fern?" Alice said.

"He's probably just picking up on the anxiety level in the house."
Melody made a flat smile. "With everything that's happened, this
morning, and with George, and... Animals are very sensitive."

Buck dropped to the floor again and let out a contented groan.

Fern went to Alice. Irresistibly, with her upraised arms and
upturned face, she asked for the quilt. When Alice handed it to her,
Fern dropped it next to Buck, then opened a fold and stretched out
there.

"I'm not sure that's such a good idea," Alice said. "Dogs can be
impatient with small children."

"My only concern is that Buck will decide to lie on that nice new
quilt with her," Claire said. "I'll be right back." She ran upstairs.

"Claire looks tired," Melody said.

"I'm sure she is. There's a lot of that going around." Alice
touched her hair as if remembering that her tiredness extended even
to the ends.

Claire returned with a blanket and two pillows. She made a sort of
nest with them on the floor by the couch, then called Buck. He
happily curled up there.

"Fern, why don't you lie down next to Buck?" Claire said.

"I'll take the other end of the couch," Alice said. "We'll all have a
little rest." She covered herself with the quilt.

Melody and Claire retreated through the kitchen to the porch.
They found Jack in the narrow back yard, staring at the ground along
the foundation.

"I love seeing these violets here," he said. "They remind me of
how much things can change." He turned. "Melody, where's Fern?"

"Fern, Alice and Buck are taking a rest."

"I wonder who will fall asleep first?"

"My money's on Alice," Claire said. "She seems beat."

"Fern's wearing her out," Melody said.

"Is this okay, Claire – us being here?" Jack stepped back from the
flowers. "It probably isn't a great time for us to impose on you."

"I invited you, remember? I'm glad to have the distraction."

"Can you tell us anything?" Melody said. "Any news about AJ's dad?"

"I don't have too many details. George has to have bypass surgery. That's definite. The surgeon the cardiologist wants – the same one they mentioned at Westerly – is out of the country, but she's due back in a few days. They're trying to work out a schedule."

"That's a pretty common procedure now, right?" Melody said.

"It's common, but it's still open heart surgery."

Jack touched the screen that separated them. "If the cardiologist wants to wait for this surgeon, she must be good. That's the important thing. Get a good surgeon."

"How's everyone dealing with it?" Melody said.

"Okay, I think," Claire said. "I could hear AJ's mom in the background, so I think he was being guarded. He didn't talk at all about recovery. I guess I'll hear about that later."

"If there's anything I can do…" Jack stopped. He looked down at the violets, and a restraint inside him seemed to give way. "I can check with a surgeon I know and make sure that George's doctor's are the best. I can arrange for a home nurse during the recovery. And I can cover the cost of staff at the market so that they don't have to worry about the business. The last thing they need is another worry."

Claire gave him a teary smile. "That's incredibly generous, Jack. But you know AJ – and George and June are the same way. They'll probably say it's too much, and they can't accept it. But I will talk to AJ."

"Okay."

"There is something else I could use your opinion on, Jack," Claire said. "Sort of a business matter."

"Sure, anything."

Melody started for the door. "While you talk, I'm going to check on our sleeping beauties." She passed Ben on the way to the sitting room.

"A beauty checking on the beauties," he said, in a whisper. "I know it's a cliché with a pregnant woman, but you really are more beautiful than ever." He followed her. "What brought you guys over here? I saw Claire texting furiously. Did something happen?"

Her hand on her belly, Melody watched the trio of nappers – Buck, sprawled on the blanket like it was the world's most luxurious bed, Alice, snoring into the cushions at one end of the sofa, and at the other end, Fern, perched with her arm dangling toward the dog.

Melody moved close to Fern.

"What happened to you, little one?" Melody said, in a whisper. "How can we keep you safe?"

20

Steering with one hand, holding a phone to his ear with the other, Chad swerved into the pull-off. He came to a stop behind Devon's car. "Make it quick," he said. In the rearview mirror, he watched Bobby get out of Devon's silver sedan then head toward the stream just beyond some trees. Chad twisted around to look into the back seat. Devon, bound and gagged, lay across the black vinyl. She glared at him.

"You're awake," Chad said. "I was starting to worry. Listen, you have to do what I say. If you do, then Bobby will leave you alone. He's got… Let's call it impulse control issues. If you make the wrong move, you could end up like Eric. He'll try to tell you that it was an accident, what happened to your boyfriend, but trust me, it was no accident." Chad glanced out the window in Bobby's direction. "Just do what I say and I'll wait for the right moment to let you go."

Devon's wide-eyed face was as still as molded plastic.

Bobby had stopped at the edge of the stream. He stood there in plain view in that unmistakable pose, feet apart, hands hidden in front of him, head down, as if in a sort of prayer.

***

The pavement had turned to gravel and then to tire-tracked dirt, and then to something between a weedy parking lot and a sparse, hard-packed lawn. That ended at the peeling skirt of a cabin. Only one of the cabin's three front-facing windows was not covered up with gray plywood. The roof was green and bumpy with moss. A crudely painted sign hung by the door – *Office.*

Bobby stopped Devon's car in as good a place as any.

Chad swung the LeMans around so that it faced the trees. "You need to come sit with Devon while I go in," he said into the phone.

"Yup." Bobby climbed out of Devon's car. He came over to the Chad's door. As they traded places, Chad passed Bobby his gun.

Bobby frowned. "I don't need this."

"You won't need it because you have it. That's the way that works."

"Chad – "

"Just keep her quiet. I'll be right back."

When Bobby was sitting at the wheel, he poked the handgun between the seats. "I've got this, so keep quiet." He watched Chad go into the cabin.

After a minute, the cabin door swung open. Chad came out brandishing a key. Bobby lowered the window.

"All set," Chad said. "Got the most private cabin in the place. You know what the guy said? It's perfect for honeymooners, cheaters, and kidnappers."

"He didn't say that."

"I'm not shitting you. That's exactly what he said." Chad smiled big.

"How are we going to get her out of the car and into the cabin?" Bobby said. "We can't let anyone see her all tied up."

"I'll park first, then you come in alongside, between me and the road."

The cabins were spaced along a loop. Theirs was the farthest away, a duplicate of the office, though without the plywood on the windows. Bobby pulled up next to Chad's car. Chad moved to his back seat, shoving Devon's feet aside. She rolled against the seat belt, which had been wrapped around her.

"I'm going to untie you and remove this gag," Chad said, "Then you're going to get out, stretch a little like you just woke up, and walk to the cabin nice and quiet. Don't forget, Bobby has the gun. Got it?"

Devon nodded.

Chad undid the rope at Devon's feet, then worked on the hands. "Damn." After a couple of minutes of tugging and prying, that knot remained as tight as a fist.

Bobby got in the front seat. "What's going on?"

"This fuckin' knot."

"You want me to try it?"

"No, I don't want you to try it."

"Did you push the rope? Sometimes you have to push and not just pull."

"Yeah, thanks."

"Sometimes you just have to give up and use pliers."

"Do you have pliers?"

"No."

"Well, good idea, then."

"There might be pliers in the cabin. We should go ahead and go in."

"Right. She'll just walk in with her hands tied. Why didn't I think of that?" Chad kept working at the rope.

"I thought we got the most private place in the camp."

"We still have to be careful."

"It's funny, when you think about it."

"Yeah, it's fuckin' hilarious."

"No, because fishermen are supposed to be good with knots."

Chad had his keys out now and was prying at the rope. "Okay, I got it. Let's go, Devon. Don't forget what I said about looking like you just woke up."

Once she was on her feet, Devon raised her arms in a sort of exaggerated gym class stretch. As they went to the cabin, she stayed sandwiched by the two men, Chad in front.

"Think you'll need help with the lock?" Bobby said, a grin on his face.

"Fuck you." Chad opened the door.

"Jesus, nice smell," Bobby said, when they were inside. "It's like this place has been closed up for a hundred years."

"That's good. It means privacy."

"It means we should open some windows."

"I need to use the bathroom," Devon said.

They moved as a group.

When Devon tried to close the door behind her, Chad held it open an inch. "Nope. I can't chance you locking yourself in there or something. Don't worry, I won't look."

Devon eyed him, then retreated inside.

Chad reached out. "Gun."

Bobby gave it to him. He went on into the kitchen. "This place is a dump," he said, from there. "How do they keep it going?"

"Same as everyplace else, the casinos."

"Guess this is where the losers end up."

"Lucky for us there weren't many losers today."

"Yep, just us." Bobby was opening drawers, reviewing the utensil situation.

The toilet flushed and water splashed in the sink. Chad yanked the door open. "We need to fix you up again."

"I won't try anything." Devon was looking at him in a mirror over the sink.

"That's what they all say." He came in after her and took her elbow. He led her to a stained couch in the living room. "Sit." He pointed. "Bobby, watch her. I'll be right back."

Bobby came in from the kitchen.

Chad left. After a minute he returned with two duffels and an old shopping bag with handles. He found a bedroom and dropped everything on the bed. Dust leapt into the air like a sudden hatch of minute insects. Carrying the shopping bag, Chad went back into the living room.

"You can have the fresh half," he said, holding the unused part of the dishtowel gag for Devon to see.

"I'll be quiet," she said. "You don't need that."

Chad didn't say anything. Slipping behind her, he did the gag first, then started in on the rope.

"You need help with the knot?" Bobby grinned.

"Fuck you."

"Just trying to make myself useful."

When Devon's feet and hands were bound, Chad stepped back. Devon looked up at the two men standing over her.

"I'm hungry," Chad said. "How about you, Bobby?"

"Starved."

"Okay then. Next thing is to go get some food. Let me have the keys."

"Why don't you just take your car?"

"I want to change the plates."

"You're going to do that in broad daylight?"

"I'll only do it if it's safe. I have no chance if I don't even have the car. So give me the keys." Chad held out his hand. Bobby slapped the keys into his palm. "I'll be back ASAP."

Bobby turned the lock behind Chad, then watched out the window as the car drove away. "Fuck this," he said, walking over to Devon.

She began to tug against her ropes, whimpering, tilting her head as if to avoid a blow that she knew was coming. As Bobby got close, she fell off the couch onto the floor.

"Jesus, calm down," Bobby said. "I just want to take off that gag. Just don't yell, all right?"

On the floor, Devon continued to struggle. When Bobby tugged the gag down from her mouth, she stopped. He helped her back onto the seat. He got in front of her, stared into her eyes for a second, then went back to the window.

"What a fucked-up mess," he said. "If I had keys I could get us the hell out of here." He turned around. "Do you want some water or something?"

"Yeah."

Bobby pulled a plastic bottle from a duffle. When he tried to tip it to her lips, water dribbled to the floor. "Damn it. Hang on." He untied her wrists, then handed her the bottle. "I'll have to tie you back up before he comes back. I can't piss him off – that will just makes things worse." He stood looking down at her as she drank. "Is there any chance that Eric hid that money somewhere around the big house where he was parking the camper? Maybe stashed it in a garden or something? You know, like tucked it under a little plastic gnome or something?"

"It's not the kind of place that has plastic gnomes," Devon said, keeping her eyes down. "Anyway, there are motion sensors all around the house. Eric knows not to go near it." She spoke in a softer voice. "I mean, he knew." She stood the bottle on the cushion beside her and rubbed her wrists. "Where's Fern?"

"What?" Bobby worked his jaw back and forth, as if loosening the joint.

"Fern – is she…" Devon stopped.

"No, no. We left her in the boat. So those motion sensors – "

"You left her in the boat? What boat?"

"We found Eric on the water. Him and Fern. They were eeling. When it seemed like he wasn't going to cooperate with us, we took him and left her. For incentive, you know, so he would give us the cash, so he could go back for her."

"How was he going to go back for her? What boat was he going to use? And then... You stopped him from he ever going back." Devon took a deep breath. "Jesus Christ, Fern's just a little kid."

Bobby moved a half step toward Devon. "Maybe I shouldn't have removed that gag."

Devon took a defiant gulp of water.

"Chad said someone would find her," Bobby said. "She was close to shore and there's lots of boat traffic."

Devon screwed the lid back on the bottle. Bobby took it from her.

"So the sensors," Bobby said, "do they contact the police, or maybe a security company?"

Devon nodded.

"So that's why Eric was running toward the house. If Chad hadn't stopped him he would have tripped the alarm, and we would have had company pretty quick."

Devon began to cry. Her hands stayed together on her lap, as if they were still tied. The tears streamed down her cheeks and onto her shirt.

Bobby made a face. "I'm sorry. Look, finish your crying, then make sure you've had as much water as you want. I need to tie you up again."

"Please just let me go," Devon said, looking hard into Bobby's eyes. "I promise I won't tell anyone. I promise."

"Do you want more water or not?" When Devon didn't respond, Bobby jammed the water bottle into his pocket, making little crackling sounds. He tied Devon's wrists again. Holding the gag in his hand, he said, "I'll just put this around your neck so we can pull it up quick. Don't try to yell for help. You'll only screw things up for yourself."

Devon had gone back to avoiding his eyes.

"Look, if I let you go now," Bobby said, "you won't get far enough away before Chad comes back. I promise, as soon as I can, as soon as there's a real chance, I'll get you out of this. I'll get us both out of it. Okay?"

After setting up the gag, Bobby went back to the window. He positioned himself so that with one turn of the head he could go from looking outside to checking on Devon. He pushed at the window frame. "Damn, painted shut," he said. "Is this cabin a piece of shit or what?"

Devon didn't say a word.

21

"I feel like I'm out on bail." George looked around the room as if to be sure it really was his own house.

He was in his favorite chair – the big recliner with the best view of the TV. June was seated next to him, straightening a stack of catalogs. All was completely normal in the Bugbees' living room. Except, on a normal day, they wouldn't have been in the living room, they would have been at the market, cleaning up after the last of the lunch rush. And they wouldn't have spent the morning talking with a medical team about the plans to remove a blood vessel from George's leg and graft it into his chest.

"You're not a flight risk, are you Dad?" AJ tried, with a smile.

"Not with your mother watching me."

"You're not going anywhere," June said. "They sent you home so that you could rest up before the surgery. You have two days of pure R & R."

"Why don't I make you guys something to eat?" AJ said. "Or I can get something from the market."

"You know what I'm in the mood for?" George said. "Some of your mother's vegetable soup. Do we have any in the freezer, June?"

"I'll go look." June popped to her feet.

"I'll get it," AJ said.

But June was already gone.

"Your mother needs something to do," George said, in a whisper. Then, in a louder voice, "You should go home and see Claire."

June's voice rang out from the kitchen. "Found some!"

"Great!" George answered. "Zap it up!"

"Maybe I should see if there are any groceries Mom needs," AJ said. "I could bring them over later."

George held up his hand. "No. You know we are never short of food in this house. If an atom bomb dropped tomorrow, we could hunker down in the basement until the radiation cleared and eat like kings all the while. Go home, AJ. Spend some time with Claire. I want to get through all of this without screwing up everyone else's lives."

"You're not going to screw up our lives," AJ said.

"You have a job. We have a business. The Daves can't pick up all of the slack. They have lives, too."

"Not sure about that," AJ said.

They laughed.

"Well, they do," George said. "So we have a few things to figure out."

"And we will, Dad. Don't worry."

"I won't. Now say goodbye to your mom."

"Call me if you need me."

"We definitely will."

AJ and his mom hugged by the counter, awkward, out of practice. When he was behind the wheel of the Jeep, AJ texted Claire that he was headed home. His phone rang as he was latching his seatbelt.

"Hi," he said. "What's going on?"

"There were some kind of explosions on Wamphassuc Point," Claire said.

"Explosions? We didn't hear anything over here." AJ had the key in the ignition now, waiting to turn it as Claire related the events of the morning. "I haven't heard anything from Sam or the chief," AJ said. "I guess I'm totally out of the loop."

They said goodbye. AJ slid his phone back into his pocket. "Maybe out of the loop is a good thing."

***

AJ stopped at the edge of the gravel. He looked across the green space in front of Claire's house – more and more like a lawn all the time. Claire was there with Fern, who had Buck on a leash. Buck swung his sharp nose in AJ's direction, and started that way, but not with his usual full-tilt sprint. Instead, he took deliberate, patient steps, checking to see that Fern was keeping pace.

AJ moved slowly, too. When they met up, he scratched the dog behind the ears. "Hey, boy."

Fern looked up at him, unsure.

"AJ, this is Fern," Claire said, joining them. "Fern, this is AJ. You met him at the hospital, remember? He lives here, too."

"Hi, Fern. Thanks for taking Buck for a walk. He loves walks."

"Fern and Buck have become good friends," Claire said.

"That's great."

Buck struck off in a new direction, his long legs executing precise, restrained steps. Fern went with him.

"I'm not sure who's walking who," AJ said.

"I know. He's being so careful with her. It's really sweet."

"Where is everybody?"

"Out back. I promised Alice I'd stay with these two. I guess she's not exactly a dog person."

"If any dog can change Alice's mind, it'll be Buck." AJ watched the girl and the dog, the lead drooping between them.

"So your dad is settling in?"

"Trying. He said he feels like he's out on bail."

"I can imagine."

"That meeting at the hospital today." AJ shook his head. "They explained all about the surgery. I guess it's good to know going in. But, Jesus. How did we get to the point where we're cutting people open right down the middle and working on their hearts?"

Claire studied AJ's face without saying anything.

"I mean, who would have the courage to do that? To take a saw to a man's body like that? To literally hold a heart in your hands?"

"The surgeon might say the same thing about what you do for a living."

AJ kept on looking across the yard. "I'm not sure I have the greatest record there. When I washed out in Bridgeport – "

"You didn't wash out. And that was a long time ago. You have a whole new track record in Stonington. I seem to remember a couple of commendations."

"I was going to say, when I came back to Stonington, I figured courage wouldn't be that big a part of my job anymore. This was a quiet town. Always had been. And the last thing I wanted was to use my…ability." He pronounced that last word as if it were in quotes.

Claire waited, giving him space.

"It felt like I cheated, to get those commendations. I wanted to do things the old fashioned way – the normal way – on the job. I was just coming around to Roland's way of thinking – being able to see ghosts was a tool, and I should use it – when Roland left."

"I don't think you should let the chief – Roland or Gaines or whoever – determine what you do." Claire slid her hand up and down his back. "You have to decide."

"You're right, as always." He kissed her.

As AJ went toward the house, Claire went the other direction, towards Fern and Buck, calling after them, "Hey, you two! Wait for me!"

AJ found Jack, Melody, and Alice on the porch. He asked if anyone wanted a beer to match the one he'd picked up on the way through the kitchen. They were more interested in hearing about his dad. He explained about the meeting with the cardiac team, which had ended with the surprise news that George could go home until the surgery.

"Good for him," Alice said. "You should spend as little time as possible in the hospital. I've heard of that surgeon. She's supposed to be very good."

"We're counting on it." AJ glanced toward the house. "Before Fern comes back, can you tell me about what happened today?"

"There was a loud boom," Melody said. "It sounded close. Then a second one, even louder."

"Like explosions you'd hear at a construction site where they're doing blasting," Jack added.

"That's right," Melody said. "Whatever it was, I didn't want any part of it. Especially for Fern."

They talked about stopping to pick up Alice, hearing sirens, seeing police cars, then the plume of smoke rising above the trees.

"I think it was coming from the Bartletts' house," Alice said. "Which is odd, because earlier in the day, I took a walk up the road, and I happened to see the girl the Bartletts have watching the house just as she was coming out of their lane. We didn't speak – I just saw her drive away. I don't know why, but I had this feeling that something was off, that there was something that should be looked into. I even called Sam Wheeler. When I got back to my house, though, I doubted myself. I decided that I had an overactive imagination, stirred up because of Fern being found the way she was. Then, a little while later, *boom!* I guess maybe my instincts weren't so bad after all."

"Do you know the girl?" AJ said. "The one who's watching the property?"

"No. All I know is that her name's Devon. She's not the person the Bartletts usually use. I understand their regular person was away on a trip. Mrs. Bartlett called me to see if I'd fill in. I did once before, years ago. I hate that alarm system, though – it's very complicated – so I said I'd only do it if she couldn't find anyone else. She called me the day before they left and said that it was taken care of. I didn't ask for details."

"Do you know how to get in touch with the Bartletts?"

"No. They're on safari. I don't have their cell phone numbers, I'm afraid."

"Who might know this Devon?" AJ said.

"Probably the landscaper. He'd have to be in touch with her, I think. The Bartletts use Always Green. And the security company – they would have her info, right? You could check with them. Or, I guess Sam could."

Away down the sloping yard, Fern and Buck, still exploring, had come into view, heading for the trees. Claire trailed behind them.

"Maybe I'll just take a run over there," AJ said.

"You don't have to get involved." Alice put a hand on his arm.

"Really, AJ," Melody said. "You just got back from the hospital."

"It won't take long." He tipped his bottle toward Jack. "You want this? I didn't touch it."

"Actually, I'd like to ride along, if you don't mind."

"I'll take care of that." Alice swiped the beer and took a gulp.

"Let me talk to Claire for a second." AJ went out the side door and across the grass. When he'd taken just a few steps, Ben appeared suddenly at his elbow.

"Hey, everything okay with your dad?"

AJ only nodded.

"You can catch me up later," Ben said. "Are you headed to Wamphassuc Point?"

AJ nodded again.

"You're going to do your sixth sense thing, right? Looking for

Eric's ghost. Would you like a second pair of eyes?"

AJ shook his head.

Ben watched Claire, Fern, and Buck move together along the tree line. "She saw me, AJ. The girl. If she's around a lot that could make things kind of interesting."

As if feeling the eyes on her, Fern looked their way.

"Gotta go," Ben said, and vanished.

AJ kept on walking.

22

The back of the pickup camper was just a sketch, a collection of charred rectangles that roughed out the shape. The cab was still recognizable, though everything not metal, even the paint, had been stripped away. The Bartletts' wooden boathouse was just gone, replaced by a mound of ash outlined by cement blocks.

From the paved drive, slightly above it all, AJ and Jack studied the wreckage and the continuous scramble of the police and firefighters.

"I'll wait here," Jack said.

AJ walked further down the hill to Detective Wheeler. "Hey, Sam. What have we got?"

"One body in the camper. Appears to be an adult male. There's evidence of a child – a kid's spoon, a toy porcelain horse, one singed pink sock."

"So the other night we found an unaccompanied girl, and now, less than a mile away, we've got a dead adult and maybe a missing child, probably a girl."

"Yeah. It sure does seem like it's all one case. We'll have a better idea when we've talked to the Bartletts, or whoever's been watching the property for them."

"I know a little about that," AJ said. "I spoke with Alice Garrison –"

Wheeler cut him off. "Damn. She called me, but between the press conference and this, I haven't been able to get back to her. I'm sorry if she ended up calling you."

"Actually, she was at my house. Jack wanted to get Fern away from all the commotion of the emergency vehicles. He thought it might be traumatic. Claire invited them over. Alice called you about something else." AJ explained about Alice seeing Devon leaving the driveway.

Wheeler took down a few details in his notepad. "We should be able to get Devon's full name and number from the security company. Either she or the security company should know who was in this camper. I'll need to track her down and talk to her. I'll need to talk to Alice, too. And Jack and Melody."

"You could talk to Jack now." AJ motioned up the hill. "He's in my Jeep."

Jack got out of the vehicle as the two cops approached.

"Hey, Jack," Wheeler said. "Thanks for calling with the girl's name. Fern is a little bit unusual."

"I hope it helps."

"Can you go through what you heard and saw this morning?"

"Unfortunately, not that much." Jack repeated his story – hearing the loud booms, scrambling to get Fern away from it all, seeing the police cars, then looking back from Route 1 and seeing the smoke rising out of the trees. "Can you tell me what happened here?"

"Not yet," Wheeler said.

"I understand if you don't want to say anything while you're in the middle of an investigation, Sam. But I need to know if it's safe to bring Melody home. And Alice. And Fern, most of all. Is this connected to whatever else happened to her? Could someone be after her?"

Wheeler was quiet for a moment. He seemed to be swallowing the scorched taste of the air. "We'll have someone on patrol down here on the point. You should be fine, all of you."

"Okay," Jack said. "You'll let me know if you learn anything that changes your mind?"

"Absolutely." Wheeler pocketed his notepad. "AJ, walk with me a minute."

Wheeler led AJ toward the house. They took a stone path through some shrubs, then climbed stairs to a vast deck that overlooked the sloping lawn and the cove.

"This whole area is alarmed." Wheeler said. "But not down there." He pointed in the direction of the camper. "This was the perfect place for someone who was lying low to hide out."

"Assuming that pile of ash was a boathouse, then the camper would have been hidden by it."

"Think Devon would even have known they were there?"

"Yes, definitely," AJ said. "If she was paying attention at all."

"I think so, too. Whoever was in the camper had Devon's permission to be here."

"But maybe they didn't have the Bartletts' permission."

"Right," Wheeler said. "Did your dad mention seeing a camper when he talked to the guy about eels?"

AJ shook his head.

"Okay. There are no plates. Whoever torched the camper remembered to take them."

The two men stared at the remains without speaking.

Then Wheeler pointed down the hill. "What do you see when you look down there?"

AJ studied the scene from this new vantage point. "I see the same thing you see."

"You sure about that?"

AJ moved right along the deck, changing his view again. "Unfortunately, yes. A burned-out camper and a pile of ash that I'm guessing was a boathouse. That's all."

"No paranormal shortcuts, then."

"Sorry, no, at least not yet."

"You mean something could still show up?"

"Look, I really don't know much more than you do about how this works. But yeah, I think someone could still show up."

"Soon would be good," Wheeler said, "if they want us to catch whoever did this to them."

23

Chad and Bobby sat at the picnic table in front of their cabin. The table had once been stained red but now the color was just a patchy rash on the cracked gray surface.

Bobby rotated a bottle in front of him. "Chad, this is totally out of control. What the hell are we going to do with her?" He pointed the neck of the bottle toward the cabin.

"I've got a couple of ideas." Chad reached into a Styrofoam cooler for a beer.

"Here's an idea – we go back to Maine."

"We're going to do that." Chad twisted the cap. "After we get our money back."

"Yeah? And how exactly are we getting the money back?"

"I have some ideas about that, too."

Bobby kept on turning his bottle. "Look, I want to get our money back as much as you do. But who knows how long that will take? We don't even know where it is. The only person who knew is dead."

"The grandfather has it. That's what Devon said."

"Yeah, okay, but we don't know where this grandfather is. Meanwhile, we're going broke. Maybe, just for a while, we need to stop thinking about the money we lost and start thinking about how we're going to get some more coming in."

"Jesus Bobby, how do you think we're going to get some more coming in? The same way we got the money in the first place."

"How was that again?"

"From elver fishing, you dumb shit."

"The way I remember it," Bobby said, "we made about half of that money from elver fishing. The other half we got straight from our broker, for hooking him up with elvers from out of state."

"Gee, thanks for reminding me of my own ideas. All of which worked, by the way."

"They worked, Chad? Maine Marine Patrol arrested our broker! They threw his ass in prison!"

"That's right. I feel bad about what happened to him. He didn't rat us out, though, did he? He's a good man. I knew it when I picked him."

"Yeah, you picked a winner all right."

"What's your problem, Bobby?"

"My problem is that working with that crooked broker – that's what kept us from going to the cops when Eric stole our elver money. It's why we're down here in Connecticut with one man dead and some girl tied up in some shithole cabin. It's why we got nothing."

Chad blew hoppy air between his teeth. "I know you would have been happy with the fifty grand you actually made with your fishing skills, Bobby, but not me. Not when some people were making ten grand a night. It's called taking on the initiative. It's called having balls."

"Yeah, well, your balls got us screwed."

"When you have balls, there's generally going to be some screwing." Chad grinned.

"That's hilarious."

"Okay, I'll make a promise to you. Next year, it'll be straight up elver fishing. All above board. We'll get a new broker who is a hundred percent swipe card business. By the book."

Bobby looked unconvinced. "The elvers won't run again until next spring."

"That's right."

"Spring is six months away. What are we going to live on for six months?"

"Jesus! I might as well be talking to this table. We're going to live on the money we made last spring. The money that Eric stole from us, and sent to Fern's grandpa. We're going to get it back."

Bobby sat mute for a second, looking nowhere. "I thought I'd ask

Rick if he'd take me back at the sawmill. Just for a few months."

"The sawmill. Right." Chad flicked his bottle cap into the dirt. "Listen, Bobby, when you won that elver license in the lottery, didn't we say we'd never work more than two weeks a year ever again?"

"Yeah."

"I don't know about you, but I meant it."

"I meant it, too. I just think – " Bobby glanced in the direction of the cabin. "I just think we need to regroup."

Chad undid the clasp on his wide watchband, shifted the band on his wrist, then closed the clasp again. "I get it. Thing's have been a little bumpy so far. But now's not the time to back off. We just need to stick it out a little longer."

"I wish the eels would run now," Bobby said. "I wish we didn't have to wait until spring."

"Yeah, if only they ran all the time, right? All year round. It'd be like having our own personal ATM."

"We could take cash out whenever we wanted."

"Yep. Unfortunately, that's not nature's way. Nature's way is you get one shot, in the spring, when the babies head upstream."

Bobby nodded without saying anything.

"It's weird, isn't it?" Chad said. "Think about it. While we're sitting here talking, the grown eels are busy making next year's cash crop. They're down there in the Sargasso Sea fucking and dying and setting us up."

Bobby seemed to be taking Chad's advice and thinking about it.

"You know what people are saying?" Chad drank. "That the price is going to be even higher next year. Twenty-nine hundred, maybe three thousand a pound. We're going to make a fortune."

"How much is a fortune?"

"I don't know. A lot. More than you've ever seen in your life, Bobby. Maybe fifteen, twenty grand a night."

"Jesus."

"Right?" Chad took a long pull from his bottle. "From baby eels. Is that some crazy shit? Thank God those Asian bastards can't get enough of 'em."

"My dad used to catch the mature ones. Firelighting, just like Eric was doing. He'd bring them home in buckets. Honestly, they always kind of scared me. Like big green snakes." Bobby held his hands in front of him, to show the size. "Ever since then, I can't stand 'em."

"Same for me. When I was like eight or nine, I caught one in a pond, on a worm. The thing pulled, and it was *heavy*. I thought I had a muskie or something. But when I got it in close and saw it – shit. It was like you said, a big green snake. I mean, *big*. It must have been four foot long. I would've just cut the line, but my dad made me pull it in. I'll never forget that slimy thing, flapping around in the grass." Chad did an exaggerated shiver.

"If it was the adults the Asians wanted, I wouldn't have anything to do with them, twenty grand a night or not."

"I hear you," Chad said. "But that's the beauty of it, isn't it? We don't have to go anywhere near those things. The babies, though – they're beautiful. Hard to believe it's the same animal. Little eels made of glass. Little glass needles."

"Almost clearer than glass, right? They disappear in your hand." Bobby finally took a drink.

"They're like glass gold."

"Yeah, except that they're clear. More silver, if anything."

"I wasn't talking about the color. I was talking about the worth."

"Oh, right, but still – "

"Here's to buckets full of glass gold in our future," Chad said.

They clinked their bottles over the table.

"So about…" Bobby gestured toward the cabin again.

"Christ!" Chad slammed his bottle on the table. "What, you want to just let her go? Give her the car keys and say, 'Have a nice day?' She'd have the cops on us so fast – "

"I'm not saying we just let her go, Chad. We could lock her in the bathroom."

"What?"

"We lock her in the bathroom, then get the hell out of here."

"Right. Lock her in the bathroom. There's a plan. It's genius."

"What's wrong with it?"

"Well, if we start at the beginning, lock her in? From the outside?"

"Okay, not lock. Nail the door, or whatever."

"Sure. With the hammer and nails we don't have."

"I guess we go buy them."

"Okay. With the money you just told me we don't have. Good, good. And how does it help us, to shut her up in the bathroom?"

"It gives us time to get the hell out of here. By the time they find her, we're long gone."

"Oh, right. So to give ourselves time to make our getaway, we drive to a hardware store, buy a hammer and nails, move her to the bathroom, and somehow nail the door shut."

"Yeah."

"Instead of just leaving her tied up in the bedroom, *like she is right now.*"

Bobby squinted in contemplation. "Okay. Maybe we don't need to lock her in the bathroom."

"Right. So anyway, we run."

"Yeah."

"And when they eventually do find her, she tells the cops everything."

"No, no, no. We threaten her, so she's too afraid to talk."

Chad seemed to be considering that. "You know, you aren't as dumb as I think you are." He stood up. "I need to take a piss." He went inside.

Bobby sat alone at the table, staring at the cabin. A crow made a rough *caw* but otherwise it was quiet. There was a hint of smoke in the air, coming from a cabin somewhere on the other side of the dirt loop.

He took out his phone. A swipe of his thumb lit up the screen. He sat there looking at it. He put the phone back in his pocket. He took a sip of his beer. The crow went on complaining.

"Where the hell is he?" Bobby said to himself. He stood up. Leaving his beer on the table, he went into the cabin.

Chad slouched on the sofa, watching the TV with the sound low.

"Chad?" Bobby said. "What's going on?"

"Shhh…" Chad pointed at the TV.

Bobby came around just as the screen switched to a commercial.

"You just missed an interesting press conference." Motioning for Bobby to follow, Chad went out through the door again.

"What?" Bobby said, following close behind.

Chad didn't answer. He went back to the table, but didn't sit down.

"Chad, what's going on?"

Chad lifted a bottle from the cooler. Smiling, he swiped the drips from the glass. "I know what we're going to do with Devon."

24

"See, I told you they'd find the kid," Chad said.

Bobby looked back at him with disgust. "She could have fallen out of that boat and drowned, Chad. It was just luck that she didn't. Dumb, stupid luck."

"What are you talking about? You didn't say anything about that when we left her in the boat."

"She's just a little kid."

"A little kid that can solve our problems."

"How's that work?"

"Devon can get her for us." When Bobby responded with a blank look, Chad arched his eyebrows encouragingly. Finally, with a sigh, he continued. "And then we trade with Grandpa. He gets the kid, we get the money that Eric sent him. Our money."

"No." Bobby sat back, shaking his head.

"What do you mean, *No*?"

"You want to be a kidnapper now? Add that to our resumes?"

"You got a better idea?"

"I told you," Bobby said. "We go back to Maine. Regroup."

They stared across the table at each other. Chad gulped his beer.

"Okay, here's an idea," Bobby said. "I go back to Maine, and you stay here and kidnap whoever the hell you want." He got up and started to walk away.

"So you're going to walk to Maine?"

Without turning around, Bobby flipped Chad the bird.

"Hey, asshole," Chad called after him.

Bobby was on the loop road now, moving away slowly, but moving.

Chad came after him. "If you keep walking, I'll call the cops and tell them you killed Eric."

"Yeah?" Bobby faced Chad. "Go ahead. I'll tell them you did it."

Chad gave Bobby a confident smile. "You could, but you're the one with a record, a history of violent behavior."

"They're not going to pin anything on me just because I got into a few bar fights. And you're not calling any cops."

"Then go ahead, walk. Do what you have to do." Chad looked back at the cabin, then took a long swallow from his bottle.

The two men stood there for a while in the quiet, not moving, nothing moving anywhere around them, on the dirt road or the shabby cabins or even in the trees overhead.

"Jesus, Chad." Bobby scuffed his feet against the hard ground. "So this idea, using Devon to get the girl… No one gets hurt, right?"

"Of course. Grandpa gets the kid. We get our cash."

"We'd probably have to pay Devon a little something to keep her quiet."

"You're right, Bobby. That's good. I can see you're thinking this through."

"You really think it will work?"

Chad's face took on the thoughtful expression of someone assessing a detailed plan. "Yeah, I do."

Bobby came back. They sat down at the table again.

"So where is the girl?" Bobby said. "How do we get anywhere near her?"

"The chief let it slip that she's still in the area. It's a small town. It shouldn't be too hard to find her."

"Okay," Bobby said. "All right."

Their bottles clinked over the table.

25

AJ found Claire in the hallway, staring at the blueprint that showed straight stairs where the winding staircase was. She stayed facing the paper as he wrapped his arms around her waist.

"Are you okay?" he said.

"I'm a little freaked out about what happened – what they found on Wamphassuc Point." Claire leaned into AJ. "Are you sure it's safe for Alice and Fern to go back there?"

"Sam thinks so," AJ said. "They'll have the area patrolled. It should be okay."

"Should be..."

"I know. Look, whoever is responsible for what happened on Wamphassuc Point is probably miles from here by now. And, if they wanted to hurt Fern – "

"They already would have done it, I know." Claire slipped out of AJ's embrace. "What a terrible thought." She looked into AJ's eyes. "When you were at the scene, were you able to make contact with anyone – any ghost?"

"Good question," Ben said, emerging from the kitchen.

"No."

"But you'll go back," Claire said. "Maybe Sam will assign you surveillance at the Bartletts' or something. That would seem like a reasonable – "

"I'm not going to be involved, Claire."

"You mean Gaines won't put you on the case."

"He won't, but that's not it." AJ stole a glance at Ben, then turned toward Claire again. "I'm going to step away for a while. Take a leave of absence."

"You've decided? I thought we were going to talk about it."

"There isn't much to talk about. Dad's going to be in the hospital for a week. It's another month or so after that before he can do any serious work. I can't leave Mom to take care of Dad, and herself, and the market, for all of that time."

"What about Sela and DaSilva? Couldn't they cover it?"

"I can't ask them to make that kind of commitment. They have their own lives."

"Do they?"

"Yes," AJ said. "For one thing, they have big dreams for Mystic Afterlife."

"Still?"

"Yeah. They want to take it from local access to real television. I guess Jack has some contacts, and he connected with The Mystery Channel. They're going to make a demo."

Claire searched his eyes. "It's not really about the Daves, is it?"

AJ stared back at her. "Mom asked for my help. She never asks. The market has been everything to them."

"So you're okay with it?"

"Honestly, lately I've been thinking that this comes at a good time."

"Because Roland left."

"Yeah."

"If having Gaines as the chief means you can't use your ability, then you need to talk to him. Even if he thinks you're crazy at first. Explain it to him. Prove it to him."

"It's bigger than that. Roland was a great chief. Really loves this community. He believes in *protect and serve*. He was old fashioned about it, you know? With Gaines, it's all about power and image. Advancing his career. You could see from his first day that he had his sights on something bigger than Stonington. With him in charge... I'm starting to think I'd be happier being my own boss."

"You're not just thinking of taking a leave, are you? You're thinking of quitting."

"AJ?" Ben said. "Gaines isn't going to last. You're right, he's looking to move up. At the first opportunity, he'll bolt."

"I wouldn't quit right now," AJ said. "Start with a leave."

"AJ, Wheeler needs you." Ben seemed to glow a little brighter as he spoke.

AJ kept his eyes on Claire. "Gaines won't put me on the case, which is just as well, with everything that's going on with Dad right now. Even if he did, I'm not sure it would matter. I haven't seen any sign of a ghost. There might not be one, this time."

Claire stayed silent, watching his face.

"There are a couple of things you and I should talk about," AJ said.

"Yes, there are," Claire said. "This is too big a conversation to have standing up in the hall." She tugged AJ toward the kitchen.

Looking at Ben over her shoulder, AJ mouthed, "Butt out."

Ben nodded but fell in behind them.

After warming mugs of coffee in the microwave, they took seats at the little table.

"You first," Claire said.

"Okay. I know you're worried about me swapping police work for selling fish. I never thought I'd want to do that, either."

"No kidding," Ben said. "You'd be wasting your talents."

"But that's not even what I'm worried about right now. Or working with my parents, or taking over something that was theirs. Or the whole thing of keeping a business going, which, even though I was raised in it, I don't know as well as I should." AJ breathed deep. "I think that will all be okay. It's other stuff that worries me."

"What other stuff?" Claire said.

"For one, I'd be tied to this town. If you decided this area wasn't right for you... I couldn't even sell the business. That would break my parents' hearts."

"Not an option," Ben said.

"I'm not going anywhere," Claire said. "I don't want to burst your bubble, but I chose to move here before I even met you, remember?"

"Right." AJ pushed his hair back from his forehead. "There's the money. My parents will still need an income, so I won't be able to take another full salary for myself. It could be tough. There might be months when I couldn't make the rent that we've agreed on. So — why are you smiling?"

"Here we go," Ben said.

Claire took a deep breath. "I've had some news that I've wanted to share. There just hasn't been a good time."

"Wait till you hear this," Ben said. When AJ shot him a look, he added, "Okay, I've overstayed my welcome." His glowing body, tattoos and all, suddenly winked out, leaving nothing but chilled air.

***

They had switched to red wine, which had been reduced to dark circles in their glasses.

"I hope I didn't seem too surprised," AJ said. "Your books are so good, and they've done so well, won awards and everything – "

"But there are a lot of good books out there."

"Not even that. I just wasn't thinking of a TV series."

"I knew that Sonia was talking to people, but I just didn't take it that seriously. That's why I didn't even mention it to you."

"So what are you going to do with it all – all your riches?"

Claire spun her glass on the tabletop. "I want to buy out my sister's share of this house. When I bought this place, it made sense financially for her to go in with me, and we both thought she'd come here often, for weeks at a time. Then her work became a lot less flexible, and…"

"The last time she was here was, what, over a year? And that was just a three-day weekend."

"Right. She could use the money for something else. And she's welcome here, whenever, anyway."

"Exactly."

"Another thing," Claire said. "I want to finally do those renovations."

"Ah, that's why you were staring at the blueprints when I came in."

Claire gave him a hard look. "This money isn't going to change things between us, is it? Because I don't want you going all 1950 on me. Remember, I was already making more money than you."

"Okay," AJ said with a smile. "I'm still going to pay you rent whenever I possibly can."

"You better believe it."

"Though I might have to pay you in lobster rolls."

"Not a problem." Her hand found his. Gently, she traced a vein between knuckles. "Now I'm thinking about lobster rolls," she said.

"Seriously? You're thinking about lobster rolls?" He rose from his chair and, in one smooth motion, lifted her up onto the table. "Let me see if I can give you something else to think about."

26

In the windowless corner of the dank bedroom, Devon was tied to a wooden chair, a sopping wet gag in her mouth. Chad stood in front of her. Bobby hung back.

"So that's the deal," Chad said. "You help us, and we let you go. And don't even think about talking to the cops. If you do, we'll get you before they get us."

Devon made a strangled sound.

"Bobby, take that gag off of her," Chad said. "There's only one right answer here, Devon."

Bobby slid the gag down from Devon's mouth, then untied the knot. "I'll get you a fresh one." He dropped the cloth on the bed but stayed where he was.

"So, Devon?" Chad said.

"I'll help."

"Right answer."

"But I want a cut of the money." Devon's cheeks were streaked from crying but there was determination in her gaze.

"Okay," Chad said. "Maybe if everything works out we'll give you back that money we found in your car. At least what's left after we take out what you owe for food, gas, and lodging."

"Right. You spared no expense," Devon said.

Chad shrugged.

"If you want my help," Devon said, "I want thirty thousand."

"What?" Chad's lips curled. "You're out of your mind! You help us, or we kill you right now, leave your body out there for the animals." He pointed toward the back wall.

Devon considered him from the chair. "If you killed me, you'd have no chance of even finding Fern, never mind getting close enough to take her. If by some miracle you did get her, then what? How are you going to find her grandfather? You don't even know his name. And besides, if you do anything to me, my dad will hunt you down and kill you himself."

Chad stepped back. For a long time he stood there looking her up and down. "You think you're so smart," he said. "Maybe you are. Maybe you're too damn smart for your own good." He grabbed the gun from the waistband of his jeans and pointed it at Devon.

"Chad!" Bobby pushed his way between them.

Chad howled. "I should shoot both of you!" He shoved the gun back into place, then went out, banging into the doorjamb on the way.

Bobby caught up with him in front of the cabin. "You need to calm down," Bobby said.

"Yeah, calm down, sure. What the fuck are we going to do?"

"We cut her in, like she says. We knew we were going to have to pay her something."

"Thirty thousand. She's playing us, Bobby."

"We can always just get the hell out of here."

"You'd love that, wouldn't you? Take off with nothing."

Bobby was silent.

"Thirty thousand. Even if things go perfect, we lose almost a third of our cash. Unless…"

"Yeah?"

"We ask for more than Eric sent. The old man will pay, for his granddaughter." Smiling, Chad went back toward the cabin. Bobby followed him through the living room into the bedroom, where Devon sat, a fresh gag in her mouth.

"Do you know much about the grandfather?" Chad said.

Behind him, Bobby nodded.

Devon did the same.

"Does he have any money – I mean, of his own?"

Again, Bobby nodded, and Devon imitated him.

"The girl knows you? She'll do what you tell her to do?"

Devon didn't wait for Bobby's nod this time.

"Okay." Chad took a few steps toward the back of the room. "Bobby, take off the gag. And untie her."

Freed, Devon rubbed her wrists. She stayed in the chair, looking up at Chad.

"All right," he said. "This is how it's going to work."

27

Despite Daniel's insistent tugging, the heavy curtain remained stuck halfway across the window. He cursed under his breath. A few feet beyond the streaked glass, a green garbage truck lifted a dumpster, motors roaring while the backup alarm beeped insistently. Daniel Junior was on the bed, flipping channels on a silent television.

"If your friend John calls now, you won't even be able to hear him," Daniel said.

"What?"

"I said, if John calls – "

"I know. I was kidding."

Daniel gave up on the curtain. "Wish we could get some air moving in here." He began fiddling with the dented unit under the window, pushing buttons, holding his palm over the vent. "John's kind of a big shot now, right? Probably too busy to call you back."

"He's a good friend, Dad. He'll call. It just may take a while."

His father kept pushing buttons. "It's either boiling hot or freezing cold. I just want *air*."

"You're going to drive me crazy." Daniel Junior tossed car keys across the bed. "Why don't you go downtown and see if you can get us a room in a nice place? Maybe that inn by the bridge?"

"Probably pricey."

"We'll split it. Won't it be worth paying a little more to have some decent air? I'll call you if I hear from John."

"Okay." Daniel scooped up the keys. "At least I'll be doing something."

***

Daniel came out of the riverfront inn with a folded brochure in his hand. He went straight for the car and dropped the paper on the dash. He checked his phone. Nothing.

He studied the backs of the shops on Mystic's Main Street, found the alley that cut between buildings, and headed for it. When he reached the street, he went left, moving slowly, scanning the windows, pausing at the whale statue in front of the bookstore.

He continued on, the shops thinning out. At a real estate office, its window covered with listings, he stopped. For a long time, he examined the ads. Then, positioning his cell phone carefully, he took a photo through the glass.

Retracing his steps, he went into the bookstore. He bought a paperback and a local map, then started back toward the car. His phone rang. "Tell me you have good news," he said, holding the phone to his ear.

"I do. John knows someone nearby who may be able to help us. He's calling her right now and will let me know."

"So more waiting."

"You're welcome."

Daniel didn't respond.

"Did you get us a better room, Dad?"

"I'd say so. And I used my charm to get us a good deal."

"By charm do you mean your senior citizen discount?"

"I like to think it's my personality. We can check in around two."

"Okay. You coming back here now?"

"I may drive around, kill some time while we're waiting for that call."

"All right. I'd tell you not to get lost, but the town's not big enough for that, even if you try."

"That's true."

"You're looking for Fern, aren't you? You think you're going to just stumble on her"

"Like you said, it's a small town. Who knows?"

28

Roland Brown parked his SUV – the same model that he'd driven as chief of the Stonington P.D. – behind the Bay Market, in the ragged space reserved for employees. As he walked toward the back door, he noticed Beth's car. "She's not supposed to work today," he said under his breath.

Inside, Beth was sitting on a stool by the sinks, holding a bag of ice to her cheek. Sela stood next to her, looking concerned. Ben hovered nearby.

Roland went straight for her. "What's going on?"

"Ray hit her," Sela said.

Beth lifted the ice from her face. "He did not hit me."

"What did happen?" Roland said.

"We had a fight." Beth lifted the ice an inch. "It got...loud. I finally just started to walk away, and he came up behind me and shoved me. I wasn't ready for it and I fell. I hit the table."

"Let me have a look," Roland said.

Beth let the ice drop to her lap. There was a red mark on her cheek. Her nose was swollen.

"When did this happen?" Roland said.

"This morning."

"Has he ever hit you?"

"No!"

"You didn't call the police?" Roland said.

"I don't want the police. Roland... It was an accident. He's been a mess ever since he lost his job. He was just out of control for a moment." Beth's lips twisted suddenly as tears began to fall.

"Oh, Jesus, Beth." Ben's arms reached, then fell.

"I'm not the police anymore," Roland said, dampening his big voice. "Is Ray still at home?"

Ben got in Roland's face, or tried to. "You're going to call this in, right? At least talk to AJ?"

"I don't know where he is." Beth said. "I just ran out of there." She took a couple of breaths. "If he's not at home, he's probably down where he keeps his boat. He's been hanging out there a lot."

"Why don't I go have a talk with him," Roland said.

Beth pressed the ice pack to her face again. "All right."

"I'll go with you," Sela said.

"No you won't. You two take care of Beth."

Sela frowned but said nothing.

"Beth, I'd like to show Ray exactly what he's done. Would that be okay?" When Beth nodded, Roland snapped a couple of pictures with his phone. "Thanks."

"No police, Roland."

"Okay."

Sela followed Roland into the lot. "I'd really like to go with you."

"No." Roland continued around his SUV. "You'll just make the situation worse."

"What do you mean?"

"That little welcome home party you threw for George and June right after their cruise? I saw the way you looked at Beth that night. I'm sure Ray did, too."

"Jesus, Roland. It was the first time anyone had ever seen her like that – you know, that green dress..." Sela seemed like he was still seeing it. "Everybody noticed her."

"Maybe. But not everyone remembers the dress." Roland opened the door. "You have two big responsibilities right now – Beth and this market. You need to be here for both of them." He didn't wait for a response, but climbed in behind the wheel. He backed up, then raced away, sending stones flying.

***

"Hey, Josh." Roland stood on a weathered dock by a small cabin boat with a bright green hull.

Josh, a twenty-something man in a flannel shirt, was working at a knot in some heavy rope. He looked up in response to Roland's greeting. "Hey, if it isn't Chief Brown."

"Well, it isn't. Not any more."

The man shook Roland's hand. "Yeah, I heard you retired."

"I did. I heard you were back from Afghanistan. Glad to see it for myself."

"I'm sure as hell glad to be home." Josh squinted under his cap. "I've been wanting to talk to you.

"Is everything all right?"

"Everything's great. I'm going to school in the spring. I plan to become a guidance counselor. I want to thank you. You straightened me out. Straightened my dad, out, too. You really helped us."

"Helping people was the best part of my job. It's the only part that I'm having trouble giving up. In fact, it's why I'm here."

"What's going on?"

"I'm looking for Ray."

"Is he in some kind of trouble?"

"Remember, I'm not police anymore."

"Right," Josh said. "I only ask because the last day or so, he's been especially twitchy. I mean, he's always been wound a little tight. But lately..."

"Did something happen recently?"

"You know he lost his job a while back, right? He's been on edge since then. And something happened a couple of days ago that seemed to throw him. Two guys were here looking to rent a boat. I knew Ray needed cash, so I gave them his number. The next day – yesterday – I saw him scrubbing down his boat. I could tell that something was wrong. He didn't even acknowledge me when I said hello. I asked if he'd rented the boat to the men I'd sent his way. He said he had. He barely even looked at me. I left him alone. With him, you have to wait until he's ready to tell you something."

"What can you tell me about the men who rented the boat?" Roland said.

"Not much. They were about my age, I guess. One was a little heavy, the other guy was taller."

Roland probed a little more but got few details about their appearance.

"Did you get their names?"

"No. I don't think they said."

"Did they say what they wanted the boat for?"

"No, I don't think so. Why?"

Roland ignored the question. "Do you know where Ray is?"

"Nah. He was here earlier, but I didn't talk to him. I figured I'd give him his space. When he took off, I waved, but he acted like he didn't see me."

"No idea where he was headed?"

Josh scratched his beard. "He's friends with some guys who run a goat farm in North Stonington. He spends a lot of time there."

"Not sure I know it."

"Black and Blue Farm."

"You're kidding."

"Nope. It's owned by Checkers Black and Skye Blue. As far as I know, those are their real names. Ray was on the crew that built their barns and a couple buildings there. It's on Hangman Hill Road. You can't miss it."

"Thanks, Josh."

They shook hands.

"Roland, if I see him, do you want me to ask him to call you?"

"It'd be better if you just called me. I'll give you my number."

Josh put the information into his cell.

As soon as he was in his car, Roland called Detective Wheeler.

"Roland," Wheeler said. "What's up?"

"How do you feel about following a hunch?"

"Is it your hunch?"

"Yeah," Roland said.

"It has to do with the case – with Eric, and the girl?"

"If I'm right, yeah."

"Okay. Maybe I've gotten too used to working with AJ and the truly weird things that come with that, but following a regular old hunch seems completely by the book."

29

Detective Wheeler drove down the narrow road, stone walls squeezing the pavement on either side. Roland Brown was in the passenger seat. "Here we are," Roland said.

They had arrived at a red barn. Mounted on the side was a sign showing a thick wedge of mottled cheese and the words *Black and Blue Farm*.

Leaving the car in a gravel lot, they followed a path to a low building. The door was open. Nearby, in a small enclosure, a man with a goatish, white beard was surrounded by goats. Detective Wheeler and Roland Brown introduced themselves over the fence.

"Checkers Uriah Black," the bearded man said. "Cubby for short. No doubt you're here to speak to Ray Williams, in regards to either the disagreement with the fiancée or the encounter with the Maineiac felons, or both."

Wheeler gave him a confused look. "I want to talk to him about a boat."

"Both," Roland said.

"All right." Checkers smiled brightly but didn't move.

Roland took out his cell phone. He found a photo of Beth's injured face. Checkers's smile faded.

"Ray wants to cooperate," Checkers said. "He can only hope that Beth is a kind and forgiving young woman. I'll go fetch Ray and meet you back in the tasting room." He motioned toward the building.

Roland and Wheeler went inside. A bar and a few pedestal tables had been set up in a small space.

Checkers entered the room, with Ray Williams – six-feet tall, short dark hair and hollow cheeks, looking very somber – right behind him.

Wheeler addressed Ray. "You know me, right? I'm Detective Wheeler."

Hanging back, Ray eyed the detective warily.

"Why don't you tell the detective about the men who rented your boat?" Checkers said.

"It was a couple days ago. Two guys." Ray looked to the side as he spoke, as if checking out the refrigerator. "They said something about it was their dad's last wish to have his ashes scattered in Mystic. On the water. They said they just wanted to go out a little ways."

"So what did you do?" Wheeler said.

"I said I'd take them out myself, but they wanted to go alone, since it was kind of personal. Emotional, I think they said. Actually one guy did pretty much all of the talking."

"Can you describe them? Both of them?"

"The one who talked was short, stocky. The other guy was tall, kind of a thin face."

"Anything else?" Wheeler had his notepad open in front of him

Ray shook his head.

"You got their names?"

"Frank – he was the talker – and Jerry. I didn't get last names. And I didn't exactly ask for ID."

"Okay," Wheeler said, after taking notes. "They didn't want you to go with them."

"No. I didn't really want to rent to them, but with what they offered to pay, I had to at least think about it. Then the shorter guy said he'd leave his watch with me. Big thing, expensive."

"So you took his watch?"

"No. Since he offered, I figured I could trust them."

"So you let them take the boat."

"Yeah. They gave me the money. I showed them to the boat. Right before they took off, the one guy asked if the eeling was any good around here. Wanted to know where the best spots were."

"What did you say?"

"I've done a little firelighting, so I told him where I go."

"Then what happened?" Wheeler said.

"Then they set out. My motor's a little tricky, but when I tried to tell them about it, the guy cut me off, said he had one just like it back home. I was feeling a little better about things then, because at least they knew what they were doing."

Wheeler wrote something. "Did they have the ashes with them?"

"They had a paper bag. I figured the ashes were in there."

"What time was it, when they took off with the boat?"

"Six, six-fifteen?"

Wheeler wrote in his pad again. "What time was it when they came back?"

"I don't know. I waited for a while, then I got hungry, so I went for a burger, stopped for a six-pack, then came back. I wasn't gone long. I parked my truck where I could see the dock. I had a couple of beers, and I waited. At some point I fell asleep. When I woke up, the boat was back where it was supposed to be."

"What time was that?"

"It was like two, two-thirty."

"In the morning. You slept a long time."

"I can sleep anywhere," Ray said. "Always could."

"So you didn't see the guys."

"No."

"What about the boat? Anything unusual about it?"

Ray swallowed. "It was dark, you know? All I had was this little flashlight that I keep in my glove compartment. I couldn't see for shit. At first I thought everything was fine, but then I noticed…"

He glanced at Checkers, who smiled encouragingly.

"I was about to head back to the truck when I noticed footprints on the dock. Muddy looking. So I went back to the boat and got in. Then I could see that it was dirty."

"Dirty how?"

"Like I said, it was hard to tell with the flashlight. There was mud, and, like, slime. I remembered him asking about eeling. I thought maybe it was eel slime."

"What did you do next?" Wheeler said.

"I cleaned it up as best I could with an old towel I had in the truck, then I drove home. I was still thinking about that mud. I started getting this weird feeling, like something bad had happened. Like it wasn't just eels."

"Something bad like what?"

"I don't know. Drugs? Some kind of drug deal, out in a boat?"

Wheeler tapped his pad. "What made you think it might be a drug deal?"

"I don't know. Too many TV shows, I guess. Well, that cash he had on him, when he paid. A big roll of bills. That seemed weird. It just seemed like something a drug dealer would do. And that watch." He pointed at his wrist. "I remember now, it had a blue face. Weird."

"Okay. You didn't call anyone?"

"You mean like the police? No. I figured I was being an idiot. It would all seem different in the daylight. So I had a couple of shitty hours of sleep. Then I went back, finished cleaning out the boat."

"How did it look in the daylight?"

"A little dirty. Not that bad."

Wheeler closed his pad and pocketed it. "So why are you hiding out here, Ray?" he said.

"I just needed to get away and think. I was starting to freak out."

"Freak out how?"

Ray didn't answer.

"Because of Beth," Roland said.

Ray stayed silent.

"We know that you hit her," Roland said.

"I didn't hit her!" Ray clenched his teeth as if fighting a scream. "I shoved her and she fell." He stared hard at Wheeler. "I've never hurt her before. You have to tell her, I won't ever do it again."

"So why did you do it this time, Ray?" Wheeler said. "Explain it to me. What was different this morning?"

"I saw the paper. The thing about the girl in the boat, with the eels. I thought, what if those guys I rented to had something to do with that? What if *I* had something to do with it, because I rented the boat to them? I even told them where the eels were. Maybe they weren't looking for eels, they were looking for someone who was looking for eels. What if something really bad had happened, you know? And I *was* a part of it. Once I started to think that way, this feeling kept building and building. Then with Beth, it just blew up in me. Just that one time, though, I swear. It was a one-time thing." Ray took something from his pocket. He slapped it on the bar – a tight roll of bills, restrained by a rubber band. "That's every dollar they gave me. I don't want it."

Wheeler left the cash sitting there. "If you were so freaked out, why didn't you come to the police?"

"I should have. But like I said, it would've looked like I was a part of whatever happened. Maybe no one would believe me when I said I didn't know anything."

"What about your boat, Ray? Where is it now?"

"It's at a friend's dock. Groton Long Point."

"We're going to want to take a look at it."

Ray nodded.

"Mr. Black," Roland said, "you referred to the men as maniac felons. What did you mean by that?"

"That's something I figured out," Checkers said. "Ray told me the man who did most of the talking mentioned the ployes he'd had for breakfast. Ployes are a buckwheat pancake commonly served in Maine."

"Ah, state of Maine," Roland said, "not – "

"Crazy maniac? Right. I checked online and found two local eateries that have ployes on the menu." Checkers took a piece of paper out of a vest pocket. He passed it to Wheeler. "The addresses of the eateries. The last address is the location of Ray's boat."

"Thanks," Wheeler said, studying the paper.

Checkers pointed at the rolled-up bills. "You want a bag for them, Detective?"

"Thanks, but I have my own." Wheeler pulled a plastic bag from a pocket, inverted it with his hand inside, closed his fingers over the bills and then flipped the bag back on itself, leaving the cash inside.

"Nice," Checkers said. "Just like cleaning up after a dog."

Wheeler slipped the bag into his sport coat. "Sometimes," he said.

30

Melody drove them home, Route 1 to Wamphassuc Point, Alice in the passenger seat, Fern in the back. A squad car was angled across the Bartletts' driveway. Fern stared at it, but her expression didn't change. Melody didn't slow down.

Just before Alice's cottage, three balloons floated alongside the road, colorful and calm. They were tied to a yard sign.

"Oh, good lord," Alice said. "An open house? Today? That's just what we need – a parade of strangers coming in and out."

"Do you think people will use the open house as an excuse to try to get a look at the Bartlett property?" Melody said.

"Some will," Alice said. "See what they can see. Which won't be much, thank goodness."

"Isn't it odd – an open house on Wamphassuc Point? Aren't realtors usually more discrete with these big houses?"

"Discretion isn't in that couple's vocabulary."

They passed Alice's cottage and rounded a bend. The handsome, solitary house came into view. Beyond it, the silver cove and the anchored sailboats were brilliant and calm.

"I'm glad you two are coming for lunch," Melody said. "The company will be nice."

"We ladies have to stick together." Alice turned around to catch the girl's eyes. "Right, Fern? We're sticking together today."

Fern gave her two thumbs up.

Alice laughed. "We just got two thumbs up."

"You get them from me, too." Letting go of the wheel for a

126

moment, Melody pointed her thumbs in the air.

***

The two women watched Fern run alongside the water, quick but jerky, her arms not quite in rhythm.

"All the excitement today doesn't seem to have set her back," Melody said.

"You're right. She's hard to predict. Last night she was very fearful. She didn't want an inch between us." Alice's tight smile softened. "Today, look at her run."

Melody's hand was on her belly. "Sometimes I think that's what's going on in here."

"May I?" Alice placed her hand next to Melody's. "Oh. She's in full sprint. Or he."

"Seems like it. Trying to keep up with Fern."

"Speaking of which." Alice called out to the girl. "That's far enough! Come on back!"

"She can look so grown-up sometimes," Melody said, as Fern changed direction. "The night that we found her, she seemed – almost a baby."

"She's a little girl today."

"I've tried asking her age, but she either doesn't understand, or she just won't answer."

"Oh, I'm sure she understands."

"Fern," Melody said, as the girl approached. "How old are you?"

Without acknowledging the question, Fern raced toward them. At the last minute, she swerved and passed by. She stopped suddenly.

A man was coming their way from the next property, walking along the water's edge. He had dark hair and a heavy face.

Without being asked, Fern raced to Alice's side.

"Do you think he's from the open house?" Melody said.

"Most likely." Alice had one arm around the girl.

The man kept coming.

"Why don't you take Fern inside?" Alice said.

"Don't you want to do that? I can stay out here and talk to this guy. I know how to get rid of him. This belly always kind of unnerves men."

"Thank you, Melody, but I can be very effective as the grouchy neighbor. I've had a lot of practice."

"All right, but I'll keep an eye on you. Come on, Fern, I'll race you to the porch."

They took off up the slope.

The man watched them but continued toward Alice. "Hello!" he said.

At thirty feet away, the gray in his hair was visible.

Alice closed the gap between them. "This is private property."

"Oh, sorry. I'm from the open house." He pointed behind him. "I wasn't sure where the property line was."

"You're well past it."

"Sorry." He gave Alice a smile. "I'm Daniel Frost. Just came down from upstate New York. Do you live here?"

Alice crossed her arms. "I'm visiting. When you go back, kindly tell the rest of the crowd not to come around that point."

"I'll do that." He turned as if to go, then faced Alice again. "A couple of women in that crowd had quite a story to tell about this place." Seeming to catch himself, he looked out at the water. "Well, sorry for the intrusion." With a wave, he added, "Beautiful spot, by the way."

"What story were they telling?" Alice said.

"They said some old Svengali lives here with a young girl he got pregnant. And that he bought his way out of a murder charge."

"I thought as much. It's all ridiculous. The real estate agent shouldn't let them get away with that."

"Not sure the realtor heard. So it's not true?"

"Not a bit of it."

"Okay," Daniel said. "I should have known better. I've had a few stories told about me, and about people I loved. Why do we take such pleasure in the misery of others? We'll even invent misery where there isn't any." He waved again, a weight in his smile. "It was a pleasure to meet you."

Alice studied Daniel as he moved away. She called after him. "The owner of this property was a murder suspect years ago, but he was cleared. They caught the real murderer red-handed. As for the rest of it – the man's not that old and the woman's not that young, and they're both very excited to be expecting their first child."

"I like that much better," Daniel said, turning around. For the first time, he faced the house. Melody and Fern had already disappeared inside. Daniel seemed to be studying the crisply painted clapboard siding, the many windows, flanked by shutters, and the sprawling deck, still set up for warm weather. "That house next door isn't really my taste. All those columns... It's a little too..."

"Greek temple?"

"Yeah," Daniel said with a chuckle. Pointing up the hill, he said, "This is more my style. My wife would have loved it, too."

Alice let a smile show. "It's a fine old house." She relaxed; her arms dropping to her sides. "So why did you go to the open house? Hadn't you seen pictures? It seems like a long drive from upstate New York to look at a place that's not your style."

"Going to the open house was just a whim. I'm on my way to visit family in North Carolina, and decided to stop and tour the Pequot Museum and Mystic Seaport. I was really just looking for a lunch spot when I saw the realtor's yard signs. 'Ocean view.' I guess I thought it might be a nice seaside cottage."

"That house is about as far from a cottage as you can get," Alice said.

"You're right. Have you been inside?"

"Yes, a few times. I always liked it there. Once you get past that imposing façade, it's very peaceful. Though I guess not today."

"No, not today."

In a long pause, they looked at each other, then looked away.

Alice's phone, tucked into a pocket, chimed. She checked the text, typed a reply.

"Your friend is wondering if I'm being a pest," Daniel said.

"More or less."

"I guess that's my cue."

"I guess so. Though the tide's coming in. You might get wet."

Daniel glanced back the way he had come. He lifted one foot. "These are my good shoes. Maybe I can beat through the bushes."

"You'll get ticks doing that. Why don't I walk you up the drive?" Alice sent another text.

"Maybe your friend should join us."

"I think we're just fine, Daniel. It's not far."

"Okay. Lead the way."

***

Alice found Melody and Fern squeezed into a single chair at the kitchen table. In front of them were a box of Nilla Wafers and a jar of peanut butter.

"I hope you're not ruining her appetite for supper," Alice said.

"Don't worry, she has more self control than I do." Melody plunged her hand into the cookie box. "Why did you reintroduce me to Nilla Wafers?"

Fern made a sign, one hand waving over the other.

Alice interpreted. "Movie."

"Would that be okay?" Melody said. "I think I can find something suitable."

"Sure." Alice signed something to the girl, who slid down from her seat.

When Melody came back into the kitchen a few minutes later, Alice said, "She's having a good day, isn't she?"

"Maybe she's turned the corner."

"I'm sure she'll be up and down for a while, still. But right now, she's like a different person."

"She is," Melody said. "So tell me about our trespasser."

"He's not going to be your new neighbor," Alice said.

"He didn't like the house?"

"No, he didn't. Anyway, he's just passing through. He's not seriously house hunting." Alice patted her hair, as if checking the shape. "I should tell you, as I expected, there are some locals at the open house, and they're telling stories about Jack's history. Or his mythology, I guess."

"That's never going to go away, is it? Even after the chief of police made a public statement."

"Well, I set him straight, at least."

"Good. Did you do the grouchy neighbor routine?"

"I didn't have to. I guess he's had some experience with people gossiping about him, or about people close to him. He knows what that's like. He seemed intelligent, a nice man. Kind."

"You got all of that from your conversation?"

"You can tell a lot about a man in the first few minutes, don't you think? It's the eyes."

"I guess so," Melody said.

"And something else, too. He's known loss."

"Really?"

"He's a widower."

"He told you that?"

"More like let it slip. I was already thinking it, because he was obviously alone, free to stop at an open house on a whim. Then, he said 'people I *loved*.' Past tense. When he complimented this house, he said his wife would have loved it. *Would have*."

"Maybe she's an ex."

"He didn't say ex-wife. Anyway, he wouldn't have brought her up if there'd been a divorce. So, she must have passed away."

Melody cocked her head. "You seem to have put a lot of thought into that."

"Just trying to get the measure of him."

"Huh. If I didn't know better, Alice, I'd say you were smitten."

"Oh, don't be ridiculous. I was just being polite." A smile that had been flickering around the edges of Alice's face suddenly took it over, for a second. Then the usual reserve returned. "Anyway, we won't see him again."

"That's good, right?"

"It's not like I gave him my number," Alice said.

"Did he give you his?"

"No. He did tell me his name. Daniel. Daniel Frost."

"Did you give him your name?"

"Well, he did ask, as he was saying goodbye."

"Really?"

"Is that so shocking? He was just being friendly."

"No, it's fine. I just expected you to be more guarded. With everything that's going on."

"Well, of course he doesn't have anything to do with that."

"Of course not, no." Melody stacked Fern's glass on her plate. "If he wasn't just passing through, I'd say you should Google him. That's what the kids do now when they meet someone."

"Really? Did you Google Jack?"

"I think I lost the kid designation a long time ago."

"Well, then, where does that put me?"

Melody only smiled.

"He might make for an interesting neighbor," Alice said. "It's almost a shame he wasn't seriously looking."

"Neighbor. Right."

Alice slid the box across the table. "Have some more cookies."

"I think I will. But you won't shut me up that easily." Melody popped the lid. "I can talk with my mouth full."

They both laughed.

Alice stood up. "I'd better go collect our girl and head home." She carried the dishes to the sink, the efficiency of her movement a reminder that this kitchen had been her own not long ago.

"Why don't I drive?" Melody said. "With all these handsome strangers wandering over from the open house, I have to keep an eye on you."

31

From across the street, Detective Wheeler studied the old farmhouse. It was so meticulously maintained that it might have been built that morning. The grass was freshly cut. The downstairs windows glowed with a yellow light. He got out of his unmarked car, then walked between trimmed shrubs to the porch. The anchor-shaped knocker clacked under his hand. While he waited, he looked at Quanaduck Cove, which was gray under the fading sun.

A man opened the door.

"Hello, Mr. Alexander?" Wheeler said.

"Yes."

"I'm Detective Wheeler from the Stonington Police Department." He showed his badge. "Is Devon at home?"

"What's this about?" The man was in his fifties, fit, wary.

"I'm hoping she can help us with an investigation. If I could just speak to her..."

"I can't imagine what you would want to talk to her about."

Devon appeared behind him. "Dad, what's going on?" She was wearing jeans and a flannel shirt. Her hair was damp, her face recently scrubbed and pink.

Wheeler introduced himself again. "You've been watching the Bartlett property on Wamphassuc Point?" he said.

"Yes."

"When was the last time you were there?"

"This morning, around nine o'clock."

"Did you see anything unusual?"

"No," Devon said.

Wheeler produced his notepad from a pocket. "I'm looking for information on the camper that was parked on the property. Can you give me the name of the owner? What was your relationship to them?"

The father's face stiffened. "Devon, did you know about this camper? I hope you didn't let someone onto the property without the Bartletts' permission." He turned to Wheeler. "What's this all about?"

"There was a fire earlier today," Wheeler said.

"A fire?" Devon said. "At the Bartletts'?"

"Even if Devon did let someone park there, surely she's not responsible for whatever accident has occurred," Mr. Alexander said.

Wheeler kept his eyes on Devon. "It would be very helpful if you could provide us with a name."

"What burned?" she said. "Was anyone hurt?"

"I'm sorry to say we recovered a body."

"Oh, God." Devon collapsed against her father. "You said a body. Just one?"

"Yes."

"Devon – " Mr. Alexander put an arm around her.

"Was it..."

"An adult male," Wheeler said.

"No more," Mr. Alexander said, shoving Devon back inside and beginning to close the door.

"Oh God, Eric," Devon said.

"What's Eric's last name?" Wheeler said through the shrinking opening. "It would be very helpful."

"I'm sorry, but that's enough," Mr. Alexander said through the half-closed door.

"I need to ask Devon a few more questions," Wheeler said, stepping up to the threshold.

"Not without a lawyer."

The door slammed shut.

"That can be arranged," Wheeler said, as he went back to his car.

***

Mr. Alexander turned away from the window, having watched Wheeler's car round the corner. "What the hell are you involved with this time?"

They were in a clean and orderly living room – stiff wingback chairs, gleaming hardwood floors, glossy white mantle over a stone fireplace.

"Devon," the man said. "What is going on?"

"I don't know." Devon spoke in a trembling voice.

"This Eric – he's the guy from Maine?"

Devon nodded.

"What was he doing in Stonington?"

"He stopped here on his way south. He needed a place to stay, so I figured, with the Bartletts away... It would be just for a little while."

"Why didn't you send him to the KOA?"

"I was trying to save him money, Dad. The KOA's expensive."

"Why didn't you bring him here?"

"Yeah, right. If I asked you to let my fisherman boyfriend camp out in our yard, you would have been okay with that?"

Her father looked out the window again.

"That's what I thought," Devon said.

"So Eric was your boyfriend? I seem to remember he was unavailable."

In an instant, Devon's face softened. She began to cry.

"I'm sorry," her dad said. "Obviously he meant something to you."

"Obviously," Devon said, getting some of the ferocity back in her voice.

Her father waved her off. "Never mind. It's your life. You have to make your own mistakes. You asked the detective how many bodies they found. Who else was staying in the camper?"

"Eric's daughter. The girl I used to babysit." Devon's mood seemed to switch suddenly to panic. "We have to find out what happened to her!"

The father abruptly walked out of the room.

"Dad? Don't just walk away." Devon followed him.

On a dining room table there were a few folders, a cell phone, a coffee cup, and the morning paper. The man picked that up and, without a word, handed it to his daughter.

She sat down, skimmed the page. "This is her. Thank God. Dad, I have to go to the police. I have to find out where she is, make sure she's all right."

"I'll call Charles. You're not talking to anyone without Charles."

"Okay. " Devon watched him take his cell phone from the table. "Will you ask him to find out where Fern is?"

"You need to stay out of this, Devon. I know you have a soft spot for people in trouble, and I usually encourage your charitable heart, but not this time. People who are in trouble cause trouble. I shouldn't need to remind you of that, after what just happened."

Devon was quiet for a second. A few tears slid down her cheeks. "I love that little girl, Dad. She's probably so scared. I just want to know that she's somewhere safe."

Her father patted her shoulder. "Okay. We'll see what Charles can find out."

Devon sat quietly, accepting the hand on her shoulder, tears following one after the other down her cheeks.

32

The Frosts drove upstream on the Groton side of the Mystic River. On their right, the water shimmered cheerily in the morning sun. Daniel Junior, preoccupied by simultaneously driving and following the map on his phone, was oblivious to the scenery. "Her office should be just a little ways ahead."

Daniel said nothing.

"I made at least one good contact at FSU," Daniel Junior said. "That year of law school wasn't a total waste."

The father kept up his silent stare.

"I was told that this woman is really good."

Continued silence from the older man.

"Dad? Aren't you going to say a single word?"

Daniel finally looked at his son. "When you're nervous, you talk too much."

"You're right, I do. But it's better to just clam up? Let me know what you're thinking."

"I was thinking that she might be good, but she's going to be expensive, judging by the neighborhood."

"Maybe not," Daniel Junior said. "I told you, she used to work for the casinos but switched to adoption law. You don't do that if you're in it for the money."

"Maybe she just figured out a different way to make money. Take advantage of desperate people."

Daniel Junior squinted at his father. "C'mon, Dad. You wanted to do this. What's got you so negative all of a sudden?"

The father didn't respond. The muscles in his face were tight.

"Well, at least try to have a positive attitude. She worked for the casinos, so doesn't that mean she's Mohegan, or Pequot?"

"The tribes only own the casinos here," Daniel said. "They don't run them."

The men were quiet for a while.

"What's her name again?" Daniel said.

"Lolly Bridgewater."

"Right. What kind of a name is Lolly? For a lawyer?"

Daniel Junior ignored the question. "So where did you go, yesterday, after you made the reservation at the inn? Besides the bookstore?"

"I drove down Route 1 a ways. Got some nice views of the water."

"Are you really thinking you'll just run into Fern, driving around?"

"It could happen."

"Even if you did – you can't just go up to her. That's why we're going to see the lawyer."

They drove on, both men silent. The father's expression grew even darker.

"I think this is it," Daniel Junior said, as they approached a small house perched on the riverbank.

"Is this her home or her office?"

"Both maybe?"

Once they were out of the car, they stood in the sand-and-gravel driveway, looking at the river. Not far out, a tall pole was topped by a huge, ragged osprey nest. Beyond that, in the current, sailboats skimmed toward the bridge.

"Nice spot," Daniel Junior said.

Daniel nodded, his lips a flat line.

They approached the house. It was low and unassuming, covered with graying cedar shakes. The door, though, was bright blue. Daniel Junior reached for the knob, but pulled back. "If this is her home, we should knock."

"Go ahead."

Daniel Junior rapped on the wood.

The woman who answered was dressed for a lazy Saturday, in jeans and a simple cotton blouse. She was also, Daniel Junior would say later, over lunch, "some kind of goddess," tall, slender, with long black hair and emerald green eyes.

"You must be the Frosts," she said, warmly. "I'm Lolly Bridgewater. Please come in. We'll be meeting through here." She led them down a half flight of stairs, into a room that was all glass on one side, with a wide view of the river.

"Wow," Daniel Junior said. "That's spectacular."

"Yes. Until there's a flood, I guess. I'm only renting, so I'm not so worried about that. I'm afraid you caught me in transition. We're relocating in a couple of weeks. I've already closed the office in town."

They all took seats at a long table.

"John said you need some advice on a custody case. He tells me you have an interesting story."

"I gave John the short version," the younger man said.

"I'll need the long version. Don't leave anything out." Lolly picked up a pen.

Daniel Junior looked from her to his father. "Dad?"

"It's about custody of a child, a young girl. She's family, but right now she's with — " Daniel hesitated. "Someone else. We'd need to get her back."

"You said she's family. What is your relationship?"

"I'm her grandfather."

"Okay. Where are the parents?"

"The father is missing," Daniel said. "Her mother is dead."

"When you say missing — "

"I don't know any more than that. But the important thing is, what are our rights?"

Lolly studied Daniel's face. "Do you have reason to believe that the father is an unfit parent?"

"We have many reasons."

"All right. Once you have established your relationship, your rights are considerable."

A smile came and went on Daniel's face. "What are our options for establishing a relationship?"

"A DNA test is the standard."

"A DNA test is no good." Daniel kept his eyes straight ahead. "Is there another way?"

"When you say it's no good — "

"It won't show that we're related. But she's my daughter's daughter. Rose was adopted." Daniel's eyes stayed fixed across the table. "The girl's mother was adopted."

"Okay," the lawyer said. "Then we need the adoption papers."

"That's complicated."

"Complicated how, Mr. Frost?"

Daniel let out a breath. "After my son was born, his mother had some problems. I guess it was post-partum depression, but back then, where we lived, they didn't call it that. The doctor gave her drugs, but they didn't help. She started drinking. It got pretty bad. She couldn't take care of herself, let alone a child. This went on for about a year and a half. Finally, I gave her an ultimatum – get herself straightened out or I'd take young Daniel and leave. I feel bad about it now, but I just didn't know what else to do. A few days later I came home from work and she was gone. She left a note saying that she was going to live with her aunt in Toronto and get well." Daniel looked down at his hands.

"What happened then, Mr. Frost?"

"She did get better," Daniel said, lifting his eyes. "But she stayed in Toronto, stayed away. Just to be sure, she said. I didn't know what that meant, but we were doing fine, Daniel and me." He glanced at his son. "Better than when she was with us. I didn't push it. Weeks went by, then months."

"How long was she gone, Dad?" Daniel Junior said.

"Five months."

"Jesus. I don't remember her being gone. Not at all. I guess I was too little."

"I'm glad to hear that."

"Mr. Frost," the lawyer said, "how does this connect up to the adoption?"

In the long silence that followed, Daniel's eyes seemed fixed on an invisible past. "This is why we need you, Ms. Bridgewater. When my wife came home, she had Rose with her. And adoption papers, a birth certificate. She said Rose was ours to keep."

"She brought a baby home with her." The lawyer's pen worked across a pad.

"Yes."

"You heard later that the mother was someone else my aunt was helping to take care of," Daniel Junior said. "A girl, too young to handle a baby." He made eye contact with his father, as if for confirmation.

"That's right," Daniel said, no longer talking to the lawyer. "I felt like I had to take the child in. Your mom was clearly so attached to her, and she seemed herself again. Like it was the baby who healed her."

"Hearing this again – it still doesn't make sense," Daniel Junior said. "You know that." He caught the lawyer's eyes. "He only just told me all of this. I still haven't wrapped my head around it."

Lolly sat back a little, as if to let that comment pass by on its way out of the room.

"Maybe it doesn't make sense," Daniel said. "But I know that Rose saved all of us. Your mother became the mother who raised you. The mother you remember."

Lolly reached out into the center of the table and laid her hand there, as if it were the furniture that needed to be reassured. "So you're not certain that the adoption papers are legal. You hadn't signed them, of course."

Daniel pressed his lips together. "I never had anyone look at them. I was afraid to rock the boat. I was afraid we'd lose both of them – my wife and Rose."

The door opened. A man in his late twenties, with unfussy blonde hair and wire-rim glasses, tapped something against the doorjamb – a small case.

"Oh, thank God," Lolly went to him. "You're a lifesaver, Jarett." She gave him a peck on the cheek.

When she was at the table again, she said, "My glasses broke yesterday, and I've been trying to get by with these old contacts. They're killing me." With a deft pinch, she removed one lens. For a second she sat there with mismatched eyes, one the dazzling green that had met the men at the front door, and the other an earthy brown. "Ahh, so much better. Thank God my fiancée's father is an optometrist." After taking care of the other contact, she put on the glasses. "Would anyone like a cup of coffee or tea?" She went to the back wall and unclenched her fist over a wastebasket, letting the contacts drop. Opening a pair of cabinet doors, she revealed a counter with a coffee maker.

As she prepared their drinks, she continued the interview. "So, do you have the adoption papers with you?"

"No, I'm sorry."

"But you can get them."

"Yes."

"And we'll want to talk to your wife."

"Dead. Almost three years ago."

"I'm sorry. What about the aunt?"

"She passed away, too."

"Okay. You said your wife was away for five months, in Toronto. Is it possible that she was pregnant when she left?"

"No. She'd been so...sick. We hadn't..."

"I understand. I have to ask you a difficult question, Mr. Frost. Is there any chance that Rose is your wife's daughter, but not yours?"

Daniel's face stiffened. "I asked her that. She told me no. I believe her."

It was quiet for a moment. Outside, the lawyer's fiancée was sitting in a wooden chair just inches from the water, talking on a cell phone.

"Nice place to work, don't you think?" the lawyer said, coming to the table with a mug in each hand. "I'm glad that he can take advantage of this warm day."

Daniel turned to her again. "Before we go any further – can someone help us with this? Can you recommend someone? They'd have to understand that we're not rich."

"I don't know anyone more suited than myself."

"Yes, but you're moving, right? You said you already shut down your office."

"My schedule for relocating is flexible. If you want to proceed, we can talk about exactly how I think I can help you. If it still sounds good, I'll give you a list of things I'll need from you."

"Let's continue," Daniel said.

"Okay. Mr. Frost, you'll need to promise me something right up front. From experience, I know this is the most important thing."

"What's that?"

"If you want custody of this child – your granddaughter – then for now, until I give you the okay, you need to stay away from her."

33

In the interview room at the station, Wheeler sat on one side of the table, with Devon, her father and their lawyer – the only one in a suit – arrayed against him on the other side.

"Devon," Wheeler said, "we're interested in any information that you can give us about Eric, the girl, and anyone Eric might have associated with. Let's start with Eric's last name."

"Mitchell," Devon said. "Eric Mitchell."

Wheeler took notes on a legal pad.

"Before we go any further," the lawyer, said, "we want to make it very clear that Devon had nothing to do with the fire at the Bartlett residence, or the death of Eric Mitchell."

"I understand," Wheeler said. "She's not being accused of anything."

The lawyer nodded at his client.

"I met Eric at the beginning of the summer." Devon's hands pressed against each other. Her voice was flat, controlled. "I was working in the Firelight Bar in Ellsworth. He came in a lot. That's how I met his whole family. Fern and her mom, Rose."

"Ellsworth, Maine, right?"

"Yes."

"Is that on the coast?"

"Not right on the coast. It's not too far inland from Bar Harbor, if you know where that is."

"What else can you tell me about Rose Mitchell?"

Devon shifted in her seat. "Well, she had a drinking problem. I heard she did heroin, too, though she never did that in front of me. A few weeks after I started working, she went into rehab. Then just a little while later, she ran off with some guy she met there. We all felt bad for Eric, and we tried to help him out, babysitting Fern."

"Who's we?"

"Me and a couple of the other waitresses. I ended up doing most of it, though. The other girls couldn't make time or were just bored with it, I guess. But I really liked being with Fern. She was so cute."

"Were you romantically involved with Eric?"

Devon's eyes went past Wheeler to the big mirror that took up most of the opposite wall. "No. I liked him, yeah. But he was with Rose, and he had Fern to look after." Her voice had stayed measured, careful, but under the table, her right leg bounced rapidly. "Can you tell me where she is? Is she okay?"

"She's fine." Wheeler wrote on the pad. "What did Eric do for a living?"

"Fishing. Some house painting."

"Do you know the names of anyone he fished or painted with?"

"There was a guy named Joe who was a fisherman. I think Eric painted by himself."

Wheeler asked about Joe's last name, and asked her to try again to remember the names of other people Eric worked with. He gave her a minute, then continued. "You said Rose ran off with a guy. Do you know his name? Do you know where they ran off to, how we could contact her?"

"No. I'm sorry. It was like, one day she was just gone. I don't think I ever saw the guy or heard his name."

"How about family? Do you know of anyone besides Rose?"

"I don't think there was any other family – not nearby, anyway. He always said how grateful he was for our help with Fern because he didn't have anyone else."

"How did he end up in a camper on the Bartlett property?"

"Eric was sick of just getting by. He was sick of Maine winters. He got in touch with a friend who works at Disney, in Florida. The guy said he could get Eric a job on the maintenance crew. Eric decided to check it out. I'd already left Maine – business was dropping off, with summer ending. So, I was home, and I told him to come visit."

"But he didn't stay at your house?"

"I figured Dad would say no." Devon stared straight ahead, avoiding her father's eyes, which were fixed on her. "The Bartletts hired me just to drive in and out and walk around the shore a little. I figured if Eric and Fern were there, they'd just be more, you know, protection. They were going to go to a campground, but I told them the Bartletts' place was free and a lot prettier." A tear slid down her cheek. "If they had just gong to the KOA, none of this would have happened. Eric would…"

Her father patted her on the arm, though his jaw remained clenched.

"What did happen, Devon?" Wheeler said.

"What?" Devon sniffled as she looked back across the table.

"Detective Wheeler," the lawyer said, "we already stated that Devon knows nothing about the fire or Eric Mitchell's death."

"Yes. But Devon, do you have any ideas about what might have happened? Any ideas about who would have wanted to hurt Eric?"

"No."

"Okay. Maybe we'll come back to that. When did Eric arrive in Mystic?"

"Monday. We met in the parking lot at the Quality Inn and went straight to the Bartletts'."

"What did you do that day?"

"I showed him around the property. We hung out, played with Fern. Then Eric was going to let Fern nap, so I left. I planned to come back later, but I got tied up."

"It was my sister's birthday," her dad said. "We were having a dinner at her house."

"So you didn't see Eric that night, Devon?"

"No. We texted. He said they were fine."

"Did he say anything about going eeling?"

"Yeah. After he bought that camper, he had barely enough money left for food and gas. He thought he could get some eels, and find someone who would buy them."

"Where would he get a boat?"

"I guess the Bartletts' boat was the wrong kind. I told him we could rent one, but I don't know…"

"Why didn't he ask you to watch Fern while he went out in the boat?"

"He knew I was busy that night. Besides, he said he'd taken her out before, and she liked it."

"Did you check on them the next day, when you went over to the Bartletts'?"

"Well, I went over there, but they weren't around."

"Didn't that bother you?"

"I just thought they went for a walk or something."

"Did you try calling Eric?"

"I texted him but he didn't answer. That was normal though. He never had his cell phone on."

"So you didn't hear from him all day?"

"No."

"And that still didn't bother you?"

"Maybe a little. I wondered if maybe he'd already taken off for Florida. I mean, this was just a quick stop anyway. But yeah, I guess I thought he'd at least call me before he left."

"You didn't see any of the news stories on the TV? Or in the newspaper?"

"I can vouch for Devon's lack of interest in news," Devon's father said. "Local or otherwise."

Wheeler jotted something down. "When was the last time you were on the Bartlett property?"

"Yesterday."

"What time?"

"I don't know, exactly. Around noon, I guess. They still weren't there."

"You didn't see anything unusual?"

"No."

"Was Eric in any kind of trouble? Had he had any arguments with anyone, that you know of? Did he owe money to anyone?"

"No. Everybody liked Eric. He was just a good guy trying to be a good dad. I don't know why anyone would want to hurt him." Her eyes welled up again.

"I think Devon has given you all the information that she has," the lawyer said.

Wheeler tore a clean sheet of paper loose from his pad. He asked Devon to write down Eric's phone number, and the names, addresses and phone numbers of anyone connected to him, the friend at Disney, anyone in Ellsworth. She worked quickly, referring once to her cell, studious and silent.

"Just one more thing," Wheeler said, as he took the paper back. "Do you know sign language?"

"You mean because of Fern? I know some. She can hear, so I just needed the signs that she uses. The main ones were food, drink, help, mommy – " Devon did the signs as she talked " – and E for Eric." After this last sign, she let her hand fall to the table. "Mostly she just pointed."

"Did Eric or anyone else ever say why she didn't talk?"

"No, and I didn't think I should ask. I figured Rose must have drank or did drugs when she was pregnant." Devon watched Wheeler finish writing something on his pad. "Can I see her? Can I see Fern? She must be wondering where Eric and I went."

"That's not for me to decide." Wheeler put his pencil down. "Thank you for your help."

Devon looked crushed. "I just want to be sure that she's okay."

"I appreciate that," Wheeler said. "I can tell you that she's in good hands." He slipped the legal pad into a folder.

"Is she with a family – a foster family or something?"

"You might be hearing from the Department of Children and Families," Wheeler said. "They might have questions about Fern. You're the one person here with any history with her."

"I do have a history," Devon said, sounding encouraged. "I hope they call."

"I might be calling again, too, if I have more questions."

"Good," Devin said. "Anything I can do to help."

Wheeler led them out of the room, to the back door that opened on the parking lot. The door was just closing when AJ came through it.

"Hey, Sam," he said.

"You're here to talk to Gaines," Wheeler said, in a low voice. "About taking time?"

"Yeah."

They went back into the station.

"Did your father get a date for the surgery?" Wheeler said.

"Not yet. I think that will happen today, probably."

"Tell him I'm thinking of him."

"I will."

They had come to a stop at AJ's desk. "The girl who was watching the Bartlett property was just here. Devon Alexander. Along with her father and a lawyer."

"She shed any light?"

"Some. She cares about that girl."

"If you have time," AJ said, "come by the market later, fill me in."

Behind them, the chief's door opened. AJ glanced toward it. "Wish me luck, Sam."

"I definitely do." Wheeler waited for AJ to disappear into Gaines's office. Then he walked past the interview room to the narrow control room beyond. He took a seat at a table there, positioned himself in front of a monitor, picked up a remote control, and pressed Play.

34

Still dressed in the clothes she'd worn to be interviewed by the police, Devon sat at a weathered picnic table facing away from the road. She'd put a plastic bag down to protect her slacks. The only other table was empty. Ahead of her, a stream made a big curve between trees. She was not watching the light play on the water, though. Her eyes were closed. Her chest rose and fell slowly and steadily, as if she were measuring her breaths. Her eyes brimmed with tears.

She turned toward the sound of a car slowing. A gold Pontiac. As the two men climbed out, Devon brushed her cheek with the soft back of her hand. It came away damp.

"So how did it go?" Chad said, when he was seated next to her on the bench. "You didn't give them anything, did you?" He grinned as if he'd made a joke.

"It went fine," Devon said. "Really good, actually. Right now, they're probably busy looking for Rose Mitchell."

"You mean Rose Frost?" Chad said. "She and Eric weren't married."

"Right. The detective called her Rose Mitchell, and I just let that go. Nobody else said anything. So, that will kill some time – they'll be looking for the wrong name. Plus, they'll be looking for a live person."

Bobby took the other bench. "Ellsworth's a small town. They'll figure it out pretty quick."

"What do mean, a live person?" Chad said.

"Yeah, that's why Eric left Ellsworth. Rose died. Drugs. You didn't know that?"

"Oh, the girl did good," Chad said, smiling at Bobby.

"I still think it won't take long to figure all that out," Bobby said.

"No," Chad said, "but you want them to find something, so they stick around. Keep them up there digging into all the details, while we're getting our cash."

"I guess," Bobby said.

"When do you think you'll find out where the kid is?" Chad said.

"My dad's lawyer said he'd talk to some people and I'd probably hear by tonight."

"This lawyer must have some friends in high places."

"He has all the best friends," Devon said.

Another car eased into the last remaining parking spot.

"Damn, popular place," Bobby said.

"It's this warm day." Chad seemed almost to be savoring the air and the quicksilvery monolog of the stream. "Everyone's out enjoying it."

The new car had barely come to a stop when the doors flew open. A young boy and girl flew past, racing to be first into the water. They splashed in, laughing.

"That's cute," Bobby said.

"Yeah," Chad said. "Long as they don't run into a big old eel, on its way out to sea. I bet they don't know anything about eels. Like they say, ignorance is bliss." As he stood, Chad put a heavy hand on Devon's shoulder. She ducked and twisted away from him.

"You call us as soon as you hear where the girl is," Chad said.

She stayed looking out at the stream as the two men drove off.

***

Devon parked next to her dad's car, grabbed her bag from the passenger seat, and walked to the front door. Her dad and the lawyer were in the living room, each with a rocks glass of whiskey – a two-man cocktail party.

"Where have you been?" her dad said.

Devon held up her bag. "Shopping."

"All this time?"

Devon shrugged.

"Just be glad she came home with only one bag," the lawyer said.

"What would make me glad is if she came home with a job. She doesn't seem to think that she needs to earn money before she spends it."

"I have a job," Devon said.

"I know you think that checking on the Bartletts' house once a day is a job. That's the problem. Moreover, I'm sure you'll hear from them soon. They can't be pleased about what went on there on your watch. You'd better start looking for some other employment."

Devon frowned at her father, then looked away. "What are you drinking, Uncle Charlie?" she said, with a suddenly girlish voice and a smile.

"Scotch. Would you like a sip?" He raised the glass as if he were about to make a toast.

"Yuk." She made a face, hamming it up. "What do we have for food? I'm starving."

"Charlie's taking us to dinner," her dad said.

"Yeah?" Devon's face brightened. "Where?"

"That fish market on Route 1," Charlie said. "We can sit outside, take advantage of this warm weather."

"I thought you only ate at four-star restaurants," Devon said.

"And four-star clam shacks," Charlie said, with a scratchy laugh. Deep in a jacket pocket, Charlie's cell phone rang. He excused himself and left the room.

Her dad gave Devon a stern look. "We're going to have a talk when Uncle Charlie leaves. This whole thing with Eric... Letting him stay on the Bartlett property – that showed a serious lack of judgment. And hiding all of it from me – "

"I didn't hide it from you. You never asked."

"Devon! Don't you see how serious this is? Whatever he was involved with got him killed. If you want me to continue to keep you under this roof, and support your adventures in Ellsworth or wherever it is next time, then..."

"Then what?"

"Then I'm going to need some guarantee that you won't seek out the lowlifes everywhere you go."

"Sure. I'll put it in writing. No lowlifes."

"Devon Whitney Louise. Don't you dare talk to me like that."

"Like what?"

"As if I don't have good reason for what I say. As if Eric were the first boy to get you into trouble. As if there had never been that boy on the Cape – "

"Jeff. Do you seriously not remember his name?"

"I remember his name. I just choose not to say it. I remember all of it, everything he got you involved in – the pot, the reckless driving, the burglary."

"It was only vandalism."

"It was burglary. Charlie turned it into vandalism."

"Isn't that why we love him?" Devon smiled into her father's scowl. "Okay, okay. I get it. I was a little out of control back then. I'm older now."

"You may be older, but you still don't seem to understand that your actions have consequences. You still haven't shown me that you know how to work towards a goal. Or that you even have goals."

"I have goals."

"You do? I'd like to hear about them."

Charlie came back into the room. "We have something to celebrate, Devon. I've located your friend's daughter."

Devon flew across the room and hugged him. "Oh, Uncle Charlie, that's the best news."

Laughing, Charlie patted her gingerly on the back with one arm. Her father, turning away, drained his glass.

"Where is she?" Devon said.

"Strange coincidence. The woman who lives at the end of Jacques Westbury's drive – he's the man who found the girl – is a former foster mom and is taking the girl in on an emergency basis."

"Where is that? Wamphassuc Point?" Devon said.

"Yes. All the way down at the end. Her name's Alice Garrison. She used to live in the big house, before Westbury bought it."

"That all sounds perfect for Fern," Devon said.

"I'd say so."

"There's more to celebrate all the time!" Devon said. "Let me go get ready for dinner."

Upstairs in her room, she studied herself in the mirror for a full minute, as if expecting to see something she hadn't already seen. She opened a dresser drawer that was stuffed with T-shirts and light knit tops and camisoles. Digging through the pile, she found a faded blue jersey. She changed into it, tucking it deep into her jeans. At the mirror again, she studied the word *Sawyers* emblazoned across her chest. With a quick twist, she checked the back – *Mitchell* over the number 24. She pulled a sweater over her head and the jersey disappeared.

She sat down on the bed. Her phone glowed in her hand. She tapped and swiped the screen, then sat looking at a photo of a man's face, youthful and rakish, stubble on a strong chin, piercing blue eyes. With the phone still lit up, she opened her handbag, slid a zipper aside, and produced a second phone – a basic clamshell, with a tiny screen and a keypad. She made a call.

"Chad?" she said. "I know where Fern is. And I've got a plan."

35

"Let me know when you're at the house," Daniel Frost said. He stepped back from the rental car, letting his son open the door.

"Should be around noon. It'll be an easy drive."

"You have the keys to the safe and the filing cabinet?"

Daniel Junior patted a pocket. "You've always been so organized, I'm sure all the papers the lawyer wants will be right where they're supposed to be.

"Okay."

They accomplished a quick hug, hands clapping shoulder blades.

When he was behind the wheel, Daniel Junior looked out the open window. "Dad, remember what the lawyer said. Even if you see Fern, or a kid who might be Fern, keep your distance. Just be patient."

"I know, I know."

"All right. I'll call as soon as I'm home." Daniel Junior drove out of the parking lot.

Daniel scanned the backs of the inn and the shops. He started toward the inn, then cut between buildings, coming out on the wooden walk by the river. The morning sun was warm on his face and bright on the boats and the water. The bridge hummed with crossing cars.

A man and a young girl, holding hands, came down from the street. She was finishing off a cupcake that was loaded with frosting, and each bite took some concentration.

"How was that?" the man said, when the girl had swallowed the last of it.

"Yum," the girl answered. "Super yum."

The man laughed.

"I'm tired," she said, looking up at him. "Can you carry me?"

"Tell you what. I'll carry you for a while, and then you carry me, all right?"

"No!" the girl said, giggling.

The man scooped her up, expertly avoiding the worst of her sticky hands. "Ooh," he said, "pretty soon you're going to be too big to pick up."

They passed Daniel. He watched them turn toward the parking lot. Moving quickly, he followed them, found his own car, and drove away.

***

Daniel stopped his car in the driveway of Jack's oceanfront house. After slipping his keys into his pocket, he reached over to the passenger seat for a pastry bag and a paper tray that held two coffee cups. He went to the front door of the house, set the tray down on the step, then rang the doorbell.

The door swung open halfway. Melody eyed him warily. "Hello." She kept her hand on the door.

"Hi. My name is – "

"Daniel Frost."

"Yes. I wanted to apologize for wandering onto your property yesterday. This morning I stopped at a coffee shop in Mystic Village and everything smelled so good…"

"Okay," Melody said, as if it were a question.

"I thought you and Alice might like some breakfast? Or a coffee break?" He raised the bag. "I was hoping that she lived close by, and if I dropped everything off here, you could… It was kind of a long shot." He continued to hold out the bag, waiting for Melody to take it. "Here," he said.

"Hold on, Daniel." Melody pulled the door closed. A minute later, she reappeared with keys in her hand. "Follow me."

She got in her own car and the two vehicles went up the hill. They parked along the hedge by Alice's cottage.

"Here's your new friend," Melody said, when Alice opened the

155

door. She added in a whisper, "I wish you had come down to my place."

"I told you, I didn't want to wake Fern," Alice responded, speaking softly. "It's fine."

Behind her, Daniel held up his cargo – the coffee, the bag. "I didn't mean to cause trouble. I would have called, but I don't have... I thought you and your friend might enjoy a treat. I was just going to drop it off."

"It's fine, Daniel," Alice said. "You know, I think it's warm enough that we can set up outside."

Daniel backed up to let her pass, then followed her around the corner to a small stone patio. Melody went into the house.

Daniel set his gifts down on a metal table. They both remained standing.

"Aren't we lucky to have this day in September?" Alice said.

"We are," Daniel said. "I feel very lucky."

"You take a seat. I'll be right back." Alice went into the house through a glass door.

A few minutes later she was back with a tray that held plates, napkins, and utensils, plus sugar, cream, and a baby monitor. Daniel hadn't yet sat down, and he helped her navigate the door. She set two places. The baby monitor went next to her plate.

"I'm babysitting for a friend," she said.

"Oh, that's a relief."

"What do you mean?"

"I have a neighbor who uses a baby monitor for her animals. She has five or six cats. I guess fights break out often and she needs to step in. She takes the baby monitor with her wherever she goes around her place."

"So you thought I might be a crazy cat lady."

With a smile, Daniel passed the pastry bag to Alice. "Isn't your friend going to come out? I really intended the coffees for the two of you."

"She just ate. Oh, apple cider donuts," Alice added, opening the bag. "Please, help yourself."

Daniel took a seat.

"So, what's kept you in town, Daniel?"

Daniel set a donut on his plate, then licked the sugar from his fingers. "A bad cold."

Alice shifted back ever so slightly.

"Not me," Daniel said. "The cousin I'm on my way to see. She asked me to hold off a day or two until she's better. And I didn't mind staying a little longer. This really is a nice place."

"It is." Alice flipped the tab on her coffee cup. "I hope she feels better soon, though."

The faint chime of a bell came from the monitor.

Alice waited, listening. The bell chimed again. "Excuse me just a minute." She went inside. When she returned, Fern hung back behind her, eyeing Daniel suspiciously. Melody hovered just inside the sliding glass door.

"Daniel," Alice said, leading the girl to the table. "This is Fern. Fern, wave hello to Daniel."

Fern let go of Alice and obliged. Spotting the donuts, she peered up at Alice and made the sign for eat, her fingers tapping twice at her lips.

"What do you say?" Alice said, as Fern accepted a donut from her.

Fern made the sign for thank you, then sat on the single step in front of the door, where she nibbled at the pastry, stealing glances at Daniel.

Alice turned her chair so that she could keep an eye on the girl. "Aren't these donuts delicious?" she said.

"Wonderful," Daniel said.

Half-eaten donut in hand, Fern came to the table. She pointed to a brightly colored plastic slide that had been set up on a level spot in the yard.

"Put your donut up here." Alice patted the table. "Then you can play."

Daniel watched Fern move across the grass.

"You look like you've never seen a child before," Alice said.

"What?" Daniel said, as if startled. "Oh, no, I guess... I've just never seen one so young using sign language. How does she know what you're saying? Does she read lips?"

"Her hearing is fine. She'll speak someday. She's just not ready quite yet. I've seen this before. I used to work with children with speech and hearing problems."

"So you're a pro. Your friends are lucky to have you as a babysitter."

Alice responded with a question. "What did you do for a living,

157

Daniel? Or what do you still do? I guess I shouldn't assume that you're retired."

"I teach, at a small college up north."

"So you're not retired."

"Well, semi-retired. I don't have any classes this semester. But I still enjoy it. Are you retired, Alice?"

"Years ago. I loved the children, but I became frustrated with other parts of the job."

"That seems to happen a lot in education."

"Sadly, yes."

They watched Fern on the slide, praised her skill between bites of donut.

"What do you teach, Daniel?" Alice said after awhile.

"I'm in the math department."

"That sounds very – "

"Boring?"

"Abstract?" Alice said.

Just then Fern came toward them, holding something small in front of her.

"What do you have there, Fern?" Alice said.

Cautiously, the girl approached Daniel, clutching a red-tinged maple leaf.

"Is this for me?" he said, taking it. "Thanks. It's almost as pretty as you are."

Retrieving her donut, Fern sat down on the step again.

"Do you have children?" Alice said.

"Yes, a son and a daughter."

Alice seemed to be waiting for details. When none came, she said, "Two is a good number. My husband and I weren't so lucky. I've certainly spent lots of time with children, but it would have been nice – "

"They can break your heart."

Alice looked across the table at Daniel. He avoided her eyes.

They sipped their coffee as the sun burned the dampness out of the air.

"Thank you for welcoming me when I arrived unannounced," Daniel said, as he got up to leave. "I saw the donuts this morning, and they looked and smelled so delicious. I wanted to share them with someone. I thought of you."

"It was a pleasure."

"It was. Can I help you clean up?"

"Don't worry about that. I hope you enjoy the rest of your stay here. I'll see you off."

"No, you keep an eye on that little girl." Daniel stared across the yard. "Could I stop by again? Maybe on my way back up the coast?"

"That would be fine."

Smiling, Daniel gave Fern an extended goodbye wave. He circled the house. Once the car key was in the ignition, he lifted the maple leaf from his shirt pocket. He took out his wallet and flipped through a set of plastic sleeves. He found a photo of a young woman with a big smile and glistening black hair that flowed out of the frame. Gently, he slid the leaf behind the photo. Then he drove away up the hill.

36

Daniel stood at the window of his hotel room looking down at the Mystic River, which was bathed in afternoon sun. His cell phone rang. "Hi, Junior. How's it going?"

"Hi, Dad. I found the paperwork, and some photos of me and Rose and Fern."

"That's great."

"I was thinking I should look for something that would have Rose's DNA."

"She hasn't been home since your mother died. That's almost five years."

"I think I should look, anyway. And I thought I should bring the money."

"Why?"

"It might be evidence."

Daniel turned away from the glass. "I suppose it could be. But I don't like the idea of you driving around with that much cash. It doesn't seem safe."

"I'll be careful." Before his father could respond, Daniel Junior continued. "I had another idea. Why don't I come back through Ellsworth."

"Not exactly on the way."

"I think it would be worth it. I checked, and there's only a couple of pediatricians in that town. Maybe I could get some information, something that might be helpful."

"The doctors aren't going to talk to you. Even if they do, they won't hand over medical records. There are privacy laws."

"Rose asked me once if she could put me down as an emergency contact. I don't know. It seems worth a shot."

"That adds another day." Daniel paused at the end of the couch.

"We're not meeting with the lawyer until the day after, anyway."

They both fell silent.

"Are you okay?" Daniel Junior said.

"I'm fine."

"What did you do today?"

"Just walked around."

"In other words, you did a lot of pacing, like you're doing now?"

Daniel didn't answer.

"I know it's slow, but we are making progress, Dad."

"Yeah."

"I'm going to get some dinner," Daniel Junior said. "You should do the same."

"I'll probably make it an early night, so, talk to you tomorrow."

"Okay."

They said goodbye. Daniel returned to the window. He watched the river. Boats glided by serenely, like clouds in a summer sky. Suddenly, he bent foreword to get a view of the walkway that ran in front of the inn. At the railing below there was a woman with a young child. Patting his pockets, Daniel spun, then dashed across the room and out the door.

***

Alice and Fern were still standing at the railing when Daniel caught up to them.

"Hello," he said.

"Daniel," Alice said, turning around.

Fern wrapped her arms around the woman's legs.

"I just happened to be looking out the window of my room." He pointed back at the building. "This is where I'm staying."

"Wonderful place," Alice said. "It's such a great location."

"Well, it certainly is tonight."

"We just came into town for some ice cream. We'd been cooped up too long, hadn't we?" Alice glanced down at Fern. "There's a shop across the street."

"I noticed it but haven't had a chance to try it yet," Daniel said. "Hello, Fern. I hope you enjoyed your ice cream."

Half hidden by Alice's legs, Fern stared at him silently.

"Can you recommend a restaurant, Alice?" Daniel said. "I'm going to grab some dinner. I'd ask you to join me, but I assume you've already eaten."

"Yes, we have." Alice described a couple of restaurants nearby.

Daniel was non-committal.

"So how's your cousin doing?" Alice said.

"Still not feeling well, I'm afraid."

"That's a shame."

"This isn't the vacation I had planned, but there have been some really nice surprises. Like meeting you and Fern."

"How nice of you to say."

"I'll have another day or two. If you have any tips for a tourist, let me know."

"Have you driven into the Stonington Borough?"

"Briefly. I went around that square – with the library? I'd like to go back and spend some time there. Maybe that should be my plan for tomorrow."

Alice described the shops on Water Street and the point with the stone lighthouse.

There was a lull in the conversation. They avoided each other's eyes.

"I should let you go," Daniel said. "It was nice seeing you again."

"You, too."

Neither one moved.

"You know," Alice said, "Fern and I were going to stop at the bookstore around the corner to pick out some bedtime reading. Do you want to join us?"

"I would love that."

Alice led them back out to Main Street. While the adults commented on the shops, Fern was subdued, clutching Alice's hand tight. She passed by the whale sculpture in front of the bookstore without taking any obvious notice. Inside the bright and busy store, she seemed overwhelmed. After some prompting, she grabbed a big picture book from a display. She offered the book to Daniel.

"She wants you to read to her," Alice said.

With the book in hand, Fern dropped into one of the beanbag

chairs that were scattered in the space.

"This could be interesting." Daniel lowered himself beside Fern with a soft grunt, the beans hissing as they were forced aside. "I got down okay, but I may never get up again."

Alice laughed.

As Daniel opened the book and began to read, Fern worked her way onto his lap. She listened raptly, glancing up at him every now and then. The moment he had finished, Fern leapt up and ran for another book.

"Oh, honey," Alice said. "I think we have to let Daniel go. He hasn't had his dinner yet."

"One more," Daniel said. "Since I'm down here."

He read a second book, then a third. Finally, with two books under her arm, Alice brought the story time to an end. When she was done checking out, they went back outside.

"You have such a nice voice for reading aloud," Alice said. "You were really good with her."

"Thank you," Daniel said. "I thoroughly enjoyed that."

The restaurant Daniel had decided on was across the street. Alice's car was back the way they had come, in the lot. They said their goodbyes.

"Daniel," Alice added, "I was planning a trip to the library in the village tomorrow. They have a book I need to pick up."

"The village?"

"The Borough. Stonington Borough. Should we meet up there? I could give you and Fern a quick tour."

"That would be great."

"Okay, then. Around 9:30?"

"I'm already looking forward to it."

37

In a cramped room at the hospital, Claire and AJ and June did what the room asked them to do – they waited. Waited for word that George's veins had been snipped, moved, and reconnected. That his heart had been unplugged from a machine and shocked back to beating life. That his divided breastbone was wired whole again and that his chest had been sewn shut, making skin once again a barrier to the world.

"I'm going to get some coffee," Claire said in a soft voice. "Do you want some?"

"No, I'm good." AJ sat upright in a lightly padded chair, hands on knees.

"June? Maybe some tea?"

AJ's mother lowered her paperback. She peered at Claire through thick lenses that blurred her eyes. "Thanks."

"Okay. I'll be right back."

AJ followed Claire with his eyes as she moved away down the hall. She had dressed up for the day in black slacks and pumps. Their hard soles clapped against the linoleum.

"Can you see a clock?" June said.

"Nine thirty-five," AJ said, checking his watch.

"Yeah, that's what I have, too. I just wanted to know the time on a hospital clock."

AJ went out into the hall. "Same out here. Nine thirty-five."

"They said eleven, right? They'd finish around eleven."

"Yep. But if it takes a little longer, don't worry. I'm sure they can't predict exactly." AJ sat down again.

June's eyes drifted toward the television that was mounted high in a corner, which played endlessly and without sound, like a kind of eternal flame.

"Do you want something to eat, Mom?" AJ said. "Just because Dad had to fast…"

"I'm fine."

"Okay."

"Your dad talked to Gus last night," June said.

"Uncle Gus?"

"Mm. They had quite a long talk. I was glad. It's a shame that they've been apart all these years. When they were young, they were as thick as thieves – your father, Gus, and Roland Brown." She looked at AJ through her thick lenses. "Then something happened to Gus. He got so… Well, something was troubling him. You could just see it in his face. I wish he would have stayed here and gotten whatever help he needed. But instead he took off for Alaska. With his dad giving him a little shove in that direction, I guess."

AJ said nothing. If he was thinking about the family secret that Roland Brown had shared with him – the gift that he and Uncle Gus had in common – he didn't show it.

"It's too bad you didn't get to know Gus better." June continued. "I think you would have liked him."

They were quiet for a long time, then. June held the magazine as if she were still reading, though she didn't turn a page. AJ sat back, looking nowhere.

June let the magazine fall to her lap. "Do you plan to marry Claire?"

"What?"

June repeated the question, giving each word space this time. "Do you plan to marry Claire?"

"I…"

"Your dad and I wanted to get married by our third date, but our parents made us put it off."

"I didn't know that," AJ said.

"If you love Claire, don't drag your feet. You never get enough time with the people you love. Nothing is guaranteed. Not a single day. Not a single hour."

AJ put his hand on her arm. "You and Dad are going to have lots of time."

After footsteps in the hall, Claire came through the doorway. "Is everything okay?"

"Yes," June said, reaching for her tea. "I'm just being a worrywart."

Claire sat down on the other side of June. The two women sipped their drinks.

"What is it?" Claire said, noticing that AJ was staring at her.

"Nothing. Sorry." He stood. "I think I do want some coffee. Be right back."

The waiting room was quiet after AJ left.

June lifted the book from her lap and set it on a nearby table. "I don't think I've understood a word I read this morning."

"I can imagine."

"What are you writing now, Claire?" June said. "What's your next book?"

"Actually, I have a new possible, ah, opportunity. I can tell you about it, but you'll have to swear to secrecy."

"Oh, that sounds interesting."

Leaning closer, Claire began talking in a hushed voice.

***

At the back table behind the Bay Market, the Daves sipped their coffees. The morning air was damp and still, stirred only by the occasional car passing on Route 1. Ben hovered nearby. On the ground, on the rim of the dumpster, and on the roof of the market, seagulls waited, facing west.

"What time is it?" DaSilva said.

Sela didn't even check his watch. "Ten minutes later than the last time you asked me."

"9:40. Do you think the surgery's over?"

"No." Sela shifted the Red Sox cap on his head. "Someone would have called us."

"This waiting around sucks," DaSilva said.

"Tell me about it," Ben said, drifting away from the table. Hands raised, he rushed a group of seagulls. At first they seemed oblivious, then a few rose into the air, complaining. "Hey," Ben said, sounding surprised.

"I know we can't call AJ," DaSilva said, "but maybe we could text

166

him."

"No, we can't," Sela said, sharply.

Ben charged a lone seagull. It stood as still as if its white breast and black-dot eyes were carved from wood, even as Ben's legs passed through it.

"So I worked on the script last night," Sela said.

"What script?" DaSilva said. "What for?"

Ben came back to the table. "You did?"

"The show." Sela took a sip from his cup. "You remember our show?"

"Yeah, I get that. But we never had scripts. I thought it was supposed to be unscripted."

"You need an intro, and some – I don't know – shape."

"Ben never used a script."

"I was a natural," Ben said. "I still am."

"And I had an idea. What if Beth did the intro?"

"Hmmm, not bad," Ben said.

"Beth?" DaSilva said.

"Yeah, why not?"

"Well, for one thing, she has a black eye."

"I bet she could cover it with make-up."

"Maybe," DaSilva said. "If we're going to just pick someone, what about Melody? She's already been working with us. I bet she'd be really good."

"That's a good idea, too," Ben said. "The camera would love her."

"She's also pregnant," Sela said. "You can't cover that with make-up."

"Why would she cover it up? There's nothing wrong with being pregnant."

"There's nothing wrong with having a black eye."

"The whole time people are going to be wondering what happened to her," DaSilva said. "It will be really distracting."

"Not if she covers it with make-up."

"Jesus," Ben said. "This project is getting off to a great start."

DaSilva turned toward the back door of the market. "Here comes Roland."

"Time to get back to work."

"That's my cue," Ben said, and vanished.

***

Melody's cell phone shimmied across the table, buzzing.

"Is that Claire?" Jack said, turning away from the view.

"No." Melody was already putting the phone to her ear. "Hi, Alice." She opened the door to the deck and went out.

Jack watched her pace back and forth, her dark hair and the distant water glistening in the sun. After a few minutes, she came back inside.

"Is everything okay?" Jack said.

"Yeah. She was just asking about George."

"Right." Jack checked his wrist. "He should be out of surgery soon."

"He's going to be okay, right?"

"Yes, I'm sure he is."

***

They had been silent for a while, sitting upright and still in the stiff waiting room chairs, not even pretending to read the magazines anymore and stymied by conversation, when the doctor finally appeared in the doorway.

"Mrs. Bugbee?"

"Yes," June said, pushing against the chair arms to stand.

"Your husband is fine," the doctor said. She was a tall woman with a high forehead and a pert nose. Next to June, she looked like a kindly tower. "The surgery went very well."

"Oh, thank goodness."

"If you'll come this way, we'll go over the recovery, hospital procedures, everything that comes next."

"All right," June said. "AJ?" She beckoned him.

As the three started toward the door, Claire said, "I'll make the calls, let people know George is out of surgery?"

"Yes, please," June said. "You have the list I gave you?"

"I do." Claire patted her purse. "I'll start with George's brother."

"That's fine. Then call Roland, then the Daves. Those boys are like family." Beaming, she followed the others around a corner.

Claire took the elevator down. Outside, she stopped under the glass awning.

Ben was loitering in the green patch across the street. He zoomed over to her. As Claire took a seat on a bench, he watched her face intently. "You look okay," he finally said. "Things must have gone well."

Reading from a paper that rested on her lap, Claire tapped out the first number. "Hi, Gus? It's Claire. George is fine. Yes. June is very relieved."

Ben pumped his fists in the air.

"Yes," Claire said. "What time is it there? Oh, four hours – so, not that early." She laughed. "Well, now you can get some sleep. All right. Yeah, that's all that I know. June and AJ are getting the details now. I'm sure someone will call you later. Okay. Yep. Bye."

"Thank God," Ben said. "AJ and his idea that I was here to... I knew he was wrong."

"Hey, Dave," Claire said into the phone.

"Oh, good! I was hoping you'd call the Daves next. I was there earlier, and they were really worried."

"All's well," Claire said. "Yep, the surgery went fine. Yes."

As Claire talked, Ben's face clouded, suddenly. He backed away. "So, George isn't the reason that I'm here," he said, softly, as if afraid to be overheard. "Why don't I feel good about that? Why do I have this feeling that..." He pressed his hands against his cheeks. "If it's not George, then who?"

38

AJ joined Clare on the couch in the living room, under the window that was already dark.

"Is your mom settled?" Claire said.

"Yeah. She's worn out."

"I'm surprised she wanted to stay here."

"She jumped at your offer, didn't she?" AJ said. "She really appreciates your company. She likes having another woman around."

"Yeah, I think she does." Smiling, Claire patted AJ's thigh. "You need to sleep."

"I know. Mom wants to leave early."

"Come on." Standing, Claire tugged on his hand.

"I'll be up in a minute."

Claire's fingers trailed across his palm and then she left him alone. As her footsteps rounded the turn in the stairway, AJ stood. He walked to the back of the house, through the kitchen and onto the porch. Ben was there, his pinkish glow bright in the darkness. AJ reached for the wall switch but changed his mind. The light stayed off.

"You figured out that my dad is okay?" AJ said.

"Yeah. Actually, I was outside the hospital when Claire called everybody. I'm so glad, AJ."

AJ sat down at the table. "It's warm," he said.

"Is it?"

AJ didn't answer.

"So you're going back to the hospital early in the morning?"

"As early as we can."

"I'd say to give your dad my best wishes, but..."

AJ let that go. "Have you been at the market at all?"

"Yes. Everything's fine there. You owe Roland. He's really pitching in."

"He's a good friend. A good man. I owe the Daves, too."

"I'd help if I could."

"I know that," AJ said.

"What you said about your mom liking having another woman around – "

"You were listening?" AJ said.

"Sorry, I just heard that little bit. I was out here, giving you two some privacy. Then I wondered if you'd gone to bed, so I slipped inside to check." Ben crossed his tattooed arms. "You don't need any advice from me, I know, but... Claire is pretty great."

"She is."

"Yeah," Ben said. "I'm just saying, I missed my chance. Don't miss yours."

AJ looked past Ben into the dark woods.

"You should go to bed," Ben said. "You look deader than me."

AJ pushed back from the table. "You're right. You're welcome to hang around here, of course."

"Actually," Ben said, "for once, I have somewhere to be."

39

It took a couple of hours to set up the cameras, audio recorders, and computers, and the cabling to connect them all. When that was complete, Sela and DaSilva switched off the lights throughout the rambling, two-story inn, leaving on only a single hurricane lamp fitted with an LED blub in the front sitting room. It gave off a cool light. Dave DaSilva sat on a high-backed chair, his laptop open in front of him. Sela and Beth had taken the sofa, an intimidating, ornate object of rosewood and red velvet. They watched another laptop, its screen divided into quadrants, each showing a different view of a moonlit bedroom.

"So this is how you do it?" Beth said after a long silence. "You sit and stare at computer screens?"

"It depends on the location," Sela answered.

"And the type of spirit," DaSilva added.

"There are different types?" Beth tucked a loose strand of red hair behind one ear.

Sela nodded. "Different personalities, for sure. Some seek out interaction. Some are more..." He glanced at Beth, then looked at the screen again. "Shy, I guess you'd say."

"What's the personality of this ghost?" Beth said.

Ben drifted into the room. "I'd call it nonexistent."

Without answering, Sela moved a finger across the computer's touchpad, zooming in on a bedroom door. He bent toward the screen. After a second, he relaxed. "Sorry, I thought I saw something."

"I'm surprised we haven't," Beth said. "With all the stories about this place." She watched Sela watching the screen. "So you thought you saw the ghost?"

"Well, no one has actually seen the ghost." Sela lifted his Red Sox cap, then settled it again. "They've found things moved around. Doors closed that were open, drawers opened that were closed, that kind of thing."

"So this is a shy spirit," Beth said.

"Maybe. They think it may be a woman because people's jewelry gets messed with."

"Hope you guys left some jewelry out," Ben said.

Beth pointed at the screen. "That's why the owners opened that jewelry box?"

"Yeah, they set that up for us."

Beth pointed again. "I love that four-poster bed."

"Oh my God, this is boring." Ben moved to the stairs and peered up into the shadow. "I guess I didn't think so when I was alive."

Sela studied Beth's face for a second. "I hope you're not too bored."

"Not at all. It's kind of exciting. Imagine if you did see something. If you got proof…" She let that drop.

"Yeah, imagine," Ben said.

"You did great with the intro, by the way," Sela said. "If we had you on every episode, people would tune in just to see you."

"Oh, brother," Ben said. "Laying it on a little thick?"

"It's true," DaSilva said. "Ben would be really happy with what you did."

"Geez," Ben said. "Sorry I missed it."

"Just past midnight," Sela said. "We may see more activity soon."

Ben started up the stairs. "I guess that's my cue."

***

In a dark bedroom, Ben stood in front of a long dresser. An ornate jewelry box was open in front of him, a pearl necklace lapped over one side.

"This may be a problem," Ben said. "I'm not too good with delicate maneuvers."

Making a hook with one finger, he reached for the necklace. It didn't budge.

"I might be able to knock the whole box on the floor, but that's no good. The innkeepers won't want people thinking the ghost is angry."

He reached into the open box, his thumb and middle finger closing on a gold band that stood upright, offering itself. He lifted his hand. The ring stayed put.

"Damn."

He tried again, scowling with the effort. Same result.

"Come on, Ben," he said. "We can't have one of the co-founders of Mystic Afterlife being sidelined just because he's a ghost."

He tried his pinky this time, slipping it through the ring, lifting slowly. The band trembled for an instant, but his finger came up empty.

"Son of a bitch!" Ben straightened up, his fist cocked behind him as if to take a swing.

A voice stopped him. "What do you think you're doing?"

Ben spun toward the sound. In a dark corner of the room, there was a woman, dressed in late 1960s garb – a wide-sleeved batik tunic over jeans, a pair of long and heavy necklaces. Her light brown hair covered her shoulders in frizzy tangles. All of it gave off a dim but colorful glow.

"Who the hell are you?" Ben said.

The woman slid toward him. "Well, who the hell are you?"

"I'm…" Ben hesitated, as if trying to remember his name. "I'm Ben. Ben Shortman."

"Okay, Ben Ben Shortman. Move aside." The woman brushed past him. Her necklaces clacked softly as she reached toward the jewelry box. "You just need to give it a little tap." As easily as flicking ash from a sleeve, she sent the ring out of the box. "Now, the drawer." She reached under the table. The drawer hissed as it slid open. "Feel free to jump in, Ben Ben," she said.

He just stared at her.

She motioned toward the closet door, which was open a few inches.

"Oh, yeah, sure." Ben went to the closet. Imitating the woman, Ben tapped the door with his finger. It didn't move. He tried again. Nothing. "Shit!" he said, swatting the door hard. It slammed shut.

"I guess that'll get their attention," the woman said.

There was thumping on the stairs. Sela and DaSilva burst into the room, handheld paranormal gadgets searching the air in front of them.

Ben and the woman retreated into the hall.

"You never answered me," Ben said. "Who are you? Where did you come from?"

The woman watched the ghost hunters. "My name's Eden," she said. "I'm from all over." She fixed Ben with her blue eyes. "I'm like you."

"Like me?"

"Yeah," she said. "You know, a free spirit."

***

From the moonlit yard, the two ghosts looked up at the dark windows of Claire's house.

"So this is it – where you died?" Eden said.

"Yes," Ben said.

"And where you saved your friend?"

"Yeah. I guess I'd call Claire a friend, even though we've never met. I mean, we have, sort of…"

"I get it." Eden touched her necklaces, clicking the beads. "I envy you, what you did for your friend. When I tried to help, it went badly."

"What do you mean? What happened?"

"I tried to help a few people – a friend with financial problems, another woman who was in an abusive marriage. I even tried to get two people together who I was sure were made for each other. Each time, things went badly. *So* badly. Like *Final Destination* badly."

"Guess I was lucky," Ben said. "Wait – you've seen the *Final Destination* movies?"

"I haunt a couple of theaters. We can go together sometime if you want. But I've sworn off interfering. Other than some poltergeist tricks at the inn, I stay out of things."

Overhead, bats zigzagged across the graywashed sky.

Eden faced the house again. "Maybe you died in this house so that you could save Claire. Maybe it was your destiny."

"I don't follow."

"You couldn't leave the place where you died, right?"

"Right. Back then, I was stuck here."

"So you were guaranteed to be around when Claire was attacked."

"Not exactly heroic."

"You saved her life! Anyway, fulfilling your destiny isn't necessarily about being heroic. You saved her, and then you…moved on, right?"

"Well, not right way. But yeah."

"Sounds like destiny to me."

Ben frowned but didn't speak. The only sound was the faint hum of the day's first traffic on the interstate coming from beyond the trees.

"But if I fulfilled my destiny," Ben finally said, "why am I back, floating around with nothing to do?"

"Hmmm… Maybe what happened before wasn't your whole destiny. Maybe it was just the first part."

"Okay," he said, "so I'm back here to do what?"

"Meet me!" Eden laughed. "I don't know. We're not supposed to know."

She put her hand on Ben's shoulder. He twitched at the contact.

"Sorry," she said, pulling away.

"No, no, it's just… You feel so solid! I almost forgot what that was like."

"You feel solid, too." Eden brushed her fingers against the back of Ben's hand. "You have a nice glow, Ben Shortman. It's very colorful, very…alive."

"Really?" Ben looked down at himself.

"My glow is just this sort of boring white."

"Like the moon," Ben suggested.

"Hmmm. The moon, worn as if it had been a shell, washed by time's waters as they rose and fell…'"

"What?"

"Nothing. A poem I had to memorize in college. It's a good one, though." Eden closed her fingers around Ben's wrist. "Come on," she said, nodding toward a pale smudge just above the trees. "Let's go watch the sun chase away the worn-out moon."

40

Standing in the chilly morning sunlight outside Alice's cottage, Melody listened through the door. On the other side, Fern was crying. Melody leaned closer, her face pinched in concentration, as if she were comparing today's sound to the wailing of a few nights earlier. The girl had been in a boat, then, drifting in the darkness with only writhing eels for company, and now she was in a comfortable cottage with a woman who wanted only to love and protect her, but the emotion was the same – a despair without bottom. The crying died, then resumed louder than ever.

Melody rapped the wood with her knuckles. More crying. The door remained closed.

Melody turned the knob, pushed the door open a little and stuck her head inside. "Hello! Alice!"

The crying stopped. Alice's voice – soothing, encouraging – emerged in the quiet. Melody stepped inside and closed the door behind her. A short while later, Alice and Fern came down the stairs.

"Look who's here," Alice said, holding tight to the girl's hand.

Sniffling, in rumpled PJs, Fern gave Melody a doubtful look.

Melody crouched down to be at eye level. "Hey, Fern. You look like you could use a hug." She held out her arms. Fern went to her and buried her moist face against Melody's neck.

"How about some tea?" Alice said. "Fern's having cinnamon, and I'm having English breakfast."

"If it's caffeine free," Melody said, "cinnamon would be good for me, too." She hung her bag off the back of a chair, then helped Fern into her booster seat as Alice prepared the tea.

Seated, Fern went on sniffling. Then, with a look of discovery, she reached for Melody's abdomen.

"I'm going to have a baby," Melody said. "That's why I have this big belly."

Fern pulled her hand back.

"You can touch it. Isn't it a big belly?"

Gingerly, Fern placed her palm next to Melody's, her eyes wide, her sniffles gone.

When Alice brought her plastic mug, Fern took it eagerly. She pointed across the room toward the television.

Alice let out a sigh. "We don't usually do videos this early…"

Fern made the sign for *Please*.

"Okay. Come along."

After getting Fern set up with a video, Alice brought the other mugs to the table. She sat down heavily.

"Rough morning?" Melody said.

"Rough evening, rough night, rough morning."

"I'm sorry. Are you okay?"

"Sure." Alice wrapped her fingers around her mug. "It's to be expected, given her circumstances."

"She's been doing so well! I thought it would get easier as time went on."

"I've seen this before. Sometimes it takes a while for them to realize something isn't as it should be." Alice checked her watch. "Oh, look at the time."

"Do you have to be somewhere?"

"I guess I should come clean. I ran into that man from the open house, Daniel, last night."

"Well, I have to come clean, too, Alice. That's why I stopped by this morning."

"I don't understand."

"I was curious about what was happening between you two. He showed up at my house with the donuts, and then you wanted to see him… I'm just being nosey."

"You are. And you're also looking out for me, which I appreciate."

Melody smiled over her drink. "So he's still in town?"

"He is. I ran into him by the inn, where he's staying. We went into the bookstore together, and he and Fern had an impromptu story time. It was so sweet. I asked him to join us at the library in the Borough this morning, but Fern doesn't want to go anywhere right now. The crying you heard when you first got here? That was her reaction when I told her about our plans. She wants to stay home – here. I wish I could call Daniel to cancel, but I don't have his number."

"When were you supposed to meet?"

"In about twenty minutes."

"Why don't I stay here with Fern? If she'll let me. You can still go."

"I think she'll be more than willing to stay here with you. But I'm sure you have other things to do."

"I didn't have anything in particular planned. Jack is gone for the day. It'll be fun to hang out with Fern."

"I can't guarantee she'll be fun today."

"Well, good practice, then."

"Yes, practice with a cranky kid – you will probably get that today."

"We'll be fine."

Alice looked toward Fern, as if unsure what to do.

"So," Melody said, "Daniel extended his stay here. Is he house hunting after all?"

"No. The cousin he was on his way to visit is ill. He's waiting here to find out if he should continue on or just turn around and head home."

"That's his story, anyway."

Alice squelched a smile.

"If he has that much flexibility in his schedule," Melody said, "he must be retired."

"Semi-retired, he says. From teaching math, at a college." Alice checked her watch again.

"You should get going," Melody said.

"If you're certain…"

"Absolutely." Melody looked into her mug. "I'm not so sure about this cinnamon tea, though."

"Let me take that from you." Alice carried the mugs to the sink.

Following behind, Melody tapped a drawing that was hanging on the refrigerator. Two more were mounted beside it. "She's pretty good with a crayon."

Alice joined her. "Yes. For her age, the drawings are quite detailed. The first one is her mother."

Melody tapped another drawing. "Is that her house? It looks like some kind of palace."

"When I asked if it was her house, she said no, then pointed in the direction of your house."

"Oh. Well, I can see that. Here's the ocean. This must be Fern."

"Yes."

"What about this last one? That's Fern again. What is that next to her, with four legs – a pony? And who's this in bright colors? At least, I think it's a person."

"I couldn't figure that one out." Alice checked her watch.

"You should go."

"Are you sure?"

"Yes, go!"

"All right. I was supposed to give Daniel a short walking tour. Maybe I'll just drive him around. That will be quicker."

"It's nice out. You should walk."

"We'll see." Alice went to Fern. They talked quietly. Fern turned around in place, found Melody with her eyes, then went back to the video.

"She didn't sleep much," Alice said, coming back into the kitchen. "Don't be surprised if she nods off at some point."

"Will that get her off schedule? Should I try to keep her awake?"

"I think it's all right. Just follow her lead."

"Okay."

"I'll be back before you know it."

"We'll be fine," Melody said.

When Alice was gone, Melody joined Fern on the couch. Fern slid close. She was warm and soft in her pajamas. On the television, over a bouncy cartoon song, an animated girl spoke words as she signed them with her cartoon hands. *Dance.* Two fingers danced on her palm. *Jump. Roll. Run.*

The video came to an abrupt end.

"That was fun," Melody said, clicking off the TV. "What next?" She spotted a pile of books on the coffee table. "Can I read you a story?"

Fern dropped from the couch and went to a basket of drawing

supplies on the far side of the room.

"You'd like to draw?" Melody said.

Fern nodded.

"Okay." Melody set Fern up at the kitchen table with the pad and crayons. As Fern got to work, Melody brought one of the earlier drawings from the fridge.

"Fern, is this a pony? A horse?" Melody pointed at the brown shape with four legs.

Fern shook her head. When she saw the puzzled look on Melody's face, she took the paper. After squaring it in front of her, she drew a red line from the two-fingered hand of her own likeness to the four-legged shape.

"Oh! It's a dog on a leash. Is it Buck? The big dog at Claire and AJ's house?"

Fern bounced in her seat.

"I guess to you he seemed as big as a horse!" Melody said. "So this is you." She pointed. "Is this Jack?" She indicated the colorful figure.

Fern's smile faded.

"No, not Jack. Is it AJ? He's the man Buck belongs to."

Fern shook her head.

"Hmmm. Is he your dad?"

Fern shook her head again, her lips pressed shut.

"Who is it then?" Melody seemed to be asking herself.

Fern looked at Melody's face, then went back to her new drawing, still just a red streak on the white page.

***

Alice took a path that cut diagonally across Wadawanuck Square toward the library. Daniel was sitting on a bench, watching her.

"Sorry I'm a little late," Alice said, when she was close.

"No problem. But where's our little friend?"

"She's home with Melody – my neighbor."

"Is she okay?"

Sitting down, Alice let out a long breath. "Well, honestly, no. She had a very rough night. Lots of tears. Bad dreams, I think. This morning I couldn't even interest her in getting out of her pajamas." Alice fixed Daniel with a penetrating stare. "I'm not just babysitting

Fern for a friend. It's more like emergency foster care. Last night, she was missing her family."

Daniel turned away from Alice's eyes. "That poor girl," he said. "We should be glad that she's just realizing that something's wrong."

"I've seen it before. If a child has been bounced around from caregiver to caregiver, it can take a few days for them to realize that Mom or Dad isn't coming to pick them up."

Daniel kept on looking away down the walk, toward the library, yellow brick with concrete columns at the entrance. "My son was bounced around when he was very young. My wife was sick, and I had to work, so my sister-in-law had him a lot of the time."

"I'm not sure I'd call that bounced around, Daniel." Alice gave him a warm smile. "But that just shows that it's not always that the parents aren't loving or that they're neglectful. People get themselves into all sorts of binds."

"You're right."

The salt air carried the clang of a harbor bell across the grass.

"Fern drew a picture of her mother this morning," Alice said. She touched Daniel's sleeve.

Daniel finally faced her. "Did she?"

"Yes. Not her father, though."

"Maybe you should go back," Daniel said, suddenly. "If she's having a rough time, should you be with her?"

"She wasn't upset when I left. I don't have your number and I didn't want to just leave you in the lurch. Anyway, Melody stopped by, and she was glad to watch Fern, and she was insistent that I go. I do want to keep it short, though."

"I'm with you. You're going to be worried and I'm going to feel guilty. We can do this another time."

"But what other time? You're leaving."

"I don't know what I'm doing."

"How many times in our lives have we said that?" Alice laughed. "At least, I have."

"Same here. Too many times to count."

"Well, I have to at least walk down Water Street," Alice said. "I promised I'd pick up a treat for Fern. There's a bakery down that way that makes the cutest little cupcakes."

"I'm always up for a walk to a bakery."

As they went down the path, Alice's phone beeped. She stopped to type something. "Sorry, I haven't mastered texting while walking," she said, when her phone was back in her purse.

"Everything okay?" Daniel said.

"Yes. Good. Melody says they did more drawing, and now she's getting Fern dressed so that they can go out into the yard. She says we should take our time."

"Should we? Take our time?"

"Maybe we can walk to the point. It's just a couple of minutes past the bakery. There's an old stone lighthouse there, and a nice view. It's pretty."

"Lead the way."

***

Melody and Fern were coming down the stairs when there was a knock on the front door.

"Wait right here." Melody went to the door. When she opened it, a young woman waited on the front step. "Can I help you?" Melody said.

"Hi. I'm Devon. I used to babysit Fern up in Maine? I heard she was here, and I was kind of hoping... Is Alice around?"

"I'm sorry, how did you find out that Fern – "

Before Melody could finish, Fern flew past her and into Devon's arms. Fern gave Devon big, theatrical kisses – one cheek, then the other. Devon giggled.

"I don't know if this is the best time..." Melody reached toward Fern from the doorway. "Could you call Alice later and arrange for a visit?"

"Please?" Devon's face was wet with kisses and tears. "Look at her. You can't ask me to leave now. Fern, do you want me to stay for a while?"

Her head bobbing, Fern wrapped her arms tight around Devon's neck.

"Hey! I need to breathe, Fern!" Devon took the girl's hand. "Why don't you show me your yard?" She looked at Melody. "We spent hours in the yard last summer."

"I don't think that's a good idea."

Tugging on Devon's arm, Fern started across the grass. Devon made a show of resisting, then went along. Melody followed them around the house. Devon and Fern, holding hands, went straight to the little slide. Fern climbed it and slid down to the grass.

Meeting Fern at the bottom, Devon tickled the girl's belly. With a squeal, Fern ran. Devon chased her across the grass. Their hair glistened in the sun.

The doorbell rang. Melody looked over her shoulder. "Now what?"

The chase was coming back this way. Devon made eye contact with Melody as Fern squealed again.

"I'll be right back," Melody said, loudly. She dashed into the house.

A man waited at the front door, holding a plant in a foil-wrapped pot. Sunglasses wrapped around his narrow face. The bill of his baseball cap was pulled low.

"Yes?" Melody said.

"I have a delivery for Rogers."

"Sorry, but you have the wrong house." Melody started to push the door closed.

"This isn't number nineteen?"

"Yes, but the Rogers don't live here. Why don't you try number nine?" Melody said. She pushed on the door again.

"Wait – which way?"

"What?" Melody paused in the doorway.

"I guess number nine would be back that way." The man pointed back up the road. "Sorry, it's my first day. I don't want to screw up."

Melody opened the door a little further again. "Did they put the Rogers' phone number on the paperwork?"

"Yeah, yeah, I think so." The man patted his back pockets. "Must have left that in the car."

"Then just call them and ask for the house number again," Melody said. "I'm sure they won't mind. Now, I'm sorry, but I have to go."

"Right. Thanks. I'll make that call."

"Good luck." Melody closed the door. She watched out the window as the man walked up the road toward a car that was parked nearby, its long, gold body mostly hidden by the shrubs at the edge of the yard. Before heading back through the house, she turned the lock.

On the way past the kitchen counter, she swiped her phone from her purse. She kept moving as she scrolled through her contacts. She had just located Alice's number when her foot landed on the patio. She looked across the yard. Devon lay on the ground by the playhouse, flat and still. Fern was gone.

41

Alice and Daniel's walking tour of the Stonington Borough came to a stop in front of a big, Georgian house with 24-pane windows and a flagpole jutting out over the entrance.

"This one took a cannonball in the war of 1812," Alice said. "It's had some famous occupants, too. Both Whistler and his mother lived here. Long before he painted her."

"I love that you're so proud of this place," Daniel said. "It makes you a great tour guide."

Before Alice could respond to that, her phone rang. "Hi, Melody." Her eyes opened wide. "What?" She froze, the phone pressed to her ear. Her face went white.

"Alice, what's happened?" Daniel said.

She was mute, stunned, on her feet only because he braced her.

"Alice?"

"Fern's missing. Devon..." Alice started down the sidewalk. "I have to get back."

"Alice." He reached for her.

"I have to go!"

She sped away, her gait a march that wanted to be a sprint. He caught up with her, fell in alongside. He tried to ask questions, but she seemed not to hear him. When she did respond, she only said, "I have to get back."

He steered her toward his car. "I'll drive."

"Okay," she said, getting in. "Let's go."

42

Ben and Eden arrived at Jack and Melody's house with the sun already sharp on the water. Ben took Eden's arm. "Come see the view."

Eden went with him, circling around to the deck in back. From there, they looked down the grassy slope and across the cove.

"It's gorgeous," Eden said. "You weren't lying."

"Right? Almost as beautiful as that sunrise from Stonington Point was."

"Oh, there was a sunrise?" Eden squeezed Ben's hand.

He let his fingers travel up her arm.

"This Jack that your Melody ended up with must be loaded," Eden said. "What does he do?"

"He owns businesses and real estate. There's family money, too."

"So is that what Melody's into? Money, material things?"

"No. She actually loves him."

"Ouch."

A smile came and went on Ben's face. "Yeah. If she was just into the money, I could say screw it, she never would have wanted me, anyway."

"But now you say, *if only I'd had more time.*"

"Do I?" Ben seemed to be considering that. "Yeah, I guess. Stupid, right?"

Eden gave him a sympathetic shake of her head.

"Well, where to next?" Ben said.

"What's the hurry? It's so nice right here." Eden closed her eyes.

"I can almost feel the sun. Do you know what I mean?"

"Maybe," Ben said, sounding unsure.

For a long time they perched there, the cove stretched out below them, shades of blue and silver, opaque and glittering, spiked with the masts of boats.

Ben broke the silence. "I heard Melody tell Claire that they might use Ben as a middle name for the baby."

"Really? That's a nice tribute."

"Your parents must have known you'd end up being a hippie when they named you Eden. Or, were they hippies themselves?"

Eden laughed. "My name's not really Eden."

"No?"

"A man gave that name to me. He gave all the girls new names... There was Harmony, Clover, Honey, Lyric..."

"Sounds like a commune or something."

"Something like that."

"Huh. I didn't know we had communes here."

"It wasn't here. I was in California then. Drove all the way out there in my VW Bug." Eden stopped suddenly, seeming lost to that memory.

"So was there lots of peace and love?"

"No. It was horrible, actually. At least I left before things got really bad."

"Oh. I'm sorry. Why do you still use the name that they gave you?"

"It's the only pretty thing I got from that time. Anyway, I never liked my real name – Louisette."

"So who was this man who was giving everybody names? Wait, don't tell me – his name was Moon Dog."

After a long silence, Eden gave Ben a hard stare. "His name wasn't Moon Dog. It was Charlie."

"Charlie and his hippy family," Ben said. He frowned. "Wait, you don't mean – "

"Do you hear that?" Eden said, cutting him off. "Sounds like a siren." She left the deck and went around the side of the house.

Ben followed. "Sounds like more than one. And coming this way, fast. What the hell is happening now?"

"I suppose you want to check it out."

"I have to. You should understand. Maybe this is why I ended up here, right here, right now. You, too. Maybe that is the reason, coming down the road, right at us."

Eden sighed heavily. "Okay. We'll check it out. But *just* check it out."

"Sure," Ben said, not even trying to sound convincing.

Up the hill, the sirens had stopped moving. They were close by.

"Come on," Ben said.

"Okay," she said. "Someone's got to keep an eye on you."

43

Emergency vehicles of all kinds crowded the road by Alice's cottage. As Alice and Daniel approached in his car, an ambulance took off for Route 1. Melody sat in the open bay of another ambulance, talking to a medic.

"Just pull over anywhere," Alice said, her fingers already closing on the door handle. On foot, she made directly for Detective Wheeler. "Did you find her?" she said. "Did you find Fern?"

"Not yet. But we will."

She tried to move past him. "I need to talk to Melody."

Wheeler blocked her path. "Let the EMT finish with her."

"I need to find out what happened. Melody called, but she was frantic. All I know is that Fern is missing."

"I'll fill you in. Let's go inside." Wheeler shepherded Alice into the cottage. They took seats at the kitchen table.

"Are your men out looking for Fern?" There was life in Alice's face again – fear, but forcefulness, too. "She's so little. She can't have gone far."

"I'm afraid it's more complicated than that."

"What do you mean?"

"How well do you know Devon Alexander?" Wheeler said. "Have you been in contact with her?"

"I don't know her well. Melody said something about her, but I didn't follow. What does she have to do with this?"

"She showed up here this morning to see Fern."

"Why did she want to see Fern?" Alice's eyes narrowed.

"She knew both her and her father. She got to know them when they all lived in Maine."

"Was that Devon in the ambulance? What happened to her?"

"She was in the back yard with Fern when someone attacked her." Wheeler paused. "And we believe that the attacker took Fern."

"Someone took her?" Alice rocked back. "Oh my God. The same people who killed her father."

Wheeler responded with a steady voice. "We don't know that."

Outside, another car arrived, brakes squealing.

"I don't understand," Alice said. "If they wanted to take that child, they would have done it the night that they took her father from the boat. But they left her. Why take her now?"

"We have a lot of questions that we need to get answers to. But we will get them."

"How do you know that Fern didn't just run into the woods? If someone came after Devon, Fern might have gotten scared and run away. You should be out there looking for her."

"We are checking the surroundings, and I hope to God we find her. But everything we know so far leads us to believe that Fern was taken."

"I need to talk to Devon."

"Remember, Devon is in that ambulance on her way to the hospital. She needs medical care."

Alice closed her eyes. "I just can't believe this. I took Fern in. She was mine to protect. But I was off..." Leaving that hanging, she stood up. "I'm going to check in the trees around here. Fern could be hiding there, still afraid to come out."

"Alice." Wheeler took her gently by the elbow. "I have officers all around this property. They're scouring every inch. Believe me, if we don't find her very soon, we'll bring every possible resource in on this to find her."

Alice's nod became a tremble that took over her whole body. She sat down again. "Melody – is she all right?"

"Yes. She wasn't attacked."

"Where was she when it happened?"

"Talking to someone at the front door."

"Someone at the front door." Alice seemed to be turning that over in her mind. "A distraction. This was planned, wasn't it?"

Wheeler said nothing.

"Did you know that Fern was in danger?" Alice said.

"Ma'am." Wheeler stopped, as if out of reassurances.

Alice went to a nearby cabinet. She came back to the table with a drawing. Crayon on newsprint, it showed a woman as a stack of shapes, an orange circle for the head, long, crisscrossing lines for hair, three dots for the eyes and nose. A big, downward curve for mouth.

Alice handed it to Wheeler. "Fern said this was her mother."

Wheeler studied it. "What are you thinking?"

"In all the years I did foster care, I never lost one of the children I took in. But I know two people who did. In both cases, a relative was responsible. The child was abducted by a parent who'd lost custody."

"You think Fern's mother may have taken her."

Just then Melody came in the front door. She stopped just across the threshold, a blank expression on her face. "Alice, I'm so sorry." She began to cry.

Alice rushed to her, wrapped her in her arms.

Without a word, Detective Wheeler slipped past them and went outside. He studied the uniformed cops swarming the yard and the lane and the thick woods on the other side.

Behind the detective, Ben and Eden emerged from the cottage.

"Seems like they've got squat, so far," Ben said. "Maybe that girl they took away in an ambulance will have something for them."

"I don't think so."

"Why? Can you sense something? Do you have some kind of a special…"

"No, no special senses," Eden said. "Did you see her head? That wound looked bad. She may not be much help for a while."

They watched the police move about the yard.

Eden turned to Ben. "So what are we going to do about this, Benjamin? What are we going to do to help that girl?"

"I thought you swore off interfering. *Final Destination* and all."

"Special circumstances – this girl. I can't just stand by."

Ben stared at her for a second. "Well, ordinarily, I'd be working with AJ already. But since he's taking time off…"

"So your specially gifted cop friend is unavailable."

"I'm on my own."

"You have me."

Ben smiled. "Okay. We need a map. A big one."

"Do they still sell those at gas stations? I guess even if they do, I

have my limitations. Getting a map out of the store? Opening it up –
all of that folding? I'd need another fifty years of practice to
accomplish that."

"We need a map that's already unfolded," Ben said.

"Like a map that's mounted on a wall."

"Exactly. I know where to go."

"Time's a wasting," Eden said, taking his hand.

44

Bobby turned into the driveway at Devon's house. Swerving right, he steered the LeMans onto the grass and around the garage. The car just fit between the building and shrubs that marked the property line.

"Careful," Chad said from the back seat.

"If you didn't drive such a boat – "

"You scratch my boat and you're in deep shit."

"Language," Bobby said, checking the rearview mirror.

Chad scowled at the rounded towel in the foot well – all that was visible of Fern.

They were motoring slowly across the back yard, now, heading toward a shed with a slanted roof.

"Park behind," Chad said.

"I got it."

Bobby swung the car around the shed. He brought it to a stop in some tall weeds. On the other side of the car was a hedge, and beyond that, a stretch of empty marshland.

"Okay," Chad said. "Let's see what Devon set up for us."

He got out of the car, circled around it, and opened the back door. He yanked the towel away from Fern. She stayed curled there on the floor mat.

"Out you go," Chad said.

Slowly, she got to her feet. She looked up at him, her eyes wide.

They went to the front of the shed where there was an oversized door with black strap hinges. Bobby swung it open. Chad dragged

Fern inside. When the door closed behind them, it was dark. The only windows were small and smudged, barely translucent. For a minute, the three of them were motionless, waiting for their eyes to adjust.

"There's the camping gear," Bobby said, nodding toward a pile of cinched nylon bags, folding chairs, a red plastic cooler.

Chad pointed. "What the hell is that?"

Next to the camping gear was a soft mound with sloping sides.

"Blanket fort," Bobby said, laughing a little. He lifted a corner of the sagging roof, showing the construction – two layers of quilts draped over saw horses.

Fern dove through the opening. As soon as she was inside, she began to cry.

"Oh, great." Chad glared at Bobby.

"You shouldn't have told her that she was going to see her family," Bobby said. "She probably thought Eric and her mom would be here."

"I didn't say when."

"Jesus Christ, Chad. You have to think like a kid. She doesn't understand the future. She only knows now."

Chad tapped the roof of the blanket fort. "If you know so much about kids, get in there and make her stop."

"I'll try." Bobby watched Chad go out through the big door. Lifting the quilts a little, he ducked under them.

***

After latching the shed door, Bobby went back to the car. Chad had a map spread out on the hood.

"What are you doing?" Bobby said.

"Right now, I'm looking at this map."

"Yeah, I can see that. What's it a map of?"

"This place. New London County."

"Where'd you get it?"

"Devon."

If Bobby noticed the purse on the windshield, he kept it to himself.

Chad pointed at a circle drawn in ink. "I think this is where she wanted us to take Fern." He traced more hand-drawn circles. "These are stops along the way. To keep us moving. Which we should probably be doing right now."

"I thought the plan was to wait here for Devon."

"It may not play out exactly like that." Chad picked up the map.

"What does that mean?"

Chad collapsed the map, making no effort to fold on the creases.

"What's going on, Chad? If you did something to piss her off… She could talk to the cops. She could be talking to the cops right now."

"Calm down. She's not talking to the cops." Chad had made the map into a bulky rectangle. He tried to flatten it. "We should move, though."

"Are you trying to cut her out? Because then she'll definitely talk to the cops. She'll tell them we kidnapped her and forced her to help snatch Fern. It's almost true, too."

Chad didn't look up. "She's not telling anybody anything."

Bobby studied Chad, his head cocked, his eyes narrow. With a sudden lunge, he snatched the map out of Chad's hands. "What the fuck, Chad? What did you do?"

Chad made a lopsided smile. "Well, I was supposed to hit her, right? I'm not so good at gauging how hard, you know?"

Bobby took a step back. "You fucking killed her, didn't you?"

Chad kept up the lopsided smile.

"Shit, Chad! What the fuck are you doing? You keep getting us into deeper and deeper shit!"

Chad's smile flattened. "Listen, when I came up to her in that yard, you know what she said to me? She said Fern wasn't in the mood for a camping trip. Maybe another time, she said."

"She got cold feet?"

"Ice cold."

"So when you hit her – "

"I might have put a little more into it than we originally planned."

Bobby was silent, as if he were trying to visualize the scene. Then, with a swift pivot, he kicked the side of the shed.

Chad dragged him backward by the elbows. "Knock it off, or you'll get her yowling again."

"Fuck! Fuck! Fuck!"

"Calm down," Chad said. "What was I supposed to do, Bobby? She was backing out. Anyway, this is better. It's simpler."

Bobby stood still. Chad let him go and backed off.

"How is killing another person making this mess simpler? We've got to get out of here now, Chad." Bobby started toward the car.

Chad blocked his path. "It's simpler because it's just you and me again. You, me and a good plan."

"You, me, and a kidnapped kid!"

"A bargaining chip. A very valuable bargaining chip. If we just follow through now, stick to the rest of the plan, we'll be fine. Come on, Bobby. Besides, what are we going to do with the kid – leave her on the side of the road? Stick her in another boat? You sure weren't happy the last time we did that."

"All right. But let's just ask for our money. We don't need Devon's share. It will probably go a lot quicker."

"No! Think of that as interest. Compensation for our pain and suffering. Look at all of this extra bullshit we're having to go through, Bobby."

"I guess."

"Don't worry. This will all be over quick. By tomorrow afternoon, granddad shows up with the cash and we make the trade. Everybody's happy. Then we get the fuck out of here."

"Unless granddad calls the cops," Bobby said.

"Do you even know how a ransom works? He won't call the cops because we tell him if he does, the kid gets it."

"Maybe granddad doesn't care. Maybe he'd rather have the money."

Chad put a hand on Bobby's shoulder and squeezed. "Man, you need to have a more positive view of people. Of course granddad loves the kid. That's what granddads do."

Bobby knocked Chad's hand away.

"Cheer up, Bobby. Devon left us everything we need. We have the camping gear." From his pocket, Chad produced a chunky phone. "I have this prepaid phone she got to make the call. I already got granddad's number from Eric's phone, and put it in contacts."

Bobby stayed silent, facing the shed.

"You pack up the camping gear. I'll make the call." Chad opened the phone. "You know, maybe it would be good if the girl cried. Have that in the background when I'm talking to granddad. That would get our message across. You want to get her riled up?"

Bobby just stared ahead.

"All right. You know me, Bobby. I'm always looking for a little extra. I just can't help myself." Smiling, Chad opened the phone and began tapping the keypad.

45

The three women sat at Alice's kitchen table, bathed in a misplaced cheerful sunlight.

Ms. Holt folded her hands on the leatherette cover of her notepad, which was embossed with *Connecticut Department of Children and Families*. "I don't know what the police have told you."

"Nothing." Alice looked anxiously from Ms. Holt to Melody and back again. "They've told us exactly nothing."

"I'm sure they'll update you when they can." Ms. Holt peeked at her watch, then tugged her sleeve over the watch face, as if she didn't want anyone to be thinking of the minutes ticking by with Fern still missing, still in the hands of her abductor. "As far as our investigation at DCF, unfortunately, there isn't much to tell yet. We've been acting on some information from the police."

"What information?"

"The police really haven't told you anything?"

"Nothing."

"Okay. We haven't independently confirmed any of it, but Devon Alexander told the detective that Eric Mitchell was Fern's father, and that the mother was a woman named Rose, who left them some time ago."

Alice leaned forward in her chair. "That's a good lead! They should be tracking down Rose Mitchell. Fern might be with her."

"I'm sure the police are looking for Rose." Ms. Holt tapped the leatherette again. "We're also trying to get confirmation of Fern's parentage, or anything about her family. So far, all we have is from

Devon Alexander."

"What about Eric Mitchell?" Melody said. "Does he have family? Do you have anything on him?"

"His parents are dead. No siblings."

"So that's it?" Alice said.

"So far. I'm sorry."

"There's got to be more," Alice said. Every muscle in her face was taut.

"There will be. But it takes time."

"We don't have time!" Alice smacked the table, making the others jump. "You're saying that even with everybody everywhere on their phones and computers" – she motioned toward the tablet computer that lay nearby on the counter – "you can't track down one relative, friend, acquaintance, someone who knows something that will help us find that little girl?"

"Alice has a point," Melody said. "There's nothing on social media?"

"We are looking everywhere we can think to look. I'm sure the police are, too. But even today, people can stay under the radar if they want to. And some people want to."

Alice rubbed one hand with the other, shaking her head.

Melody patted her on the back. "Are you all right?"

"I need a moment. Will you excuse me?" Alice went out of the room and up the stairs, her footsteps heavy and slow.

Melody slumped in her chair. "This is my fault."

"Fern was Alice's responsibility," Ms. Holt said.

Melody snapped upright. "She was supposed to have eyes on Fern every second of every day? No one expects to have a child snatched out of their own back yard."

"Of course you're right. I just meant, don't blame yourself. Ultimately, Fern is my responsibility. So if you want to blame anyone…"

"I'm sorry. I guess we all played a part." Melody spread her fingers on her belly. She slid them up and down, following the shape. "Do you think you'll be able to identify Fern's parents?" Melody said.

"Not as quickly as I want to, but yes."

Melody nodded. "Do you think the police will find Fern?"

Ms. Holt met Melody's gaze then looked away. "I really don't know."

The house was quiet after Ms. Holt left. Alice hadn't yet come back downstairs. Melody stared out the window at the grassy slope, as if trying to imagine what had happened there. She went to the counter, where she picked up the tablet computer. After pressing a button to bring the screen to life, she opened a web browser. She typed in the search field. *Eric Mitchell.* She deleted that, then typed something new. *Daniel Frost.*

46

At the counter of the Quinabaug Diner, where Wheeler's attempt to follow a lead had taken him, every surface was spotless, but the air was a mess of mingled smells — frying onions and eggs and coffee and ground beef and clam chowder.

"It would have been four days ago," Wheeler said. "Two men. Maybe from Maine. At least one of them ordered ployes."

The response was a perfect set of blank stares from the wait staff, who had gathered around the cash register.

"Just think back to anything from that morning and work from there."

At first he got only more blank stares. Then a waitress with a round face raised her hand. "I could have waited on them." She wore Boston Red Sox earrings — two pairs of tiny red socks with white heels and toes.

"All right, Trisha," Wheeler said, reading her nametag. "Tell me what you remember."

"Most people who order ployes eat them just like pancakes — stacked, with butter and syrup. They even ask sometimes why they're so thin, and why the cook didn't flip them over. I have to explain that that's what makes them ployes. The guy I'm thinking of put butter on them and rolled them up. He seemed like he'd been eating them his whole life. We call them Maine ployes right on the menu — so, like you said, he could have been from Maine."

"Okay." Wheeler opened his notepad.

"Are you talking about the eelers?" the busboy said, looking at

Trisha.

"I don't know anything about eelers," Trisha said.

Wheeler turned to the busboy. "Tell me about that."

"Well, the one guy asked me if there was any eeling around here. I said there was, but I didn't really know much about it, except that a couple of years ago they tried to set up commercial fishing for glass eels here like they have in Maine. The governor vetoed it. I said something about that and the guy said it was another case of the government trying to screw people over. He said glass eels were the best thing that ever happened to fishing. I said I'd heard that the eel population was in trouble, so I wasn't so sure. He said from what he could see, there were plenty of eels to go around and always would be."

"Did you happen to get this guy's name?" Wheeler said. "Either one of them?"

"One guy was named Bobby," the busboy said. "The taller one. I heard the other guy call him that. Bobby's my name, too. Well, Bob. So when I heard the name, I thought for a second that he was talking to me."

Wheeler addressed Trisha again. "Did they pay with a credit card?"

"No. The one guy had a wad of cash. He kind of flashed it, like he thought he was a big shot. That reminds me – he was wearing a big fancy watch, too. Then he barely tipped me." She laughed. "I hope you put them both in jail."

"Did anyone happen to notice their car?"

Trisha and the busboy shook their heads in unison.

"Let's just see what you can give me in the way of a description." Wheeler took notes as Trisha and the busboy recalled what they could. It didn't add up to much more than what Wheeler already had – two men, thirties at the oldest, one taller and thinner than the other – Bobby. A vague take on the hair. The shorter man wore a golf shirt. He did most of the talking.

After leaving a card with the hostess, Wheeler went back to the car. He had just put the key in the ignition when his phone rang.

"AJ," he said. "How's it going? How's your dad?"

"He's coming along. He's still in intensive care, but that's just the normal process."

"When I talked to Claire yesterday, she said the doctors were really pleased with how the surgery went."

"Yeah. Everything they're telling us is that he's doing really well. They're moving him to a regular room today. They'll even have him out of bed, sitting in a chair. Tomorrow, he'll walk."

"Amazing. Tell him I'm thinking of him. June, too. I'd like to get up there to see him, but – "

"I know, Sam. Claire told me. That girl from the boat has been abducted?"

Wheeler pressed back against the seat. "Yes."

"Jesus. How did it happen?"

Wheeler explained – the man coming to Alice's front door, Devon playing out back with Fern, someone else assaulting Devon there and snatching the girl.

"So two men – one at the front door, one at the back," AJ said. "You heard from Ray Williams that two men rented the boat the night that Jack found the girl."

"That's right."

"So it could be the same two men."

"It could be related," Wheeler said, "but doesn't make a lot of sense. First they leave the girl in the boat, then they kidnap her?"

"You're right, it doesn't make sense." AJ shook his head. "Have you been able to talk to Devon?"

"No. She was still unconscious when they took her to the hospital. They're supposed to call me as soon as she comes to."

"Let's hope that's soon."

"Yeah."

"What's been done so far to locate Fern?"

"We canvased and searched the neighborhood. Didn't turn up anything. There's going to be a complete search of Wamphassuc Point. That's probably already underway. Gaines issued an AMBER alert, and he made a statement to the news media. He contacted the FBI. The state's doing roadblocks. The Coast Guard is doing extra patrols. It's a full court press."

"Good."

"Gaines sent Nardi up to Ellsworth, Maine."

"What's in Ellsworth?"

"Sorry, I forgot I haven't talked to you." Wheeler recounted the interview with Devon. "Rose Mitchell is the mother's name," he said. "Gaines's theory is that the men who abducted Fern might be working for her. He thinks the clues to finding her are in Ellsworth."

"How does Gaines fit Eric's murder into that theory?"

"Maybe she just wanted him dead. Or maybe that was an accident."

"Okay," AJ said. "But if they were here to take Fern, they can't be the same guys who left Fern behind in the boat."

"That's right. It gets more complicated."

"Well, he's right about sending someone up to Ellsworth, no matter what," AJ said.

"Yes."

"Who's running the command post?"

"He is."

"What does he have you doing?"

"Talking to some people about ployes."

"What?"

"I guess it's a Maine thing. Buckwheat pancakes." Wheeler recounted the events of the morning – Beth's black eye, Roland's search for Ray leading them to the goat farm, Ray telling him that he'd heard the man who had rented the boat use the word *ployes*.

"Is that getting you anywhere?"

"Well, I think we know that our guys were here at the Quinabaug Diner. Four days ago. One of them asked about eeling in this area."

"Maybe he thought that might be a way to find Eric."

"Maybe. And we have one first name – Bobby."

"That's something."

Wheeler squeezed the steering wheel. "It's too slow," he said. "This isn't a case we can put together piece by piece. With the girl missing, we need something to happen fast."

"I want to help."

"AJ, you've got to look after your dad. That's why you took time off, remember?"

"Yeah, but now that I see things in motion... He's got a whole staff looking after him. Twenty-four seven. Not to mention Mom, who won't leave the room. I'm a third wheel. I definitely don't need to be there every minute."

"What about the market?"

"The Daves have stepped up, and Roland – when he's not acting like he's still a cop, he's doing a pretty good impersonation of a fishmonger. Anyway, I'm talking about right now, until we find this girl."

Wheeler sat there looking across the parking lot. "Okay. When do you want to start?"

"As soon as I can. I need a few minutes to fill everyone in here. And I have to stop in at the market. Then I can meet you wherever."

Wheeler had just ended the call when the dashboard radio came to life.

"Wheeler."

Sam clicked the mic. "Chief?"

"You're going to get a call on your cell in five minutes. Be ready to take it."

"Okay," Wheeler said. "Who is it?"

"A man named Daniel Frost. He asked for you specifically. He says he's the girl's grandfather."

47

The long-hooded sedan bumped along a farm road that skirted an overgrown field. Chad was behind the wheel, cursing softly with every bounce.

"C'mon, Chad. Language." Bobby motioned toward the back seat, where Fern sat wrapped in a quilt from the blanket fort.

"She's fine. But I'm going to need a new suspension after this."

"How many times have I told you, a truck is way more practical."

Chad only scowled.

Bobby went back to studying Devon's map, which was open on his knees. "Okay," he said. "The road should turn into the trees right up here."

The car sank into a rut, then jumped out of it, sending everyone back in their seats.

"Jesus Christ!" Chad said. "You call this a road?"

"You want to turn around?"

Chad smacked the steering wheel.

"Fern, are you okay?" Bobby peered over the seatback.

She stared blankly from the quilt.

"Hang on," Chad said. He pulled on the wheel.

They dropped down a hill, toward the edge of a small woods. Chad killed the engine.

When they were out of the car, Bobby held the map in front of him. "There should be a trail."

"Right here," Chad said. "Looks like there are even steps." He pointed to an opening in the bushes, where a path led further downhill. "You wait with her." Chad nodded toward the car. "I'll check it out."

Bobby watched Chad disappear into the greenery. He looked through the car window. Fern sat motionless, wrapped in the quilt. Bobby stuck out his tongue. Fern didn't respond. Bobby stepped back, pulling his phone from his pocket.

Just then, Chad came crashing out of the bushes. Bobby slipped the phone back into his jeans.

"Who are you calling?" Chad said.

"Just checking the time. What'd you find down there?"

"There's a campsite – it's been used before. It's a good spot. Lots of cover. We need to carry the stuff down."

"I suppose that's my job."

"We'll take turns." Chad opened the big trunk. He began tossing gear onto the ground.

"You think we'll be safe here."

"For as long as we need to be, yeah."

"Because we're only a few miles from the nearest house." Bobby motioned back up the farm road.

"We're fine here for today."

Bobby scowled. "So when are you going to call the grandfather again?"

"That first call was just to get his attention," Chad said. "I'll call again after we're settled in. Start to talk specifics." Chad straightened up, a cinched canvas bag under each arm. "I'm going to take this stuff to the site. Have a load ready when I get back." He plunged into the leaves and disappeared.

Bobby tapped on the car window. When Fern turned toward him, he smiled. She faced straight ahead again.

Bobby picked up another cinched bag from behind the car. He stood there holding it, looking toward the path. "I am so screwed," he said.

48

Melody was bent over a tablet computer in Alice's kitchen when the stairs behind her creaked, then creaked again. After glancing over her shoulder, Melody put the tablet to sleep with a few taps.

"Ms. Holt is gone?" Alice came across the living room, jabbing at her hair where the pillow had flattened it.

"Yeah, a few minutes ago." Melody filled a glass from the faucet.

"Sorry to leave you alone. I felt like I might be sick. I just had to lie down. And then I just – " Alice stopped with one foot on the kitchen tile. "Why are you looking at me like that? Did you hear something? Did someone call?"

"No, I didn't hear anything…"

"But?"

Melody made a face. "I looked up Daniel Frost on the internet."

"Why?"

"I don't know. Just a funny feeling."

"And?"

"You should see."

"See what?"

Melody picked up the tablet again, then brought up a web page.

Alice came around to face the screen. "'*Kawenni*,'" she read, slowly. "What is that?"

"It's the newsletter of the Saint Regis Mohawk tribe."

"Okay, what about it?"

"Just look."

Alice began reading aloud, with the confidence of a longtime teacher. "'We sat down with Daniel Frost in his office on the campus of the State University of New York at Potsdam, where he is a professor of Anthropology specializing in Native American studies.'" Alice stopped reading. "Didn't he say mathematics?"

"That's just the beginning." Melody scrolled deeper into the text. "Read this. Here." She touched the screen with her finger. Without waiting for Alice, she read aloud. "'He's the father of a son, Daniel, and a daughter, Rose, and has a granddaughter.'"

"Ms. Holt said Fern's mother's name is Rose. Is Daniel Fern's grandfather?"

"Unless it's a different Rose."

"That would be a big coincidence," Alice said.

"But if Fern is his granddaughter, why wouldn't he just say so? Why wouldn't he just claim her – why isn't she already with him?"

"Something's not right. Maybe it's a custody situation – a legal complication of some kind." Alice took in the kitchen with a glance. "I had them both here in this room."

"How did Fern act around him?"

"She gave no indication that she knew him. Maybe I just missed it but... No. I don't think she recognized him."

"In the interview," Melody said, "he says that he and Rose had had difficulties, and he hadn't spent much time with her once she was grown. That would explain why Fern wouldn't know her own grandfather."

"Okay. But he surely knows who Fern is. He didn't just stumble into my yard that first time. He was looking for her."

The two women stared at each other.

"So you think Daniel could have had something to do with the kidnapping?" Melody said. "Is that what you're thinking?"

"Well, that's why you looked him up, isn't it? That was your funny feeling."

"Alice, I... I just want to find Fern."

"Of course. We have to call Detective Wheeler. Or did you already call?"

"No. I wanted to talk to you first."

"Well, we can't wait any longer," Alice said. "Would you call the detective, please? I'm going out for a second." She made a direct line for the door. It slammed shut behind her.

49

There was a knock at the door to the Frosts' room, loud and urgent. Lolly Bridgewater let Daniel Junior in. He was carrying a cardboard box with a lid. Daniel Frost remained motionless at the end of the unmade bed, a vacant look on his face.

"Let me take that," Lolly said, lifting the box, revealing a leather case that had been hidden underneath.

"I'll keep this." Daniel Junior tucked the case under one arm.

Lolly carried the box to the sitting area – a sofa opposite a fireplace, with a small table in between. She began sorting through the contents of the box.

"The adoption papers are in that top envelope," Daniel Junior said to her. "I brought everything else that I could find. There's a lot of stuff Mom saved. All of Rose's school pictures and report cards. Some pictures of Rose with Fern, too."

"Good," Lolly said.

Daniel Junior moved toward the bed. "Are you okay, Dad?"

Daniel shifted, making room for his son, though Daniel Junior stayed on his feet. By the headboard, a dark blue throw pillow decorated with an anchor tipped off the edge of the mattress and fell to the floor.

Lolly held a small plastic bag up to the light. Inside it were a hair brush and hair clips.

"That was in Rose's bathroom," Daniel Junior said. "There's some hair on the brush, and I think on the other stuff, too. I figured,

DNA."

"Excellent." Lolly set the bag aside. She picked up the oversized manila envelope. Sitting back on the sofa, she undid the clasp. She slid a sheaf of papers onto her lap.

"I'm glad you're here, Junior," Daniel said.

Father and son hugged quickly, awkwardly, Daniel clutching his phone, Daniel Junior with the leather case pinned under one arm.

"How are you holding up?" Daniel Junior said.

"Honestly?" Daniel said, pulling back. "I'm not. This is all my fault. I should have listened to you and gone to the police as soon as we got here."

"Not going to the police right away was as much my fault as yours. Anyway, you've talked to them now, right?"

"Just got off the phone with the detective. He's on his way here."

"Right. Good."

"I should have tried to get Fern as soon as she was born," Daniel said.

"Dad, don't beat yourself up. We all agreed – not just you and me, but Mom, and the aunties – Fern was exactly what Rose needed to stay straight."

"And it worked. For a while."

"You couldn't have just taken Fern," Lolly said from the sofa, without looking up. "It would have been a long, legal battle."

There was another knock on the door.

"That will be our food." Lolly opened the door for the second time. "Come in," she said, stepping aside for her fiancée.

When the door had closed behind him, Jarett held out a greased-stained paper bag that gave off the unmistakable smell of burgers and fries.

Lolly peeked inside. "Perfect. Thank you."

"Sure thing. Let me know if there's anything else you need."

"We will," Lolly said.

After giving the Frosts a tight smile, Jarett went back out the door. Lolly pulled something from the takeout bag – a fat, plastic-wrapped bundle of one-hundred-dollar bills.

"What is that?" Daniel Junior said.

"I should have thanked him." Daniel rubbed one cheek. "I just can't think straight."

"I'll thank him for you." Lolly brought the two bags to Daniel

Junior. "Your father needs to eat. You probably do, too."

Daniel Junior's eyes stayed fixed on the cash. "Is that the extra fifty thousand that they asked for?"

"Yes," Lolly said.

"Where did that come from?"

"It doesn't matter."

"Lolly – or Lolly's fiancé – is loaning it to us," Daniel said. "To keep things moving."

Lolly held the bundle out to Daniel Junior. "Put this with the rest. Then eat something, please."

Daniel Junior slid the bundle into the leather case, where it bulged like a rat in a python's belly. He sat down on the edge of the bed with his father.

"You hungry?" Daniel Junior said.

"I want you to hear the second call."

"You recorded it?"

"After the first call, I started recording everything." Daniel worked an app on his phone, then pointed the device at his son. A voice came from the tiny speaker.

"We have her."

"Who are you? What do you want?"

"One hundred fifty thousand. Cash. Get it, and be in Mystic, Connecticut tonight."

"Okay. Don't hurt her."

"And no police. We will know."

For a long time fter the ending beep, no one in the room made a sound.

50

In the front room of the Bay Market, Beth wiped down the counter while Sela ducked underneath her to freshen the ice bed. Eden watched from nearby.

"Your friends are kinda cute," she said. "I can see tuning in to their show."

Ben, who had positioned himself before a large, vintage map that was framed and mounted on the wall, responded without turning to her. "Beth wasn't on the show originally, but Dave is trying to work her in."

"Good. They're a cute couple."

"They're not a couple."

"No? He keeps looking her way. I'm pretty sure he has a thing for her."

Ben smiled. "Yeah, he does. Has for a long time."

"Huh. Like you and Melody. You guys and your torch carrying."

Ben went on examining the map. "Geez, they could be anywhere," he said under his breath.

Eden moved a little nearer to the counter. "She has a black-and-blue mark. She's hiding it well with make-up, but it's there."

"Ray did that," Ben said. "Her boyfriend. I guess it was an accident. "

"An accident?" Eden made a face. "Maybe so, but I'm rooting for your friend Dave." She came over to Ben. "So what exactly are you looking for?"

"A hiding place. Somewhere you would take a little girl that you kidnapped and not get found."

"What makes you think they're even still in the area? Connecticut's so small, they could already be out of the state by now."

"You heard the cops. They set up roadblocks. They must think the guys haven't gone far."

"There are an awful lot of little roads. The police can't block them all." Eden edged forward. "This isn't the most up-to-date map in the world, either."

"It's just to help me visualize."

The plastic-strip door to the kitchen rustled.

"Who's that, with DaSilva?" Eden said, turning toward a pair of men coming into the front room.

"Roland Brown. Ex-chief of police." Ben looked toward the counter, where Roland spoke quietly to Sela and Beth. "What's he saying?" Without waiting for an answer, Ben zipped across the room. With a sigh, Eden trailed behind.

"That poor girl," Beth said, just as Ben and Eden joined the group. "What are you going to do, Roland?"

"There's not much that I can do. I already talked to Gaines. All he offered was to add me to a search party that they're planning for later today. He said he'd call me."

"Sam has your number," Sela said. "He'll call."

"Yeah." Roland ran his hand across his scalp. "Yeah."

"We got a text from AJ," DaSilva said. "His dad is doing really well."

"Yeah. That's good news, at least."

"Actually," Sela added, "AJ is stopping here in – any minute."

Eden nudged Ben. "AJ – he's the one who can see us?"

"Yeah."

"We should go."

"Well, no. I want to talk to him. See what he's heard. Tell him what we know."

"We don't know anything, and he's been with his family, so he probably doesn't know anything, either."

"I still want to talk to him. What's the problem?"

"It's weird, being seen. Actually talking to someone who's…"

"Alive."

"Yeah."

"So you haven't run into this before? AJ's not the only guy in the world to see ghosts, right? Hell, DaSilva could, too, for a while."

"You didn't tell me that!" Eden ducked behind Ben. "He can't see us now?"

"No. It was temporary. Calm down. AJ's great. You'll like him. Let's go outside, though. It's always tough trying to communicate in a crowd." As Ben started toward the back door, Eden seemed frozen in place. He reached for her. "Come on, free spirit."

Ben waited by the picnic table, looking out toward the access road. Eden stayed with him.

"This is him," Ben said, as AJ's Jeep approached.

Eden touched her hair. "Do I look okay? I've let myself go, haven't I? Being invisible."

"You look great," Ben said. "You haven't aged a day."

AJ's Jeep slowed suddenly. It rolled past the table, crunching gravel. AJ's head was turned their way.

"Damn," Eden said. "He was looking right at me."

Ben touched her arm. "Let me go talk to him." He went around to where AJ waited behind the wheel. "Hey!" Ben said, through the open window. "I'm so glad to hear about your dad."

"Thanks. What's going on, Ben? Who is that with you?"

"Someone I want you to meet."

"Is she okay? She looks a little – "

"Faded, I know. But believe me, she's all there."

"I was going to say on edge."

"She's fine," Ben said. "She's never met anyone like you, so, yeah, she's freaked out. But you'll like her. She's a free spirit. That's what she calls one of us who's not attached to a place."

"I'm kind of in a hurry, Ben."

"I know. You have to get back to your dad. It'll just take a minute."

As AJ was climbing out of the Jeep, Ben told him to take out his cell phone.

"I know the drill." AJ walked toward the table, the phone to his ear.

Ben tugged Eden toward AJ, saying, "He has to pretend to talk on the phone so that he doesn't look crazy."

He did the introductions. "Eden, this is AJ. AJ, my friend Eden."

"Hi, Eden, It's nice to meet you. I'm glad that Ben has company."

Eden stared back at AJ with wide eyes. She turned to Ben, who made an encouraging gesture with his hand. "It's nice to meet you, too," she said. She went back to staring.

AJ kept on pretending to talk into the phone. "Ben, I'm sorry, but there's an emergency. We're going to have to do this properly another time."

"You know about the kidnapping? We were there right after it happened. Are you helping with that? We want to help, too."

"That's good, but I'm not even sure how I can help yet. First, I need to talk to the guys."

"Roland's here, too. I was looking at the big map because I'm thinking the kidnappers must be hiding somewhere in the area."

"Ben, that's great, but this is just a quick stop before I meet up with Wheeler. I'll let you know what you can do as soon as I can."

"How?"

With no answer, AJ hurried toward the building.

"Okay," Ben called after him. "We'll just wait here." Ben watched AJ disappear through the back door. "Well, I feel friggin' useless."

Eden seemed to have come out of her trance. "They're probably all feeling useless right now."

"Yeah, I guess."

"Let's go look at that map again. I know some places where kids used to hang out and drink, back in my day. And while we're at it, we can eavesdrop."

"Okay," Ben said. "But remember, AJ can see us and hear us."

"Yeah." Eden was already moving toward the market. "That's going to take some getting used to."

51

AJ parked in Mystic's main downtown lot, behind the shops. As he walked to the inn, which stood between him and the river, two bright shapes waited in the shade of the building, one grayish, one more colorful. Eden and Ben.

"Hey," Ben said, as AJ got close. "Sam's right behind you." Ben pointed across the lot at Wheeler.

"Look, Ben," AJ said, softly. "It's going to be crowded in there. I'd really rather – "

"We don't take up much space. Or any space, really." Ben sunk his hand into the nearby wall.

AJ said nothing.

A few minutes later, Lolly Bridgewater opened the door to the Frosts' room. It stayed open just long enough to let AJ and Wheeler in, leaving Ben and Eden in the hall. They slipped through during the introductions.

Raising his left hand, which was clutching a cell phone, Daniel said, "Can we get to the call?"

Lolly directed everyone to the sitting area by the fireplace. She and the Frosts took the couch. Wheeler sat at a small desk. Staying on his feet, AJ backed up against the fireplace mantel, with the ghosts at his side.

Daniel studied his phone. "Weird. My battery's almost dead. I just checked it."

AJ found Ben with his eyes. He scowled.

Ben motioned to Eden. "That's us, draining the battery."

Eden nodded.

They moved to the far wall, by the window.

Daniel played the recording. Chad's voice blared from the tiny speaker, making demands. One hundred fifty thousand in cash. Be in Mystic. Then came the beep, then silence.

"You don't recognize the voice?" Wheeler said. "Either of you?"

"No," Daniel said.

Daniel Junior shook his head.

"And you were already here when you got the call? In Mystic?"

"Yes," Daniel said. "I was right here in this room."

"Let's go over that again, how you came to be here, for Officer Bugbee's sake."

Daniel stiffened, hands on his knees. "We thought she might be in Mystic, because of the postmark on a package that we got from Eric."

"Why don't you back up, Mr. Frost." Wheeler flipped open his notepad.

"Daniel."

"Okay. How did this all start?"

Daniel exhaled heavily. "My daughter, Rose – Fern's mother – died recently. Eric called to tell me."

"Eric is Fern's father?" Wheeler said.

"Yes. They've been together for a while."

"Tell me about him."

"I don't know a lot, other than he never held down a job, was always hurting for money. I think he was good with Fern. And he tried to keep Rose off drugs and alcohol."

"Tell me about Rose's substance abuse."

"That started when she was a teenager. Her mom and I – we tried everything we knew. Strict rules, loose rules. Counseling. Doctors of all kinds. Books. Other drugs. Nothing worked. Then, her mom got sick, and I didn't have the time or energy that Rose demanded. I sent her to a rehab center. She fought it, every step of the way, and she hated me for it. When they let her out, she took off. Said I'd never see her again. I told myself that I didn't believe her. But I second-guessed myself many times. As it turned out..."

"So you lost touch with her?"

"Yes. She must have been in touch with one of her cousins, because she showed up when her mom was... at the end. Rose stayed until the funeral, then she took off again. I didn't hear from her after that until she had Fern."

"So Rose got back in touch with you when Fern was born?"

"Not when she was born. Fern was two years old before I even heard of her. I got a picture, in an email, of a little girl having a birthday party. Cake, candles. Little pink dress with a white collar." Daniel smiled. "Icing all over her face. After that, yes. Rose and I were in touch a little more. Emails, photos. Sometimes phone calls."

"Did you visit them?"

"We had one visit. Fern was two and a half years old. They just showed up at my house one day. They stayed for a few hours."

"You never went to see them?"

"I didn't have their address. Rose said she wasn't ready to tell me."

"Where did she die, Daniel?"

"Medway, Maine. I could have driven there in a day."

"How did it happen?"

"Car accident – DUI. She ran into a tree. When they found her, she had a syringe in her leg."

"Was Fern with her at the time of the accident?"

"No. She'd left them – left Fern, and Eric – a little while before. She went into rehab. Then I guess she met this guy there, and..." Daniel's shoulders dropped. "Eric said she'd left before. She always came back."

"Eric never called you, when Rose took off?"

"Once. He thought maybe she was with me, or that I might know where she'd gone. I tried to get him to tell me where they lived. I would have hopped in the car right then, that second. But he wouldn't tell me. He said he wanted to tell me, but he'd be betraying Rose. And he had someone he trusted who helped out with Fern."

"Did Eric give you a name for whoever was helping out with Fern?"

Daniel and Daniel Junior exchanged looks. "I don't think so," Daniel said. "I've been trying to remember. But I don't think he ever told me."

"Does the name Devon Alexander sound familiar?"

Daniel gave Wheeler a blank look. "No. Sorry."

"So, Eric called after Rose died?"

"A few days after. That time, he did give me the address."

"Did you see Fern at the funeral?"

"No funeral," Daniel said. "Eric had her cremated. He said that's what she wanted. It had already happened when he called me."

"So, no funeral. But you did see Fern?"

"When we got to Ellsworth – Junior came with me – Fern and Eric were already gone. I learned this from a neighbor. Eric hadn't told anyone where they were going, at least anyone I talked to."

"Is that when you came to Mystic?"

"I didn't know anything about Mystic yet. I stayed in Ellsworth, hoping Eric and Fern would show up."

"I rented a car and drove home," Daniel Junior said. "The next day, a package arrived, postmarked Mystic. That's when we decided to come here."

"We didn't know if they were traveling and long gone," Daniel said. "But Mystic was the last place we had any information about."

"What was in the package?"

"Some traditional clothing that I had made for Rose, years ago – a buckskin tunic and a skirt."

Daniel Junior jumped in. "Cash. A hundred thousand dollars."

Wheeler gave him a long look. "A hundred thousand dollars."

"Yes," Daniel said.

"From Eric? You said he was always hurting for money."

"That's right. There was a note from him saying the money was for Fern, that we were to keep it safe for Fern."

"Did you have any idea how Eric got his hands on that much cash?

The Frosts exchanged glances again. "No," Daniel said.

"You didn't think that maybe there was something going on that you should be concerned about?"

"We did," Daniel said. "That's why we came to Mystic."

"But not to the police," Wheeler said.

"My dad isn't big on the police." Daniel Junior avoided his father's eyes. "That's kind of his specialty."

"I'm sorry, I don't follow," Wheeler said. "What do you mean, his specialty?"

"He writes about the relationship between law enforcement and the Native American community. He doesn't have a lot of good to say."

"Junior." The elder Frost shook his head.

His son continued. "Did you know that Indians are killed by

police at a higher rate than any other racial or ethnic group, Detective? More than three times the rate of whites."

Wheeler looked back and forth between the two men. "No, I didn't know that."

"It doesn't make the news," Daniel Junior said. "But it's true. You can go to one of Dad's lectures. Or read his book."

"Let's get back to finding Fern," the father said.

"Okay," Wheeler said. "What did you do when you got here?"

"We kept our eyes and ears open," Daniel said. "We showed the picture of Fern around town a little bit. Then I saw the article in the paper about the girl who was found in the boat."

"But still you didn't go to the police."

Daniel stared hard at Wheeler. "No."

"That's when they came to see me," Ms. Bridgewater said.

They described the conversation of that morning, their concerns about establishing a relationship to Fern because Fern's mother, Rose, had come into the family through adoption papers that Daniel had never fully trusted.

"So you can't prove that you're Fern's grandfather?" Wheeler said.

"You can say whatever you want, Detective, but I know I'm her grandfather as surely as I know anything in this life."

"And being in Mystic," Wheeler said. "Keeping your eyes and ears open – that paid off, right?"

Daniel was slow to answer. "Yes."

"What do you mean?" Daniel Junior said.

Lolly Bridgewater seemed especially on alert now, her eyes moving back and forth between Daniel and the detective.

"Why don't you tell me how you came into contact with Alice Garrison?" Wheeler said.

"Dad?" Daniel Junior said.

Daniel explained how he'd found Wamphassuc Point, near where Fern had been rescued from an eel boat by Jack Westbury. How he'd lucked into the open house nearby and used that as an excuse to wander onto the Westbury property. How he'd gotten really lucky, then, and found Alice and Melody there.

"And Fern?" Wheeler said.

Daniel answered with a nod.

Daniel Junior rose up in his seat. "You saw Fern?"

Wheeler continued. "Did you have any further contact with Fern after that?"

"A couple of other times." Daniel described bringing coffee and donuts to the cottage, then seeing Alice and Fern from his room, joining them by the river, visiting the bookstore. "I was with Alice when Fern was taken."

Daniel Junior swore softly.

"Tell me about that," Wheeler said.

Daniel recounted the plans to meet at the library that turned into a brief tour of Stonington Borough, ending with a phone call from Melody.

Wheeler closed his notepad. "So you were using Alice Garrison to get close to Fern?"

Lolly put her hand on Daniel's arm. "Are you comfortable with these questions?"

Daniel kept his eyes on Wheeler.

Outside, heavy clanging warned that the drawbridge was about to open.

Wheeler stood up. "You know what? This is taking longer than I expected. I'd like to be in the station when you get the next call. Why don't we head over there now – as soon as the bridge is down? AJ, can you step outside with me?"

AJ gave Ben a look, then followed Wheeler into the hall. Eden moved to join them, but Ben blocked her.

"Don't we want to hear their conversation?" Eden said.

"I think AJ wants us to watch them." He pointed toward the Frosts.

A tense silence had taken over the room. Standing in front of the fireplace, Daniel ran a hand through his hair. "I know, I should have told you," he said. "Both of you."

"You have really complicated things," Lolly said. "You didn't think this would come out? What were you planning?"

"I…" Daniel stood there were his palms up. "I wasn't planning anything. When I went to that open house, and then into the neighbor's yard, I only knew that Fern had been found nearby, by the people in that house. I just wanted to be where she had been. I guess I thought I might learn something, if I was really lucky, from talking to people there. I sure as hell didn't expect to see Fern."

"And you thought it was a good idea to keep this a secret," Lolly said.

"I didn't know what to do."

"Jesus, Dad," Daniel Junior said. "When were you going to tell me?"

"I'm sorry, Junior. You have every right to be mad. I can only say I was desperate." Daniel turned to the lawyer. "How bad does it look? I know you told me to stay away from Fern, but the contact I had was all public and proper. Doesn't it bolster my case, in a way, show that I can be trusted, that I could make a reliable guardian for her?"

"You were much less than forthcoming about your actions. It could look like you were plotting something."

"Like what?"

"Like luring Alice away from Fern, then taking advantage of that."

"Shit." Daniel looked toward the door. "The cops left the room to talk about us. What are they saying out there? How much time are they going to waste checking me and Daniel Junior out? Every minute that those kidnappers have Fern..."

"The police have to consider all possibilities," Lolly said. "Fortunately, it doesn't make much sense for you to arrange to kidnap your own granddaughter, *then* alert the police. Furthermore, Daniel Junior was on the road when it happened. It will help if we can verify that."

Daniel Junior had been pacing in front of the window. He froze with an expression of alarm on his face. "Oh, God."

"What is it?" Lolly said.

"I stopped on the way back here. I'd barely slept the night before, and I just got so tired I couldn't keep my eyes open. I was maybe twenty minutes away, but I got off the interstate. I found a place to pull over. I thought I'd just close my eyes for a few minutes, but I went out like a light, slept for almost two hours. Dad's call woke me up." His eyes went from his dad to Lolly. "So the timing – is that going to be a problem?"

"When you pulled over," Lolly said. "Were there people around?"

"It was a park and ride. There were cars, but I didn't see anyone. Maybe while I was asleep..."

"It will be all right," Lolly said. "You can explain it to the detective just like you did to me."

"I'm sorry, Dad," Daniel Junior said.

Daniel nodded, his lips tight. "You have nothing to apologize for.

Me – I should have known better. But we're going to get her back. We have to."

***

AJ and Wheeler stood just outside the front door of the inn. The sun warmed the yellow wall. Somewhere out of sight, seagulls argued.

"What do you think?" Wheeler gestured back inside.

"My gut tells me they're telling the truth."

"Yeah, mine too."

"The cash gives us a motive for Eric Mitchell's murder," AJ said. "It could mean that his killers are also Fern's kidnappers. When they found out that Eric didn't have the money, they decided they could use Fern to get it."

Wheeler glanced back toward the bridge. "I don't like that Frost had figured out where the girl was staying."

"Yeah, and he wasn't going to tell you anything about that. You had to call him on it."

"With that knowledge, he could have pulled off the kidnapping," Wheeler said.

"What are you thinking?"

"What if the kidnapping and ransom is a cover story? Frost knows he can't prove a biological connection to the girl, so he gets scared that he'll never get custody. He hires two guys to snatch Fern for him and then make that ransom call. Now it looks like a kidnapping that's connected to Eric and the money. We spend all of our resources on the fake kidnapping. The fake kidnappers deliver Fern to the Frosts, and then everyone takes off."

"That's a pretty good plan, if maybe a little complicated. Frost seems smart enough to come up with it, too."

Just then Ben and Eden appeared through the front door. "AJ, if you were wondering, these guys are totally legit. They're really hurting. Really worried about the girl."

AJ turned his head just enough to make eye contact with Ben. Without words, his eyes said, *Keep going.*

Ben continued. "The son, coming back from Ellsworth, got tired and ended up sleeping at a park and ride. So, it may look like he has some time that's not accounted for. But you can believe him."

"I should talk to Gaines," Wheeler was saying. "See what he wants to do with Nardi. He's still looking for whatever he can find about Rose Mitchell – I mean Rose Frost – in Ellsworth. Maybe we should have him start looking into Daniel Frost and his son."

"Guess I'm not much of a witness," Ben said.

"I think we need Nardi here," AJ said. "Why don't I look into the Frosts? I need something to do."

"Okay," Wheeler said, "as a start. I'll confirm with Gaines."

Wheeler and AJ headed back inside.

"Shouldn't we follow them?" Eden said.

Ben took a moment to answer. "I'm thinking maybe we should do our own thing."

"Yeah," Alice said, her eyes bright. "That sounds good to me."

52

In a quiet, spotless room at the Westerly Hospital, Roland watched Devon breathe. She was squared on the pillow under a light blanket that rose and fell in a regular rhythm. She might have looked peaceful except for the bandage that covered her head and the plastic tube that snaked from one arm.

A nurse in crimson scrubs hurried into the room and checked the IV. "Have you tried talking to her?" she said, without looking at Roland.

"I called her name a few times, didn't get an answer. Since I know it's not protocol anymore to keep the concussion patients awake, I figured if she was unconscious, it was for a reason."

"She was awake before, when she came up from radiology." The nurse had gone on to straightening the bed covers. She focused her eyes on Roland. "You *are* the chief of police in Stonington, right?"

"I was. I retired."

"So you're not here as the police."

"I've been deputized."

"Okay." The nurse dropped the bedrail on his side of the bed. "Because I wanted to know if anyone saw this." She turned Devon's arm. There was a faint pink line across the white underside of the wrist.

Roland's eyebrows went up. "Thank you."

The nurse raised the bedrail again. Without another word, she dashed out the door.

Roland went around the bed and slipped Devon's other arm from under the covers. He examined the wrist. It had the red mark, too. He went out into the hallway and made a call. "Hi Sam. Do we know anything about Devon being tied up?"

"Tied up?" Detective Wheeler said. "What are you talking about?"

"She has abrasions on her wrists. They look like rope burns. I couldn't check her legs without disturbing her, but I wondered if she'd been bound."

"You're with her at the hospital?"

"Yeah. Still waiting for her to come to." Roland was quiet for a second. "The nurse pointed out the marks on the wrists, and I'm not sure how they fit in. If they fit in. Who would have tied her up, and why?"

Wheeler blew out through his teeth. "That is strange. Maybe whoever took Eric Mitchell out of the boat got their hands on her, too."

"You mean, they snatched her that night in the boat? But then later she got free, and never said a word about it to anyone?"

"I don't know," Wheeler said. "What if it was the kidnappers who had her tied up? They came up with a plan to snatch Fern that required her help – "

"She wouldn't help them willingly," Roland said, "so they kept her tied up until it was time for her to do her part."

"Okay," Wheeler said, sounding unsure. "I have another question that I want to clear up with her."

"What's that?"

"Why, when I used the name Rose Mitchell – why didn't she correct me and tell me the last name was Frost?"

"Maybe she just didn't think it was worth mentioning. Maybe she didn't know Rose used that name."

"Okay, maybe," Wheeler said. "But why did she never mention that Rose was dead?"

At the end of the hospital hallway, an elevator chimed. Roland glanced toward the sound. "She didn't just forget to mention that."

"I don't think so."

"So you think, with the wrong name for a dead woman, she was trying to send us off track?"

"I don't know."

Roland went to the doorway. As he peered in, the clear plastic saline bag hanging behind Devon suddenly caught the sunlight and lit up like an enormous crystal. "We need her to wake up," Roland said. "Now."

"Call me as soon as she does."

"You can count on it."

53

Ben followed Eden over the treetops. They flew side-by-side, tilted slightly to better study the ground beneath them.

"This is crazy," Ben said, looking down as the lawns and streets rolled by.

"You seriously have never done this before?"

"No. I guess that shows a lack of imagination."

"Or fear of heights?"

Ben shook his head.

Eden swooped close to him. "This is the one thing that's better," she said, "about the afterlife."

"It is pretty cool."

"It's nice to have someone to do it with. I've always been on my own before." She touched his hand. "I feel a little like Chagall's flying lovers."

"Who?"

"A Russian painter named Marc Chagall painted couples floating in the air."

"Huh. I'd like to see those paintings."

"Okay," Eden said. "Maybe we will one day."

Ben resumed scanning the landscape below. "They're going to be hard to spot. And there is so much ground to cover. Even like this."

"A gold car should stand out."

"I hope so."

They traced a small road through woods. Now and then the trees reached across it, hiding it completely.

"We're coming up on that location that I want to check out," Eden said. "There's a field, and an old shed. It seems like a natural place to hide."

"Here," she said a moment later, where there was a break in the trees. She descended. Instead of a clearing, she was met with a tangle of shrub and saplings. "Geez," she said, instinctively raising an arm to protect her face, as branches whipped through her. "There's not much of a field left." She turned around, searching the chaos. "That jumble of rotting wood used to be the shed." She pointed. "I'm just wasting our time, aren't I? My knowledge is out of date."

"Come on," Ben said, tugging on Eden's hand. "On to the next place." Rising, he found the road again.

"Why don't we take a straight line?" Eden said. "You know, as the ghost flies?"

"I want to keep a lookout for that gold car. We might catch them traveling."

Though they picked up speed, the air rushing past didn't disturb their hair or their clothes. Everything remained perfectly in place.

"When we find them, what do we do?" Eden said after a while.

"What do you mean?"

"These men are kidnappers, murderers. We're a couple of shades. We're going to have to do more than close a door or pull some jewelry out of a box."

For a long time, Ben was quiet as they sped over the curving road.

"I don't know what we're going to do," he said, finally. "But it seems like the times that I've been able to touch things or move things have been when I was most worked up. The emotion somehow makes me more solid or something. So when the time comes, when we find these guys, I think we'll be able to do what we need to do."

"Well, I know what I *want* to do," Eden said.

"Yeah? What's that?"

"I want to make those bastards pay."

54

"Do you have the cash?" As he talked on the phone to Daniel Frost, Chad stood by the car, looking away into the trees where the tent was hidden.

"Yes," Daniel said.

"Be in Mystic tonight."

"Let me talk to my granddaughter."

"Tonight. You do your part, you can more than talk to her, you can give her a big hug."

"Where? Where do I meet you?"

"When it's time, I'll let you know."

Chad ended the call and slipped the phone into his pocket. He went down the slope to the tent, which was just tall enough for him to crouch inside. Fern was curled up under a blanket in one corner, facing the sunlit canvas, a thumb in her mouth. Bobby sat next to her. Cross-legged, he looked particularly long-limbed and insectlike.

"He says he has the cash," Chad said.

"So you set up the meeting?"

"Not yet."

"Why the hell not?"

"In case he's talking to the cops. I don't want to give them any extra time to get ready for us."

"I thought you already told him no cops, in the first call."

"I did. But maybe he went ahead and talked to the cops anyway. We've got to be ready for that. It's like chess. You've got to anticipate, be two moves ahead."

"Uh huh. I'm sure you're a regular grand wizard at chess."

"It's grand master. And I sure as hell could beat you."

Bobby stared at the girl, who lay motionless, slightly bent, her back to him. "You really think you know how to pull this off?"

"I'm sure I do."

"Yeah, I guess because you handled everything so well up till now."

"Fuck you, Bobby."

"Yeah, fuck you, Chad."

"What is your problem? We're about to get our money back – all of it."

"My problem is we don't have the money yet. What we do have is a live girl. And I don't think you know how to swap one for the other without something going wrong."

"Nothing's going to go wrong."

Bobby stood and led Chad out of the tent. He said, "What happens after we turn her over? She can identify us. We haven't even been hiding our faces from her. We should have been wearing masks this whole time."

"How's she going to identify us? She can't talk. Or maybe you haven't noticed."

"There could be ways. Pointing at photographs, or drawing us."

"Sure. She's going to turn out to be a regular Rembrandt."

"Maybe she is! There's just too many questions, Chad. What makes you think you have them all figured out? When did you get to be such a criminal mastermind?"

"When did you get to be such a goddamn wimp?"

"There's a difference between being a wimp and being careful."

"You're careful, all right. If it was up to you, we'd be back in Ellsworth right now without a penny of our hundred grand. So, you're welcome."

"Yeah, if it was up to me. Like you've done everything."

"Everything that took any balls."

"Like with Devon. That went perfect."

"Exactly, like with Devon." Chad's voice rose. "We keep moving, and wrap things up tonight, and we're fine."

"And Eric, too," Bobby said. "You handled him perfect, slamming him into that lamp pole."

"It all worked out. I just went on instinct. You got to, at a time like that."

Bobby gave the other man a long look. "You are one badass, Chad. The way you took care of Eric."

Chad allowed a little grin on his face. "I'm not going to say I'm badass. But I do what needs to be done."

"Even if it's killin'."

"Sometimes."

"You are so full of shit," Bobby said. "You didn't fuckin' kill Eric."

"Yeah? Who did then?"

"I did, you asshole."

"What the hell are you talking about? I shoved him, he hit his head on the lamp pole, he went down. You were standing back out of the way, doing nothing, as usual."

"Eric was still alive after that," Bobby said.

"I know, he was still breathing when we put him in the camper. And then he wasn't."

"Except, he was. Because he was still alive the next day when I went back looking for the phone."

"What the hell are you talking about?"

Bobby glanced at the tent. "When I went into the camper, he was lying there like he was dead. But then he moved. And he made a sound."

"What kind of a sound?"

"Like, uhhhhhh."

Chad just looked at Bobby for a moment. "So what did you do?"

Bobby didn't answer.

"You finished him off?"

"He was freakin' me out. It wasn't even like he was Eric. It was like this dead body came back to life. Like a zombie or something."

"The fuck did you do, Bobby? We could have talked to him. He could have told us where the money was."

"Oh, I see, now it was a mistake to kill him. When I did it. When you killed him, it was badass."

"Well, since he was still alive, you could have adapted to the situation. See what he could tell us."

"He wasn't going to tell us anything, Chad. That's why you shoved him in the first place – because he wouldn't tell us anything."

"Jesus Christ, Bobby. I can't fuckin' believe you."

Neither man spoke for a while, long enough for a noisy plane to pass by overhead and leave silence behind.

"How did you do it?" Chad said.

"There was a pillow next to him. I..." Bobby held his hands in front of him like he was pressing down. "It was like I didn't even think what I was doing. I just wanted it to stop."

They were silent again.

"Good old Bobby." Chad shook his head. "So I'm supposed to believe all that."

"Believe whatever you want. It's what happened."

"And you just now decided to tell me."

Bobby didn't respond.

"What am I supposed to do with that news?"

"You do whatever you want with it," Bobby said. "Just quit saying that you're the one that's doing everything."

"Okay. I'm not the only badass, then."

"Guess not."

Chad laughed. "The Stonington P.D., if they do get involved, they are going to have their hands full, with us two badasses."

Bobby wiped sweat from the back of his neck. "So do you want to tell me your plan?"

"What do you know about inflatables?" Chad said.

"Inflatable what? Dolls?"

"Right. That's what we need right now. Sex dolls. Jesus."

"Well, I don't know. Inflatable what?"

"Boats, you dumbass. We're going to get us an inflatable boat."

55

Roland was looking directly at her when Devon stirred and opened her eyes.

"Where am I?" Her eyes rotated, vaguely, as if she were not just confused but half blind.

"Westerly Hospital," Roland said.

Devon reached across herself and touched the tape on her forearm, then noticed the tube. She let her arm fall back to the bed. "Who are you?"

"My name's Roland Brown. I recently retired as chief of the Stonington Police. I'm helping them now. Do you remember what happened to you?"

"How long have I been out?"

"A few hours."

Devon stared blankly across the bed toward her toes. "I don't know... I can't..." Her voice was slow and clumsy, as if every word were as thick as clay in her mouth.

"Try to remember. I know you're tired. But it's important."

"Shouldn't you call a nurse?" Devon sat up a little straighter.

"There's a button on that big remote-control — right by your hand."

Devon found the control but didn't press the red button in the center of it. Abruptly, she sucked air in between her teeth. "Did someone call my dad?"

"Yes. He got on the first flight. Shouldn't be too long."

Devon seemed to be thinking about her dad, but when she spoke again, it was to name a different man. "Chad."

"What about Chad?"

"He knocked me out." Devon reached gingerly for the back of her head, switching arms when the IV line pulled on her skin. "Shit," she said, when she found the bandage. Her fingers traced the gauze all of the way around her head, felt the hair lap over it.

"Why did Chad do that?" Roland said.

"Fern." Devon struggled suddenly on the mattress, fighting with the blanket, trying to rise up. "Fern. He took her, didn't he?"

"Chad and Bobby – they were at Alice Garrison's house today?"

Devon nodded. "Chad's in charge."

"Okay. We think Chad and Bobby have Fern. Do you know where they would have gone?"

"I might. Shit." Devon touched her IV. She seemed to be considering ripping it out of her arm. "You have to find her."

"Where would they be?"

"They had a map. They made me mark some places on it, where they could hide."

"What spots did you mark?"

"I don't know. It's too hard to describe."

"Are they close by?"

"They're all here in Stonington."

"If I showed you a map on my phone, could you point them out?" Roland produced an enormous black phone from a jacket pocket. "Could you show me on the screen?"

"I'll try." Devon finally looked at Roland directly, her eyes focused and clear. "They killed Eric. They'll kill Fern, too. We have to stop them."

56

AJ got the call from Wheeler as he swerved into the parking lot of one more motel, one more mostly empty parking lot with no gold car. Because of what Ben had told him, he hadn't been checking into the Frosts, as he'd promised Wheeler he would. Instead, he'd been scouring the county for the big gold sedan that Melody had seen outside Alice's cottage just before the kidnapping.

"I sent you a map," Wheeler said. "Roland marked it with the places that Devon said to try."

"Okay, let me look at that. Hold on one second." AJ pulled the phone away from his ear. With a few taps on the screen, he found the map. He studied it, zooming in on the marks Roland had made, then zooming out again. He put the phone back to his ear. "I can read that. He marked some spots off of Deans Mill Road, and on either side of Pequot Trail."

"Yeah, off of that power line."

"I'll start checking them out."

"Adams will be with you," Wheeler said.

"Adams? Do you think that's a good idea? I mean, do you think he's ready to handle this kind of thing?"

"Not on his own. But he'll be with you. I don't have to tell you how careful you have to be, AJ – we don't want to do anything that endangers the girl."

"That's exactly why I think Adams should sit this one out."

"I know he rubs you the wrong way."

"He does, but that's not what I mean. He's not just a rookie, he's an overconfident rookie. His cockiness could get Fern into trouble."

"You keep him in check, AJ. Keep him on the sidelines if you have to, but he's going with you. Gaines wants all of our guys to have a partner. No exceptions. And he's right. These men are murderers."

"So Adams is my partner now."

"For tonight."

AJ looked out the window at the long motel porch, lined with plastic chairs. "Okay."

"I wish I could be with you, but I have to stay close to the Frosts. They got another call."

"What happened?"

"The guy just wanted to know if Frost had the money. He told Frost to be in Mystic tonight – said he'd call later with details."

"So Devon said she knows these guys? Bobby and – "

"Chad. Yeah, she knows them a little. Based on what she said, that would have been Chad on the phone. He's the leader. I think he's the one we have to worry about."

"As long as they have Fern," AJ said, "I'm worried about both of them."

Immediately after ending that conversation, AJ called Adams. They arranged to meet at Claire's house, which was located near the center of the marks that Roland had made on the map. Adams would come in street clothes and an unmarked car.

"I can be there in fifteen minutes," Adams said.

"You're going to beat me. Just wait in the car."

"I can do that."

"Good. You're going to be doing a lot of it."

***

"That's quite a place," Adams said, looking out through the windshield. The dark façade of Claire's house loomed over them. "I've heard some stories," he added.

"Not now, Adams." AJ settled into the passenger seat.

Adams kept staring at the house. He hadn't yet turned the key. "I'm going to be up front, AJ – this scares the hell out of me. Two killers holding that little girl... I've never done anything like this. I don't want to make the wrong move and cause something bad to

240

happen."

AJ was silent while he buckled in. "That's the right attitude," he finally said.

"You sound surprised."

"I didn't take you for someone who ever worried about doing the wrong thing."

"I know I come across as cocky."

"Could be. A tad."

"I get that from my father. But really – I just want to do a good job. In this case, I just want to keep that girl safe."

"Listen to what I tell you and you'll be okay."

Adams gave AJ a tight smile. He pulled a couple of sheets of paper from the dash and handed one to AJ. "I printed Roland Brown's map."

AJ pointed to a dot. "Let's start here."

57

"Hi Sam. What's up?" As he spoke into the phone, Roland stood just outside of Devon's hospital room, watching her confer with the family lawyer from her bed.

"Have you gotten any more out of Devon?" Detective Wheeler said. "Is she still talking?"

Roland turned and headed down the hall. "Not to me she isn't. Ever since her lawyer showed up."

"Great."

Roland ducked into a stairway and descended quickly, landing heavily on each step.

"Do you think she's told us everything she knows?" Wheeler was saying. "Or is she still holding out on us?"

One floor down, Roland opened a door. "She's holding out. I'd bet my life on it." He jogged around a corner and stood in front of a vending machine. "One sec." Juggling the phone and his wallet, he fed the machine a credit card, then punched some buttons. A soda can dropped. He put the phone to his ear again. "You have AJ checking the spots on her map?"

"Yeah. AJ and Adams. Nothing so far."

Roland went back around the corner and started up the stairs. "Maybe it occurred to the kidnappers that Devon might be talking to us. If so, then the places on her map are the last places they'll be."

"These guys aren't familiar with the area. We should ask Devon, see if she has any ideas about where else they might go."

Roland was in the hallway again, moving toward Devon's room. He looked in. "Shit. That just got a little more difficult."

"Why? What happened?"

"I don't know. I was away from her room for a few minutes – just long enough to get a soda. She's gone."

"Check with a nurse. Maybe they took her out for an X-ray or something."

"I will. But I don't think that's what happened." Inside the room now, Roland had opened the door to a small closet. "Unless she took her clothes to Radiology."

58

AJ knocked on the shiny wooden front door of Devon's house. Adams stood next him, one thumb hooked on his belt just above his holster.

"No one home," AJ said. He called Wheeler.

"Stay there," Wheeler said. "She might still show up."

"Okay. I'll let you know. There is a car here. I assume it's her dad's. No word on him getting back yet?"

"No."

AJ and Adams left the porch and got into their car. AJ leaned close to his window. He lowered the glass. "Those look like tire tracks." His eyes were focused on the lawn next to the garage. "Let's see where they go."

He opened the door and stepped out onto the driveway. Adams followed him on foot around the garage. Faint parallel lines led away across the back yard.

"Straight toward that shed." AJ pointed.

"Probably from hauling something there," Adams said. "A piece of equipment, or bags of fertilizer."

"One way to find out."

AJ paused at the closed door to the shed. The two cops stared at the latch.

"There's definitely imminent danger, right?" Adams said. "We don't need a warrant."

"No doubt." AJ flipped the latch. He swung the door open.

Once their eyes had adjusted to the dim light inside, they saw a riding mower and some yard tools, sacks of chemicals for the lawn, a bird feeder on a pole. There were a couple of paint-spattered saw horses. Blankets draped over something. AJ lifted a corner.

"That almost looks like the blanket forts my sister makes for her kid," Adams said.

AJ let the blanket drop.

When they were outside again, AJ slid the heavy door across the opening. The latch closed with a *clack*. AJ circled the shed. He faced the garage, seemed to be mentally following the tire tracks that crossed the grass. He walked a little further past the shed and looked around him. "A car was parked here," he said. "This grass is all flattened."

"The kidnappers?" Adams said. "Was this their first stop?"

As Adams studied the ground, AJ got a call. "Sam," he said into his phone. "I was just about to call you. Did Devon mark her house on the map? Or say anything about sending the kidnappers here?"

"No. Why?"

AJ explained about the tire tracks and the trampled grass. "We really need to talk to Devon. I bet she's coming here. I'll wait for her."

"You can't wait there for her. I need you at the precinct."

"Why? What's up?"

"The feds have arrived."

"The FBI is here?"

"Yeah. They want everyone at the precinct for a briefing. Now."

"But Devon could be headed this way. We've got to talk to her. Adams can leave me here, go to the briefing, come back for me when it's over, and fill me in."

"I already tried that with Special Agent Corso. He wants you here."

"Can you get Gaines to talk to him?"

"Tried that, too. Gaines wasn't exactly eager to fight for the idea. With you on leave, then back – I think he already feels like there are too many exceptions being made."

"For me."

"Yeah."

AJ let the phone fall away from his ear. He took a deep breath. Then he spoke into the phone again. "Okay, Sam. We're on our way."

59

"Sorry, Ben. This was a big waste of time." Eden circled around a stone chimney – all that remained of a cabin at the end of a narrow, leaf-covered dirt road. "My ideas about where they might hide out are all obsolete."

"Hey, knowing where they aren't helps, too. We can tell AJ some places they can eliminate." Ben came over to her. "I wish there was some way I could carry a cell phone," he said. "It would be nice to be able to call AJ rather than having to track him down."

"If he's out looking, like us, he could be hard to find."

"I think we should head to the station. Even if he's not there, maybe we'll overhear something about where he is."

"Okay. Let's go."

They went over the treetops, sticking to the roads again so that they could keep an eye out for AJ's Jeep and the kidnappers' gold car. It wasn't long before they reached Route 1. They went north over the road, the water glistening on their right.

"Hey, look," Ben said, pointing down at the traffic. "I think that's Melody."

He did a quick about-face and tracked the car as it went south.

Eden came up alongside him. "Where do you think she's going?"

"Don't know."

"You sure it's her?"

"Pretty sure. I've never seen her car from this angle before." Ben dropped down, swooped alongside the car, and peered in the window. He joined Eden again. "It's her."

"I thought we were headed to the police station."

"Let's just follow Melody for a bit. She might know something, and be headed somewhere relevant."

"Seems like a long shot, but okay."

The car continued on into town. It rounded the Civil War monument. At the flagpole just before the drawbridge, it took a right onto Holmes Street, which ran alongside the river – only a sidewalk and a low stone wall separated them.

"It almost looks like she's sightseeing," Eden said.

"This is one of her favorite places."

Slowing further, Melody took the left on Bay Street. There, the sidewalk disappeared and the stone wall gave way to a white wooden fence in a narrow strip of ground. Melody pulled to the right and stopped behind another parked car.

Ben and Eden hovered over her.

On foot, Melody crossed the street and stood at the fence, staring out at the water.

"I think she's just grabbing some time for herself," Ben said. "I'm suddenly feeling like a stalker."

Where Melody stood, a couple of short docks stretched out into the river, ending in floating platforms with slant-backed chairs that faced the current. Seagulls claimed the pilings. To the right, the red wooden buildings of the Mystic Seaport Museum shipyard were visible behind a flapping American flag. White houses lined the opposite shore.

"I can see why she came here," Eden said. "This is such a nice spot."

"Right?" Ben watched Melody watch the river. "She's into history. She has a degree in it. One of the reasons that she likes this spot is because it feels so connected to the past, with the Seaport and the old sailing ships right there, and the captains' houses across the way." He pointed. "She helped us – Mystic Afterlife – with some historical research. She was really good. So smart. I used to love to hear the words that came out of her mouth."

"So she's not just a pretty face."

"No, that's for sure."

"Tell me more, Ben Shortman."

"Yeah? Okay. She'd had some tragedy in her life, and it made her – I don't know – brave. No bullshit, you know? She had this way of

248

really looking at you. She'd stare at you, and let you stare right back at her, like she was asking you to see whatever you could see in there."

"Why are you using past tense to tell me this?"

"I guess because I'm...dead. It's over."

"Is it? And if it is over, is that why?"

Without saying anything, Ben suddenly dropped lower, toward Melody. He took up position next to her at the wooden fence. Together, they watched a boat moved silently across the sparkling surface of the river toward the bridge.

Ben looked at Melody. He saw her belly press against the rail, saw her breathe deep, turn her eyes back and forth. With her, he looked down Bay Street, the way she had come. Just then, moving past on Holmes Street, there was a flash of gold.

"Did you see that?" Ben said.

"What?" Eden hung above them.

"A gold car. Melody saw it."

Melody had her keys in her hand. She ran to her car, jumped in behind the wheel. Juggling her cell phone and the keys, she managed to start the engine and initiate a call, all the while whispering, "Shit shit shit shit shit." She clutched the cell phone with one hand. With the other, she gripped the steering wheel, which she turned with a jerk. The car leapt forward, starting a U turn that was cut short as the tires resisted, tugging the wheels, straightening. The phone fell. "Shiiiit!" Melody shouted, reaching. The engine raced. The car shot across the street and the narrow strip of grass. "Shiiiit!" The grill struck the wooden fence, burst through it. The front wheels cleared the stone wall, and the whole thing tipped, hesitated, then plunged into the river.

60

The water found cracks and holes everywhere. It quickly swamped the foot wells, swallowed the pedals and Melody's feet. Ben raced to her headlong, skimming above the surface. Through the window, he could see Melody, slumped against the sagging air bag, out cold.

The car continued to sink. Soon the water was up to Melody's lap. Ben grabbed at the door handle. He couldn't take hold. He dipped lower, half in the water, tried to pound the glass with his fist. His hand passed through. He swung his arm again. This time, the window blocked him.

He dove. At the river bottom, his fingers closed on a rock, lifted. First try, his grip held, the rock came free from the mud. He shot back toward the surface, the kick of his feet finding purchase, propelling him upward. When his head was above water again, he swung the rock. It bounced off the window, throwing his arm back. A second blow broke through, shattering the glass into a thousand sparkling beads.

Ben reached through the opening. His hands sunk into Melody's shoulder. She shuddered. Ben tried again. This time, he managed to take hold of her.

She stirred, bleary eyes opening. "What the hell?"

"Come on!" Ben said.

Melody shifted, angled her body toward the window, pushed with her feet. Her head slipped through the opening. Her swollen shape just fit. Then she was in the river.

She bobbed, went under, came up coughing right next to Ben.

They were face to face. Ben stared into her unfocused gaze. She squinted, then began to wave her arms, flailing, as if trying to free herself from an unwelcome grasp. She dipped under again, resurfaced.

"Come on, Melody, swim," Ben said.

Melody's motion became more organized. She found the direction of his gentle pull. Her stroke was labored but there was not far to go. Struggling and slow and gasping for air, she climbed onto the dock. She collapsed there, staring up at the sky.

"Ben?" she said, when she could breathe normally again. "Are you really here?"

"Yes," he said, from beside her. "I'm here."

"I don't understand. Am I dead?"

"No!" Ben said. "No."

"But you – "

"Yeah, *I* am. I mean, I definitely died. I'm a ghost."

"But just now, in the river, I felt you. You were real – "

"I've been real."

"You were solid. Does that mean you're back? You came back to life somehow? You saved me and now you're alive again?" Melody still hadn't looked in his direction. She put one hand on the downslope of her belly.

"Actually, I think..." Ben left that thought unfinished.

"You saved two lives." Finally looking at him, Melody reached for his hand. He bent down. For a moment, their fingers were intertwined. "You're cold," she said.

"I just came out of the river..."

"How did you happen to be there to save me? Have you been watching over me or something?"

"It was just luck. Just good timing."

They were quiet. The soft air around them was quiet. The water sliding off of them darkened the weathered boards.

From somewhere near the bridge came the opening wail of a siren.

Melody smiled up at Ben. "I'm so glad you're back."

He touched her knuckles with his lips. "Just rest. Help is on the way."

Melody tried to give Ben's hand another squeeze. Her fingers closed on her own palm. "Ben?" She peered into a suddenly empty space.

Glancing down at himself, Ben backed away. "You're going to be a great mom."

Melody turned toward him. Her eyes pointed directly at him but kept moving, kept searching for the thing they could no longer find. "Ben?"

"I'll always love you, Melody," Ben said.

The ambulance roared up Bay Street.

***

"Well, that was dramatic." Eden looked down on Melody from high above.

Ben had joined her. Together, they watched the EMTs tend to Melody.

"Sorry I didn't try to help," Eden said, "but I went after the gold car for a minute. When I got back here, things were already happening, and – "

"I know. You don't like to get involved. *Final Destination* and everything."

"I might be rethinking that. You saved her life, Ben. And the baby's."

"I did." Ben raised one hand in front of him, turned it back and forth. "You know I'd never even held Melody's hand before? When I first got to know her, she used to let me stay after at the Honey B, when she was alone counting the tips. We'd talk and laugh for hours. But that was as far as it went. When I'd ask her out, she'd always have some excuse. Today, though, I held her hand. I kissed her hand. I had to die and come back, twice, and she had to almost die, for it to happen. But I kissed her hand."

Eden seemed to be barely holding back an eye roll. "Seems like an awful lot of work for not so much. Was it worth it?"

Ben let his arm drop to his side. "So, that was it. That was my destiny."

"What are you talking about?"

"That's why I came back. I've been wondering all this time why I was here – now I have the answer. I came back so that I could save the woman I love, and have one last moment with her. I'm going to move on now. I'm sure that's it."

Eden stared at him without saying anything.

"I don't know how this goes," Ben said. "The last time I moved on, I was with someone."

"Ah. If only we had more time, you could tell me about that someone."

Spreading his arms, Ben lifted his face to the sky. He closed his eyes. "It will probably happen any minute now."

This time Eden did roll her eyes. "Do you feel anything?"

"I don't know. Maybe something. Like I'm getting lighter..."

Eden kept on staring at him. Nothing changed.

Ben opened one eye. "Goodbye, Eden."

"Well, I'll just leave you to it, then," Eden said, moving away. "I'll go check on the love of your life."

61

Adams drove up Route 1 toward the precinct. In the passenger seat, AJ talked to Wheeler on the phone. "Is Melody okay?" AJ said.

"Sounds like it. She managed to get out of the car and get to shore."

"How did she end up in the river?"

"I don't know."

"We're not far from there," AJ said, glancing towards Adams.

"You'd better be going north on Route 1, heading to the briefing."

"Shit." AJ pushed the hair back from his forehead. "It's Melody. She almost drowned. Couldn't you catch us up later on the briefing?"

"I told Gaines and the special agent that you'd be here."

"Melody's accident could be related to the case."

"How do you figure?"

There was a long silence on the phone.

"I'll think of something," Wheeler said. "If you get there in the next few minutes, you might catch her before they take her to the hospital."

"Thanks, Sam."

"As soon as you've talked to her, I want you here."

"You got it."

AJ explained the change in plans to Adams. One perfectly executed U-turn later, they were heading toward Mystic at speed. AJ didn't object when Adams switched on the lights and the siren. Soon they were turning onto the little side street by the Seaport Museum.

Adams went to check on the retrieval of the car. AJ found Melody on a gurney. He put a hand on her shoulder. "How are you?"

"He was here, AJ," she said. "He saved me."

"Who?"

"Ben. He pulled me out of the car. I would have drowned."

"Melody, you've just been through a trauma. Maybe you're – "

Just then, Eden slid into AJ's sightline. "That's not going to work, AJ."

Melody was giving AJ a hard stare. "Don't bullshit me," Melody said. "I talked to him, just like I'm talking to you."

"Told ya," Eden said.

"Okay." AJ glanced at an EMT who was just out of earshot, readying the ambulance. "Why don't you give me the quick summary of what happened?"

"I came here to clear my head. I got a glimpse of a gold car driving past, like the one I saw at Alice's. I'm almost positive it was that car. I was frantic trying to follow it, and I guess I lost control and went into the river. I woke up in the water with Ben holding onto me."

"Holding onto you?" AJ said. "What do you mean? You could touch him?"

"Yeah. I'm sure he pulled me out of the car."

AJ stared across the river, silent.

"You don't believe me," Melody said. "I thought you of all people…"

"I do believe you."

She looked back at him, unconvinced.

"So the gold car," AJ said, "where did you see it?"

"It was heading that way." She pointed.

The EMTs came alongside the gurney.

"Can you call Jack?" Melody said.

"I will. I'd come to the hospital myself, but – "

"I know. Fern is your priority. Anyway, it's just procedure. I'm fine. I'm sure I'll be out of there in a few minutes."

The gurney slid through the bay doors.

Eden came over to AJ. "Is she okay?"

"Yes, I think so." AJ was punching Jack's number into his phone. "Where's Ben now?"

Eden nodded across the street. "He's having a moment. I think we need to leave him alone for a bit."

"Hey, Jack," AJ said into the phone, at the same time turning his back on Eden, as if to focus his attention on the call. "Melody has been in an accident. She's okay." He described the events as he knew them, minus the ghosts. "I'll let her tell you the whole story when you see her."

When AJ had put his phone away, Eden was gone. There was no sign of Ben, either.

AJ's phone buzzed. He put it to his ear. "Sam?"

"It's happening," Wheeler said. "You're going to have to leave Melody."

"She'll be on the way to the hospital in a second. Where do you need me?"

"At the flagpole, by the bridge. Quick as you can."

"Be right there."

62

"You're the best, Kashmira," Devon said, as they rolled into the driveway. "Thanks so much for coming to get me."

"I'm glad to help." Kashmira gave Devon a perfect smile. "I mean, after what you went through today, a hospital is the last place you should be. You need to be home."

"Yeah, definitely." Devon got out of the car. "I'll talk to you later," she said through the open door.

"You want me to hang out until your dad gets back?"

"Thanks, but I'm going to crash."

"I could make you some chicken soup or something. If you have a can." Kashmira flashed a smile again. "I mean, you need to take care of that." She touched her own head where Devon's was bandaged.

"I just need to rest."

Kashmira leaned across the seat. "You sure you don't want some company? Listening is my superpower. Tell me about Eric. The way you looked when you mentioned him earlier – I have this feeling there was more – "

"I said, not tonight!"

"Okay," Kashmira said. "Just trying to help."

"Just trying to pry, more like it."

"Sorry. Jesus."

Devon closed the door. As the car moved away, Devon seemed to be taking stock of her own vehicle situation. Her dad's BMW was there – he'd driven a rental to the airport. Her silver car was absent, still in the possession of the police.

The porch light was on, and so was a lamp in the living room, telling the lie that all was normal. She went in. After grabbing a key from a hook just inside the door, she went to a neat office in back of the house. She unlocked a desk drawer. Inside was a thick folder. Underneath the folder was a compact, black handgun. A minute later she was outside, heading for her father's car, wearing a jacket that sagged on one side. As she slid into the driver's seat, she tapped the pocket once. She was ready.

***

The campsite was the second place she looked. As the BMW crept down the dirt lane, Devon caught the glint of dying sunlight off of chrome. She cut the engine and got out of the car. She patted the jacket pocket.

She set her feet down carefully in the dusty tire tracks. She breathed in little bursts.

Up ahead, under the trees, the long sedan became clearer, its color more distinct. There was some kind of artificial light coming through the leaves to the left. Devon kept to the edge of the lane, in the shadow of the shrubby woods.

As she got close, from the direction of the light, she could hear men's voices. She stood for a long time behind a tree trunk that was half her width – a make-believe blind. The louder voice continued, giving orders.

"Chad," Devon whispered.

She left the tree, slipped toward the sound, located the source of the soft light – a tent, at the bottom of a small hill.

She took a few more steps, moving with exquisite care. A break in the shrubs revealed itself to be a path, heading down to the tent. She took it.

The men's voices came from the tent.

"Okay, Chad," Bobby was saying. "How many times do we have to go over this? First, It's…" The rest of what Bobby said was inaudible.

"As many times as I tell you," Chad said. "You can't screw this up."

At the bottom of the path, Devon stared at the tent's glowing canvas wall. The door was to her right. She took the gun out of her pocket. She waited.

The growl of a zipper tore a hole in the silence. Its pitch rose as the teeth were split apart with increasing speed. The tent shook, then spit out two men. Chad and Bobby.

Bobby turned and bent into the opening. "Come on, Fern."

"Leave her," Devon said from behind the barrel of the gun.

"What the hell?" Chad spun around. "Devon! You found us."

Bobby pulled his head out of the tent. "Shit."

"I didn't think I should call you," Chad said, "in case you were with the cops."

"Or in case I was dead." Devon kept an unsteady aim as she spoke.

"That's quite a bandage," Chad said. "Are you okay?"

"No thanks to you."

"Can you put that thing away?" Chad pointed at the gun with a gun-shaped hand. "You're going to hurt somebody by accident."

"You mean like the way you almost killed me by accident."

"Listen, I'm sorry about that. It's kind of a hard thing to judge how hard to hit someone, you know? And in the moment, when it's all happening so quick... Is that what this is about? I'm really sorry. But it worked, didn't it? You're in the clear with the cops, and you're okay. I mean, here you are up and around. Everything's going just like it's supposed to."

"Is it?" Devon said. "It's all going according to plan?"

"Well, yeah. We were actually about to – "

"So the way things happened with Eric," Devon said, "that was according to plan, too? You just hit him a little harder than you meant to?"

Chad's forced smile faded. "Well, that was actually Bobby. He was just telling me all about it."

Devon swung the gun to the left, toward the taller man. "You killed Eric?"

Bobby raised his hands. "I didn't mean to."

"You didn't mean to?" Chad said. "You didn't mean to suffocate him when you pressed the pillow down on his face?"

"Chad!" Bobby said, his hands wavering.

Devon aimed the gun first at Bobby, then at Chad. When the gun was off of him, Bobby said, "You screwed up the plan, Devon, when you told Chad you changed your mind. That's why he had to hit you so hard."

Devon scowled. "What are you talking about? I never told him I changed my mind."

"Look," Chad said, spreading his arms wide. "Maybe things haven't gone exactly according to plan. But we're about to collect the money from Grandpa Frost. You'll get your cut. And no one will be any the wiser."

"And Fern will be back with her grandpa," Bobby said.

"All's well that ends well," Chad said.

"All is not well!" Devon said. "Jesus! Eric is dead. You hit him and I guess suffocated him and burned him. You fuckers." She pointed the gun down, suddenly, and shot a bullet into the dirt.

"Damn!" Chad jumped back. "Okay! Okay! I thought you were working with us."

"I was never working with you!" The tendons were practically popping out of Devon's neck. "Jesus! Haven't you figured that out? The only thing I was working on was how I was going to do this, right now."

"Do what?" Bobby said.

"No, no, no, no, no," Chad said. "You were working with us. You did your part exactly like you were supposed to."

"I know! It was my fucking plan, you asshole!" As Devon's voice got more agitated, the gun seemed steadier. It stuck unwaveringly on Chad.

"It was *our* plan," Chad said. "We worked it out together."

"But then she changed her mind, right?" Bobby said.

Chad ignored him. "*Our* plan got Fern to us, and it got you in the clear for the kidnapping. And it got us all a pile of money."

"I don't care about the fucking money!" Devon said. "What the plan did was it got me in the clear for you two. It let me take my revenge for what you did to Eric. I loved him – don't you get that? You bastards."

Chad seemed to be thinking that over. "No, see, because if you wanted revenge, you would have just turned us in."

Devon shook her head. "Why the fuck are you trying to explain my plan to me?" She looked ready to shoot another bullet, this time into Chad's chest. "I couldn't turn you in because the cops were never going to give me what I wanted. There's no death penalty in Connecticut. I Googled it. How screwed up is that? Cause here's a couple of guys who definitely deserve it – who deserve to die – and we can't execute them. All we can do is put them in prison. Not good enough."

Chad looked unconvinced. "If you just wanted us dead, you would have shot us that day in the woods, when we met to talk about the plan."

"We didn't meet to *talk about* the plan, we met so that I could *tell you* the plan. You asshole. I couldn't just shoot you that day, because it would've seemed premeditated. Like I arranged the meeting just to take care of you. I needed something that looked more spontaneous."

Chad stared at her without speaking for a moment. "More spontaneous?"

"Sure. I came here to save Fern. Then it got ugly. I think I look pretty good in that scenario."

Chad seemed to be turning that over in his mind. "Have you ever shot something with a gun before?" he said after a while. "Besides the ground? It's a lot harder to hit what you're aiming at than it looks."

Devon's gun hand was dead steady now. "My dad, you know, he's kind of into guns. We have a bunch of them in the house. So, yeah, I know how to shoot. Have since I was a little kid. Don't count on me missing."

Chad nodded slightly, as if trying not to. "You'll never get away with this."

"Like you're one to give advice on that topic," Devon said.

The air had grown darker and damper as the sun dropped. The black gun was already harder to see than it had been when this all started.

There was a scraping sound from the tent. The flap flew open against the side. Fern hurtled out, headed for Devon. The little girl on her little legs didn't make it past Bobby, who snagged her easily, as easily as a fyke net might catch an eel. Bobby pulled her close.

"Well, that changes things," Chad said. "Nice work, Bobby."

Devon still pointed the gun at Chad. "Tell him to let her go, or I'll shoot you."

"No, I was thinking more like, you put the gun down, or Bobby will do to your little friend what he did to the love of your life. Like you said, Bobby has a history."

"You won't hurt her. You need her."

"Are you sure?"

Chad took a quick sidestep that put him behind Bobby. Tracking him with the gun, Devon found herself aiming at Fern, who was still in Bobby's grip.

"Shit!" Devon yelled, letting the gun droop toward the ground.

Chad shoved Bobby, hard. Lurching forward, Bobby tripped over Fern and stumbled into Devon. The three of them fell in a heap.

Chad pounced on the girl, grabbing her elbow and dragging her backward.

Suddenly there was a high-pitched, ear-splitting sound. A scream. Fern's scream. Everyone froze.

The first to recover, Devon rolled free of Bobby. She felt around in the dirt with empty hands.

Chad pointed. "Bobby! Get the gun!"

Bobby and Devon lunged at the same time. Though the gun was right next to Devon, Bobby, stretched out, his long arms over his head, got there first.

Immediately, Devon was on her feet. "I'm sorry, Fern."

The girl wriggled and kicked against her captor. Chad's hand clamped tighter, and the scream died. In the new quiet, the only sound was the drumming of Devon's rapidly receding footsteps.

"Shoot her, Bobby!" Chad yelled.

Barely taking time to aim, Bobby fired a round. Devon disappeared up the path.

"Jesus Christ, you idiot! Get her!"

Bobby took off. When he got to the top of the hill, Devon was already pulling the door of her dad's BMW closed. Bobby kept after her. As the car spun around and accelerated, he stopped running. He raised the gun. For a few seconds, he held it that way – not quite level, not quite pointed at the car that was speeding away.

"I am so screwed," Bobby said. He shot twice into the twilight. Then he turned and jogged down the hill to where Chad waited for him.

63

AJ and Adams raced toward the flagpole. Wheeler's voice came from AJ's phone. "He got Frost to agree to drop the money even without getting the girl in exchange. He said he doesn't trust Frost not to have gone to the police, and so Frost will get the girl when he feels safe, when he's sure that they're not being followed."

"Frost is giving up the only leverage that he has," AJ said.

"He's desperate. He said 'Yes' before we could get a word in."

"How does the drop work?"

"Frost is supposed to leave the money by the flagpole. That's all we know."

"The kidnapper isn't afraid to be out in the open picking up the money."

"No, he isn't," Wheeler said. "As long as they have the girl, he knows we can't touch him."

"So does it matter if they make us at the drop site?"

"Special Agent Corso talked about that. He said we can't depend on the kidnappers acting rationally, because if they were acting rationally, they wouldn't have tried kidnapping in the first place. Even with the girl as an insurance policy, the kidnappers are unpredictable. We don't want them to get wind of any law enforcement at any point. We're going to be there in force but we have to stay invisible."

Adams spoke for the first time. "That's not going to be easy."

"You're right," Wheeler said. "Much easier said than done."

"Can we even tail the guy," Adams said, "after he picks up the ransom? I mean, whoever does that had better be good."

"Corso has designated people for that," Wheeler said. "Himself, Gaines. And me."

"Who else is going to be there?" AJ said.

Wheeler explained the positions of the players – nearly every cop on the force, plus Special Agent Corso. "This is one time that I'm glad to have the Bureau's help." Before ending the call, Wheeler added, "We need every single kind of help we can get."

Adams, if he wondered what Wheeler meant, kept any questions to himself. Following AJ's directions, he drove past the flagpole, which stood off-center in the disjointed intersection near the bridge, where Main Street and Holmes Street, and a little closer to the river, Cottrell Street, collided. He took the left onto Cottrell. After swinging the car around, he parked by some bike racks, facing out. From there, AJ and Adams had a view of the intersection, and beyond it, Wheeler's plain gray sedan, which was backed into the last parking spot in front of a row of shops.

"Now what?" Adams said.

"Now we wait," AJ said.

Adams settled back against his seat.

After a few minutes, AJ got a call.

"Am I on speaker?" Wheeler said.

"No." AJ kept his eyes front.

"Have you had any help?"

"What do you mean?"

"Special help. Maybe from Eric Mitchell."

"No. A friend of Ben's was in the area, but she's gone now."

"A friend? He has a friend? Another ghost?"

"Yeah."

"Was she any help?"

"Not really."

"Well, keep your eyes out," Wheeler said. "That kind of help has come to the rescue before, maybe it will again."

"Right."

"Adams doing okay?"

"So far, yeah."

"Keep him on a tight leash."

AJ didn't respond. Next to him, the young patrolman sat with his hands balled up on his thighs.

Without ending the call, AJ went back to watching the intersection. "What if our guy comes up the river?" he said.

"Manzella's on the river," Wheeler said.

Twisting in his seat, AJ peered down Cottrell toward the park that ran along the water. He swore under his breath. "You know what you were just talking about? About getting all kinds of help? I need to check something."

"What is it?"

"I don't know." AJ was moving to open the car door. "I got to go."

"AJ, if the kidnappers see you – "

AJ had already slid the silenced phone into his pocket. "Adams," he said, giving the man's arm a firm squeeze. "Don't do anything without being told to by Wheeler or someone in command." Then he was out and moving quickly down the street.

Adams's phone rang. He fumbled it out of his pocket.

"Adams," Wheeler said.

"AJ just took off."

"Let him go. The Frosts got the call. They'll be here in a few minutes to drop the ransom. I expect the kidnappers to follow right after that. So be ready."

"Be ready for what? What do I do?"

"Just be ready for whatever Corso, or Gaines, or I tell you to do."

"That's what I keep hearing." Adams put the phone down on the seat. He took one last glance down Cottrell Street behind him. AJ was nowhere in sight. Breathing deep, Adams counted slowly, *one two three four one two three four...* His back pressed hard against the seat. His hands made white-knuckled fists in his lap.

64

AJ ducked under the porch roof of a small building. "Hello?" he said, in a whisper. There was no answer. He kept moving. As he came around the next building, he caught a glimpse of something – a gray light sliding into the park. "Hey," he said again, a little louder. "Eden? Ben? Eric?" He chased the light. But when he reached the park, there was nothing, just a row of trees still in full leaf, their circular shadows softened by the lamps that had just now switched on. He continued on into the center of the grass. "I just want to talk to you," he said, turning slowly, checking the gloom in all directions. He waited. He heard nothing. Then, closer to the river, he saw the glow again, gliding around the next building. Running after it, AJ risked a louder voice. "Wait! Whoever you are! I need your help. Fern needs your help!"

***

The sky was a deep blue, already showing a few bright stars, when the Frosts' car finally drove down Main Street. It swerved close to the flagpole and came to a stop. An SUV behind the Frosts edged to the left. Daniel's hand reached out the open window, waving it past. When the intersection was empty, the passenger door of the Frosts' car opened. Daniel Junior got out, holding a thick mailing envelope, the kind with bubble wrap built in. He placed it at the base of the pole, tucked in next to one of the fins that sloped toward the heads of huge bolts. He got back into his seat and closed the door. The car continued past the pole, then drove over the bridge and away.

***

Chad crossed the drawbridge on foot. He was alone. The clear air had cooled quickly and he was dressed for it, in a heavy sweatshirt with the hood up.

When he was on the Stonington side, taking advantage of a break in the traffic, he made straight for the flagpole. He picked up the envelope. He moved quickly back the way he had come, not visibly checking out his surroundings, like a man with ordinary but urgent business, a courier with an express delivery, and not a kidnapper making off with the ransom in plain view of the police.

65

"Should we go after him?" Adams said into the mic that he kept low, out of sight.

A new voice – smooth and confident as a news anchor – came through the speaker. Agent Corso. "We'll pick him up on the other side. I don't want to risk trying to follow him across the bridge on foot. We're too exposed."

Adams gripped the mic. "Jesus, don't you want to just take the guy down now? He's right in front of us."

"It's Officer Adams, isn't it?" Corso said. "You know we can't move on him. They still have the girl. You're with Officer..." He paused. "Bugbee. You follow his lead. Your job is to sit tight."

Adams glanced at the empty seat beside him.

Chad was on the bridge now. He still hadn't once looked around him. His eyes were locked straight ahead.

"Fuck!" Adams said, without clicking the mic. "Damn it all, AJ, where the fuck did you disappear to?" His fingers were on the door handle. "Fuck!"

His phone rang again.

"Adams!" Wheeler said. "Do not move. You got that? Do not move."

"But Detective – "

"We have the guy covered. You just stay put."

Adams's hand fell to his side. "Okay, okay." He sat back.

Chad reached the bridge house and faded into darkness.

"That gold LeMans we're looking for just pulled into the parking lot and is sitting right here in front of me." This was Gaines, over the radio. "Huge old sedan. 1980, '81, I think."

"So that's where Chad's headed," Wheeler said.

"Looks like I got lucky," Gaines said.

"I have eyes on him." This was Nardi, from his position on the far side of the bridge. He was standing in a doorway on Main Street, nursing a cigarette, talking into his sleeve.

"Keep your distance," Corso said.

After a long silence, Nardi spoke again. "He just passed me. I'm following."

More silence. Then Nardi's voice. "He just went into a restaurant. The Honey B Dairy."

"Chief," Wheeler said, "the doors in front of you – one of those belongs to the Honey B."

"If he comes out of any of these doors," Gaines said, "I'll see him."

"He's wearing a sweatshirt and jeans," Nardi said.

Minutes passed.

"Any sign of our guy, Chief?" Corso said over the radio.

"Nothing," Gaines said. "What'd he do, hit the john?"

"Nardi?" Corso said.

"I'm still in front of the Honey B. Do you want me to go in? This is getting to be a long wait."

Gaines cut off the response. "Shit. The gold car is moving."

"You follow it," Corso said. "Nardi, go ahead into the Honey B, get eyes on the man in the sweatshirt. Wheeler, you come take Gaines's place."

Gaines said, "He turned left out of the lot. I'm following."

Wheeler, already racing toward the bridge, picked up the mic. "On my way. You should send backup for Adams."

Corso's reply was immediate. "He's got Officer Bugbee. I'm going to count on the two of them to handle that side of the bridge."

Wheeler clicked the mic, then put it down without another word.

66

They went around the building – the gray light and AJ. The light was too fast – AJ caught only glimpses. He lost it, then chased a hint across the street. Out of breath, he went back to where he had started – the low building with the short porch. Nothing. He made the loop again, through the park, around the taller building. He cleared the corner.

The light was waiting for him.

***

Chad came out the back of the Honey B. Having dropped his sweatshirt on the way through, he was now underdressed for the fall chill, in just his golf shirt. He wore a cap with the brim pulled low. He kept his head down.

With Gaines gone and Wheeler still on his way, no one watched Chad swing around behind the shops and take the alley that cut between them, back to Main Street. There was no sign of the envelope. In one hand he held a cell phone. He took a right when he reached the street. Nardi was not there to see him pass the Honey B, moving with purpose, heading for the bridge.

***

"I thought you were leading me somewhere," AJ said in a hushed voice. "But we're just going in circles." He stood close enough that his face was lit up by the ghost's otherworldly glow.

"I'm just trying to stay out of things." Eden twisted the beads of her necklace between her fingers, making a clicking sound that only AJ could hear. "I didn't think you'd follow me. I'm still not used to being seen."

AJ blew air between his teeth.

"Did I screw something up? See – this is why I don't get involved. Even trying to stay away I screw things up."

"It's all right. Where's Ben?"

Eden looked back toward Bay Street. "I'm not sure. After he saved Melody, he was sure that he was moving on, to wherever. When it didn't happen right away, he decided to go back to Claire's. He said something about a doorway that he'd used before."

AJ only nodded.

"Look, if I screwed something up by being here, can I make it up to you? I can look for anything you might need me to look for. I can get to places that you might not be able to get to." She smiled. "I can cross the river even when the bridge is up."

AJ's eyes narrowed. "Shit." He checked his watch, then pulled his phone from his pocket. It took a while for Wheeler to answer AJ's call. "Sam," AJ said in a voice that was urgent but muted. "The bridge – the last scheduled opening for the day is just about – "

"What?"

"Where are you?" AJ said. "It sounds like you're driving."

"I'm heading out of town, towards New London. Following Gaines, who's following the gold car. Chad is in the Honey B. You should go back to your car."

"Turn around," AJ said.

"What? Why?"

Before AJ could answer, the warning bells started, a combination of ringing and clanging that told everyone on both sides of Main Street that the level grate across the Mystic River was about to break free at one end and tip up into the sky.

***

Alone now, Adams inched his car closer to the corner, until he was just clear of the single-story shop that stood between him and the bridge. He had a view across the deck into Mystic. He heard the bells, saw the last pedestrians quicken their pace. One was a squat man holding a phone, coming straight at him.

"I think that's our guy," Adams said to himself. "Jesus." He dug in his pocket for his phone.

The man left the bridge and veered right into the small riverside park. He disappeared behind the buildings.

Adams got out of the car. He reached for his phone again. "Shit," he said, letting the phone go. Then he took off running.

***

From the other side of the park, AJ watched it all unfold. Adams coming up alongside Chad, who turned toward the approaching footsteps. Chad brandishing a phone, as if warding Adams off with it. Adams knocking it from his hand. Words, then a scuffle. Chad reaching to his waistband. Something new in Chad's hand. Glinting steel. A gun. Adams grabbing for it. Chad pulling free, redirecting the barrel. A pristine crack. Adams going down.

AJ and Chad raced past each other, one headed toward the body, the other one toward the dock along the river.

"Adams," AJ said, reaching for the wound in the center of the spreading bloodstain.

"Go after him, AJ. I'll be all right."

AJ found his radio. "Shots fired," he said. "Mystic River Park. Officer down."

Adams pointed toward the dock. "AJ, go!"

AJ sprinted across the grass. He saw nothing at the dock ahead of him but pleasure boats, quiet at the moorings. Then something shifted in the shadows. It was a man, turning the blunt nose of an inflatable dinghy out into the open water.

Seeing AJ racing toward him, Chad drew the gun from his waistband again. He aimed across the few feet of water that had opened up between the dock and the boat. AJ reached the brink, jumped. Chad squeezed the trigger. The blast cracked the night. AJ's legs made one big bicycle kick and then he hit, tossing gold beads of river water into the black air. AJ grabbed the dinghy just as the pain found him. He cried out.

More gunshots rattled the darkness. AJ ducked under, resurfaced, ducked again, using the tube as a shield. Chad's next bullet nicked the fabric, tearing a hole the length of a table knife. The air escaped the tube with a moan. Chad lurched backward toward the bow. The hull flattened, became a mat. Then the whole thing flipped, dumping Chad into the water. He set off for the shore, dogpaddling, taking big, watery, walrus breaths.

AJ followed him, fighting against the cold and his heavy clothes and the burning in the center of his being. The water churned under his shoes, the slap of his hands. With each stroke his movements were more labored, his kick slower, his reach shorter, until his arms just broke the surface. The water trailing after him had a different quality to it, not so slick, not so black. It was mixed with blood.

With each stroke, he disappeared a little more, and a little more of him mixed with the river. He sank and he swam. His hands no longer cleared the water. Only the top of his head broke the surface. Still he moved forward in the water, in the dark river of freshwater and saltwater and blood. Then the Mystic River claimed him.

***

AJ came out coughing. Crawling, he was pulled across the wood. Letting go, Manzella fell back, breathing hard.

Not three feet away, Adams lay on the grass, pressing his thigh with both palms. "I tried to get to you. Manzella got there first."

AJ rolled to his side. "Where is he?"

Adams pointed toward the bridge. "Nardi got him."

Across the park there were two figures, the shorter one in the clip-winged posture of a man in handcuffs.

AJ tried to get to his feet, staggered and fell back, his face scrunched with pain.

"What are you doing?" Manzella stood.

"Finding out where they have the little girl."

"The only thing you're doing is keeping still. Until an ambulance arrives, I need to keep pressure on that wound." Manzella held out a balled-up shirt.

In the light from a nearby pole lamp, AJ saw the growing red at his waist. He stared at it, as if fascinated by the color. Leaning over him, Manzella pushed the shirt onto the source of the blood.

From close by came the overlapping wails of emergency vehicles.

"AJ," Adams said, "I hope I didn't get the girl killed. I just couldn't stand to watch that guy go right past me."

"What did he say to you," AJ said, through a grimace. "Just before you knocked the phone out of his…" AJ's voice faded.

"He said if I made another move he'd call his partner and that would be the end for the girl."

AJ almost smiled. "Good job, then."

Sirens tore across the park.

67

In the precinct's big meeting room, the Frosts sat alone at an oval table. The whisper of the ventilation was interrupted now and then by bursts of a harsh, inscrutable voice over a radio. The TV mounted on the nearby wall was black.

Daniel Junior let his eyes sweep the table, then the empty rows of double desks. "I wish they'd left someone here to tell us what the hell is going on."

"Why haven't we heard from the chief?" the father said. "I thought he was going to be giving us regular updates."

"If they had good news, they'd tell us."

"I'm going to go find Romano." Daniel stood up.

"I'm here," Romano said, coming in.

"What's going on?" Daniel said. "Where's Fern?"

"There have been some developments. We have one of the kidnappers in custody."

"One of the kidnappers. But not her."

"Correct."

"What the hell? Isn't that exactly what we don't want?" Daniel took a step toward the officer. "Doesn't that put her in even more danger?"

Romano raised his hands in front of him. "We made contact with the other kidnapper, too. Chief Gaines and Detective Wheeler followed him. They figured he had her, or he would lead them to her."

"And?"

"They were being very careful not to be seen."

"Okay."

"They lost him."

"They lost him." Daniel Frost was in Romano's face now. "He's gone, with Fern. He probably knows that you got his partner."

"I guess they think he doesn't know. Either way, it's still in his interest not to harm her. She's his only bargaining chip."

"A *Bargaining chip*. That's my granddaughter. You guys are a fucking disaster. I should never have called you."

The two men were close enough that the heat from their faces mixed somewhere between them. Romano's cheeks flushed red.

Romano took a step back. "I understand how you feel, Mr. Frost. But you should know, two of our guys are on the way to the hospital. They were shot stopping the one kidnapper from fleeing."

"Who?"

"Officer Adams – I don't think you've met him. And Officer Bugbee."

"Bugbee," Daniel said. "He was at the hotel. Are they going to be all right?"

"I think so."

Daniel swept a hand across his heavy eyelids. "So the guy you arrested – is he here? I want to talk to him."

"They're bringing him in. But you can't talk to him."

Just then there was the sound of people entering the station. The Frosts got to the hallway in time to see a handcuffed man in soaking wet clothes being escorted into an interview room. Romano blocked the Frosts' path.

"You have to let me talk to him," Daniel said.

"The best thing for you to do is go back to the meeting room and wait. They might have questions for you." Romano herded the Frosts toward the big room. "Can I get you something? Coffee?"

Peering in the direction that the cuffed man had gone, Daniel shook his head.

"I'll check on you in a minute." Romano left them.

"This could be a good thing, Dad," Daniel Junior said. "If this guy cooperates to get a deal, he could tell the cops where Fern is."

For a moment, Daniel looked like his son's words had given him some hope. But then his face grew darker again. "This is taking too long," he said. "That can't be good."

Special Agent Corso entered. He wore a white shirt and tie. He had a young face, bright eyes. When they were seated at the table, he filled in the details of what Romano had told them.

"What can we do to help?" Daniel said. "Officer Romano said you might want to ask us a few questions."

"Not at this time," Agent Corso said. "I'm afraid all you can do is be patient."

Daniel, who had seemed to calm in Corso's presence, pushed his chair back from the table with a screech.

Daniel Junior stood. "Let's get out of here."

"It's better if you stay," Corso said. "There's a chance that the kidnapper who is out there with your granddaughter could still contact you. We want to be nearby if he does."

"What would he want? Now that you blew up the deal."

"He might want to negotiate a new ransom."

"Yeah?" Daniel said. "And what am I supposed to do then? The only money we have is at the bottom of the river."

"Actually, it's not. Not all of it. The man we brought in had some of it on him."

"Great," Daniel said. "That's great. Come on, Junior." He got to his feet.

"You have our numbers," Daniel Junior said.

"What are you going to do if you leave?" Corso said.

Without responding, the Frosts headed for the door.

"Don't try to make yourself useful," Corso said, sternly. "Just go back to the inn. We'll call you."

Silent, Daniel Junior led his father out.

They didn't go back to the inn. They'd heard about the gold car, and so they searched for it, winding through woods and farmland, down narrow roads lined with stone walls, hoping desperately for a stroke of wild good luck. In the dark, they had difficulty making out vehicle models and paint colors. The unfamiliar roads were even stranger at night, and they kept having to backtrack. Frustrated, exhausted, they argued.

"We should never have gone to the police," Daniel said.

"No, we should have gone to them a lot earlier. You think it would have gone better if we'd handled it ourselves?"

"How could it have gone any worse?"

"It could have gone a lot worse."

"How, exactly?" Daniel said.

"Fern is still alive."

"We don't know that."

"I know it."

"You do? You know it?"

"Yes! If you're thinking different, Dad – just don't. Don't even fucking think it. But that's what you do, isn't it? Think the worst. Use it as an excuse to do nothing."

"What are you talking about?"

"It's the excuse that you always use – you don't want to make things worse. It's why you didn't question Mom about where Rose came from – you just went along with that crazy adoption story. You never even checked out the papers! And it's why you didn't try to get Fern away from Rose when you knew Rose, knew her problems. You didn't want to make things worse, so you didn't do anything. Look what happened! How much worse could things get, Dad? How much worse could they get?"

For a long time, Daniel drove without saying anything. He went slowly, ignoring the suggestions that Daniel Junior occasionally gave him after consulting the tiny illuminated map on his phone.

"I'm sorry," Daniel Junior said. He had let his phone go dark on his lap. "It's not your fault."

His father was silent.

"Maybe we should go back to the station."

"So we can sit in an empty room and be ignored?" Daniel said.

They kept on. Down Route 1, going toward Mystic, one more time on a route that they'd traveled many times that night. Daniel took a left onto a side road.

"Where are you going?" Daniel Junior said.

No answer. They drove deep into a point that stretched out into the sound. They passed the lights of houses that were set well back and spaced far apart.

Daniel slowed, pulled onto the grass in front of a simple cottage that was half hidden by a hedge. Lights burned brightly in the downstairs windows.

"She's still up," Daniel said.

"Who?" Daniel Junior said. "What are you doing?"

"We need a break. And I want to introduce you to someone."

Daniel Junior followed his dad to the door. "Where are we?"

Daniel rapped firmly on the wood.

The door opened. Alice stood in the empty frame.

"I'm sorry," Daniel said. "I know it's late."

"Very," Alice said.

Jack Westbury had come up behind her. "Can I help you?" he said.

Daniel kept his eyes on Alice. "I wanted to explain."

Jack touched Alice lightly on the arm. "Alice, do you want to talk to these people?"

Melody had come to the door. She peered over Jack's shoulder.

"Hi," Daniel, said, hopefully, as if Melody's might be a friendly face.

"Jack, meet Daniel Frost," Melody said. "Fern's grandfather."

68

Wheeler caught up to AJ as he hurtled down a gleaming hallway at Lawrence and Memorial Hospital. "AJ," Wheeler said, running alongside the gurney. "Where were you hit?"

The medic answered for him. "Abdomen."

AJ looked up, his eyelids half closed. "Hey."

They all raced down the shiny corridor. A pair of swinging doors opened and two men in hospital garb took charge of the gurney.

"Hold up," AJ said. The gurney did not stop. "Sam, do we have the girl?"

Wheeler yelled through the doors. "No. But we will."

AJ struggled to raise his head. "Go. Find her."

***

Outside in the hospital parking lot, Wheeler got Gaines on the phone.

"How is he?" the chief asked.

"He was conscious. Looked like he was in a lot of pain. They took him right into surgery."

"Did you talk to a doctor?"

"For a minute. He said they really won't know what the damage is until they get inside."

"One of my buddies in Norwalk took a bullet to the gut last year," the chief said. "They sewed up his stomach, pumped him full of antibiotics. It was a long recovery, but he came out of it okay."

"How long until he was back on the job?"

"He took the pension," Gaines said. "But I hear he's doing great. Spending a lot of time with his grandkids."

Behind Wheeler, the glass doors of the hospital opened with a hiss.

"Did you see Adams?" Gaines said.

"Yeah. They already have the bullet out of his leg. He'll have some rehab, but they're hopeful for a good recovery."

"I hope 'good' means 'full.'"

"Yeah, me too."

"Ordinarily," Gaines said, "I'd tell you to stay there until AJ comes out of surgery, but – "

"It's all right – they're going to call me with any updates. So where are we? Is the guy we have in custody giving us anything?"

"We know the girl is with the accomplice – Bobby – in the gold car. We got our guy – Chad – to call him, but Bobby isn't answering his phone. They were supposed to meet up on Mason's Island, so we went there. We didn't find anything, though. Bobby must have taken off. Or Chad is lying to us."

"Do you think he's lying?" Wheeler said.

"No. He seems like a man who understands what kind of trouble he's in and is desperate to help himself by helping us."

"That's what we want."

"Yes, it is," Gaines said. "One thing has been bugging me, Detective. Can you explain to me how AJ happened to be right there in the park when everything went down?"

"AJ has good instincts. You can't always explain it."

"You know, Chief Brown said something a lot like that. He said AJ has *special* instincts. Said he is a unique asset to the SPD. I remember it because I thought it was a weird thing for Chief Brown to say. I thought it was weird at the time, and I think it's weird now. What the heck are special instincts? I don't really know how to deploy special instincts, Detective."

"I understand."

"It doesn't seem like these special instincts served him or anyone else well today."

Wheeler didn't respond.

"What I'm asking, Detective, is, is he in control? Or is he too much in love with his special instincts? Does he think the rules don't apply to him, because he's special? He missed the briefing, then he went off script at the bridge. In a situation like he was in tonight, when there are a lot of moving parts and everything can go haywire at any moment, AJ needs to be able to do exactly what he's been told to do. We had everyone else in place. Manzella was on the river, Nardi on foot. AJ should never have gotten out of that car. He should never have left a rookie alone in the car. Because he was out of the car, and Adams was alone, we're here right now with them in the hospital. And we lost the girl."

"Chief, AJ did tell me what he was doing when he went into the park."

"I didn't hear that on the radio."

"He used the phone."

"Did you okay him taking off?"

Silent, Wheeler turned back to the hospital, letting his eyes search the grid of illuminated windows.

"Don't even answer, Detective. There will be a thorough review, when AJ and Adams are up to it. We're going to know everything that happened tonight, and why."

"Sounds good, Chief."

"We have a chopper in the air," Gaines said. "We're getting more help from the feds. You'll get most of that from the radio on your way back. Check in with me at the precinct ASAP."

"Okay, Chief. Will do."

Wheeler wound his car through New London to Interstate 95. As he crossed high above the Thames River, the submarine shipyard was lit up as bright as any casino. In front of it, long, yellow, rippling fingers stretched across the black surface of the water.

Over the radio, he heard from the others who were out scouring the countryside. One after another, they reported back the bad news of the fruitlessness of their efforts. No gold car. No kidnapper. And no Fern.

69

They'd fallen asleep where they were – Daniel Frost in a recliner, Melody and Alice on the sofa, Jack in a wooden rocker. Only Daniel Junior was awake, on his feet. He stood at the sliding glass door, staring into darkness.

That darkness was just beginning to soften when, as if communicating in their sleep, as if dreaming the same nightmare, the women woke with a start. Melody sat up, touched her belly, and looked across the cushions at Alice, who returned a tight-lipped smile.

They stood, each slow for her own reasons. They nodded at Daniel Junior, who returned the nod, then went back to staring into the yard. They went into the kitchen. The smell of slightly scorched coffee filled the space. The green light of the coffee pot glowed.

Without a word, the two women embraced. Wet cheeked, they slipped mugs from the cupboard and filled them from the pot, found milk in the refrigerator and sweetener in a bowl – each movement careful, stealthy. They whispered only the essential words.

They offered a mug to Daniel Junior. All three drank at the sliding glass door, staring out into the yard where Fern had last played. Mercifully, the plastic slide was barely visible in the dim light. They stared through the glass as if waiting for the sun to reveal a different world. The quiet kept on, an edict, a covenant.

Then, a knock. A quiet knock. Like something a bird might make, pecking a seed on hard ground. Like a tree branch pushed against the house by a breeze.

Tap tap tap.

"Did you hear that?" Alice said.

"Yes," Melody said in a whisper.

"Was that the door?"

"I think so."

They stayed where they were, as if paralyzed by the sound. It continued.

Tap tap tap.

Everyone was awake, now, on their feet.

"What is that?" Jack said.

Daniel was already heading for the door. "There's someone here!"

Tap tap tap.

They all converged on the sound, on the glossy six-panel front door that separated them from the maker of the sound.

Tap tap tap.

Gentle but insistent.

Jack turned the knob, pulled back, opened the house to the world.

On the step, staring up at them with wide eyes, alone as she had always been, was Fern.

70

AJ spent his first recovery day dozing between visits. June, Roland, DaSilva and Wheeler all came and went. Sela and Beth showed up together. Visiting by video, George Bugbee bent so close to the laptop screen that only half of his face was visible. "I wish I could be there," he said. "These damn doctors won't let me leave."

"I feel bad that I took Mom away from you," AJ said.

"Ah, she needed an excuse to get out of here for a while. Though I can think of better reasons than you getting shot in the stomach. So how are you? The news we've gotten is all good. You look good."

"I'm about three quarters antibiotics right now. They're fixing me right up." AJ gestured toward the IV bags that hung on a pole behind him. "I'm lucky the bullet missed the arteries and the spine."

"Lucky? I guess that's the way to think about it."

AJ shifted in bed. A twinge crossed his face. "How are you doing? You look good."

"They tell me I'll eventually feel better than I have in years. So I'm looking forward to that."

"Yeah. Me, too."

The two men were silent. As if freed by the cameras and screens between them, they held eye contact for a long time.

"I heard they got the girl," George said.

"Yes. Still one kidnapper left."

"They're waiting for you, I guess."

AJ let that go. After the video chat, AJ slept soundly. Claire kept her chair close to the bed, watching him, reading, watching him again.

When he woke, AJ looked past Claire to the window, which was filled with late afternoon light. "Guess I wasted your whole day."

"How are you feeling?"

"Like I got shot in the stomach," AJ said.

"I can't imagine."

"I don't know if you can, but I wouldn't try."

Claire squeezed his hand. "You need to eat."

"Later." He swiveled the tray to the side.

Standing, Claire leaned over AJ and gave him a long kiss. With a series of subtle shifts, he made room for her, and she climbed into the bed next to him.

She stroked his chin. "You need a shave."

"I'll shave in my own sink. Or, your sink."

"Why are you going to use my sink?"

"Your house, your sink."

"You know it bugs me when you do that. It's our sink. Our house."

"I'd like to be able to say that, but – "

"What? You want me to make an honest man out of you?" Claire raised herself up on one elbow.

"Funny you should say it that way."

"Why?"

"I haven't been completely honest."

Claire waited, looking down at him.

"It's about Ben."

Claire stiffened but didn't speak.

"He was back. While all of this was happening."

"Back where? In the house?"

"He was all over. He could move around."

"But he was in the house, wasn't he?"

"Yes. Sometimes."

"I thought maybe... But then I thought no, you'd tell me. Why didn't you say anything?" Claire's voice was suddenly sharp.

"We decided not to – Ben and I. He didn't know why he was back, or for how long, and we remembered how hard DaSilva took things, last time. Both times. We wanted to spare him. Spare everybody."

"That makes no sense to me. But even if I accept why you didn't tell DaSilva, I still don't understand why you didn't tell me."

"We didn't want anyone to have to keep a secret."

"I'm not just anyone." Claire started to make her exit from the bed.

"I was protecting you! I know you don't like having a ghost around."

"You're right, I don't like having a ghost around. Even if it's Ben. But you can't just lie to me. That's not the answer." Claire remained poised to swing back over the bedrail.

"You're right. I should have told you. I should always tell you."

"Maybe you don't have to tell me about every ghost that you pass on the street. But you have to tell me about Ben. And you definitely have to tell me if there's a ghost in my house."

"Okay," AJ said.

"Okay."

"I want us to be close, Claire. I want us to tell each other everything. Life's too short not to."

"Okay. You're starting to come around." Claire stared back at him. "Is this what happens when you get shot in the stomach?"

"Maybe. Maybe you should shoot me in the stomach every now and then."

Claire stretched out next to AJ again, cautiously laying an arm across his chest. "That's a terrible thought."

"Our house," AJ said after a while.

"What?"

"You said 'you have to tell me if there's a ghost in my house.' You meant, if there's a ghost in *our* house."

Claire laughed. "Right."

"When I get out of this place, let's talk some more about that."

"Yes," she said. "Let's."

71

A cry, sharp with misery and fear, tore through the peaceful darkness of Jack and Melody's bedroom.

Melody's face remained planted in her pillow. She moved only her mouth. "What time is it?"

Jack picked up the alarm clock up from the nightstand. He held it close to his squinting eyes. "After nine."

"You're kidding me. He let us sleep until nine?"

"He learns a new trick every day. You want me to bring him in? Maybe you can doze a little longer."

"No, I'll get up. We have to start getting ready for Claire and AJ, anyway."

"Right." Jack slid out of bed and went to the nearest window. "Brace yourself," he said. He pushed the heavy curtains aside. Brilliant sunshine assaulted the room.

From close by, the cry continued, gaining in intensity, as if some long-anticipated calamity were finally at hand.

"I'm coming, I'm coming," Melody said, moving quickly toward the sound. "Poor little Ben, you must be starving."

Within seconds, quiet reigned again. Jack turned to look out through the glass. Sunshine flooded the green lawn and sparkled on the cove. He slid the window open a crack. A curl of spring air, cool and salty, reached for him. "Beautiful day," he said. "Beautiful, beautiful day."

***

The sky had stayed cloudless and the temperature had shot well past warm by the time Claire and AJ arrived, allowing the party to take place outside on the sprawling deck. Cut daffodils brightened the table. Jack manned the grill. The others took turns bouncing the happy baby on their knees, a practice that continued as they talked and laughed through the meal.

They had just cleared away the dishes when AJ got a call.

"Sorry to bother you," Wheeler said. "I wanted to share the good news. It's about our friend Bobby."

"Hold on." AJ left the deck and started down the hill. "Okay. Fill me in."

"They brought him in this morning."

"Ellsworth Police?"

"No. Department of Maine Resources. He showed up at the Bangor office to renew his elver license."

"You're kidding me."

"No. The elvers have been running for a few weeks and he just couldn't stay away."

"That shouldn't surprise me, I guess."

"We knew that he lacked a little in both the brains and the impulse control departments."

"Yes, we did." Having reached the water, AJ stood looking out across the cove, a silver plain dotted with the masts and shiny hulls of moored boats.

"We got 'em both, AJ," Wheeler said. "And they're going to go away for a long time."

"It's funny," AJ said. "To get Chad, Adams takes a bullet in the leg, I take a bullet in the gut and almost drown. To get Bobby, someone just had to sit behind a desk."

"Good argument for an office job, isn't it?" Wheeler said. "Just sit there and wait for the bad guys."

"I'm sure there would be some slow days."

"Yeah," Wheeler said. "You wouldn't catch a bad guy every day."

The water slapped just short of AJ's feet. He looked down. Floating in the foam that advanced and then retreated was a one-hundred-dollar bill. AJ bent to pick it up.

"It might be a good place to start," Wheeler said.

"What might?"

"The office job. Sit behind a desk for a month or two."

AJ pinched the sodden bill between his fingers. "Oh, I see. That's what we're really talking about."

"I don't want to hurry you, AJ. But we need you down here."

AJ didn't respond.

"Don't tell me it's about the market, and your parents wanting to retire. I was just there last Friday. It seemed to me that your mom and dad were running the place like they always did. Maybe better. I'm not sure I've ever seen them look so happy."

"Yeah. They're sort of having a second wind."

"And you're back to a hundred percent."

"Just about."

"Look, I know that internal review was pretty rough, but Gaines will tell you the same thing – we need you back."

"Yeah. He called me last week."

"He's not a bad man, AJ. He's no Roland Brown, but he's starting to act like a human being, at least. I think that night humbled him."

"Losing a kidnapper you're supposed to be tailing will do that."

"I think it was Adams and you getting hurt, on his watch."

"Right now, Sam, I'm thinking of another career."

"Yeah? What other career?"

"Sitting in a lawn chair at the water's edge and waiting for money to come rolling in."

"What are you talking about?"

AJ told him about the hundred-dollar bill. "Maybe it's the ransom money, that's been floating around until this morning. Maybe a lot of hundreds are about to come drifting in to shore."

"Even if that did happen, that money's evidence. You'd have to turn it in."

"You know Alice and Daniel Frost have kept in touch?" AJ said.

"No, but I'm not surprised."

"Maybe she could invite him and Fern down for a little beachcombing."

"Uh huh. And maybe Jack could get back some of the fifty grand that he gave to the Frosts' lawyer."

"The lawyer's fiancé. Sure. This could be good for a lot of people."

"We can talk it over when you come in to see Gaines about your desk job."

AJ flipped the bill over again, studied Benjamin Franklin's slightly peeved expression. "Yeah," he said. "Maybe."

"Why do I feel like I'm missing something?"

"I am coming in to the precinct tomorrow," AJ said, "to talk to Gaines."

"Okay. About coming back to the force?"

AJ looked across the water again. "There's another opportunity."

"What kind of opportunity?"

"Mystic Afterlife?" AJ said, as if it were a question.

"That cable access show that Ben used to do with Sela and DaSilva?"

"Not exactly that. I guess you haven't heard, but Jack helped them get a deal with The Mystery Channel. It's been on and off for a few months, but it looks like it's really on, now. A regular show on regular cable."

"Wow. So you and Claire will both be into television. You took her move as inspiration."

"Maybe it was partly that. You want to be able to keep up with your wife, you know? And Ben coming back – the way I hid that from everyone... Maybe I feel like I owe him something."

"Did you say *wife* ? Is there something else that I should know?"

"No, no, not – I'm just saying that Claire sets the bar high."

"She sure does," Wheeler said. "So will Ben be involved in the show? Is that how you pay him back?"

"I wanted him to be, but he's not ready. Not for now."

"I thought the show was his dream."

"It was. He's having some kind of afterlife crisis – trying to figure out why he's back, and why he didn't move on after saving Melody. He says he's pretty sure it's not so he could have a job in television."

"So what is he doing with himself? Just drifting around?"

"Eden's trying to convince him to go with her to visit some of her old haunts – L.A., Marrakesh, India. Actually, I haven't seen either of them for a little while – maybe they already left."

"Would Ben leave without saying goodbye?"

"I'm beginning to think that with Ben, there is no goodbye."

"Only 'see you later.'"

"Exactly."

"Well, big changes for everyone, I guess," Wheeler said. "Going public with your ability – that's a bold move, AJ. Have you even talked to your parents yet?"

"No, I haven't. Once this gets rolling, I'll be committed."

"I doubt that it will go that far."

AJ smiled. "I meant, I'll be committed to being a ghost hunter, a psychic, or whatever the network wants to call me. I'll burn a few bridges."

"You might. I'll be proud of you, though."

"Thanks."

"I'll see you at the precinct tomorrow, AJ."

"Yeah. See you tomorrow." AJ slid the phone into his pocket. He looked across the cove to his right, toward the spot where, six months before, Jack had found Fern drifting in a boat, her feet in a tangle of eels. "I'm glad you're safe, Fern," AJ said just above a whisper. "But look at the trouble you've gotten me into."